ALIEN SHADOWS

ALIEN SHADOWS

ALIEN HUNTERS, BOOK III

DANIEL ARENSON

CHAPTER ONE
THE HOLE IN THE UNIVERSE

Siyona was walking through the shadowy, twisting corridors of the observatory when she first saw the ghost.

She had always found Kaperosa Observatory creepy. The station was dark, claustrophobic, a place of sterile hallways, flickering neon lights, and windows gazing out into the unbearable black soul of the galaxy. The observatory was more like a surreal labyrinth than a scientific outpost, Siyona had always thought. The sort of place that trapped you in your nightmares, leaving you to search eternally for an exit that didn't exist. It didn't help that the observatory was marooned on a distant, desolate planet--a sole patch of life on a rock light-years from Earth.

But worst of all was the view.

Since Siyona had arrived here, it was that gaping abyss outside the windows that left her always trembling, always glancing over her shoulder, always feeling trapped somewhere between wakefulness and dreams.

Oh, she had known long before coming that planet Kaperosa orbited a black hole. It was why the observatory even existed. It was why Earth's top scientists flew here. A black hole that was not quite a black hole. A black hole that spewed out inexplicable data as if something was awry within its emptiness, a chunk missing from its shadows, a broken darkness. Yes, that's how she had come to think of it. Broken darkness. An impossible nothingness. Perhaps almost as empty and cold as the place inside of Siyona's chest where her heart had been broken.

But reading the data back on Earth had been one thing. Coming here to the observatory on rocky Kaperosa, actually gazing into that black hole every day--that was something quite different. Quite too real. Quite too . . .

"Too broken," Siyona whispered, walking through the corridors that night everything changed. "Too *wrong.*"

The others had gone to sleep in their quarters. Seventy-three of the galaxy's brightest minds, now at rest. During the artificial days, when the neon lights were brightest, when the sounds of conversations filled the corridors and laboratories, it wasn't too bad. During those days Siyona could almost turn away from the pit outside, almost forget the terror of it. Yet now, at night, the lights were dim. The halls silent. The comfort of other living souls gone from her, leaving her shivering and cold.

Walking here, there was no buffer between Siyona and the emptiness outside.

She should have stayed in her quarters, even if she could not sleep. She would have rolled over in bed, pulled out her phone, perhaps watched an episode of *Space Galaxy* or read a couple technical manuals. Yet she had left her bed, had come here to wander the halls, feeling somehow drawn here, drawn by a presence she could not comprehend.

She was a scientist. She had always worked on the border of the unknown. She had never feared to gaze into the darkness.

She kept walking down the corridor. A light flickered above. She rounded a corner, entering the dark lab, and found herself staring out a window . . . and into the thing's gazing, consuming soul.

Yurei was not a large black hole, not as large as the behemoths in the centers of galaxies. It was no larger than the sun back home. Yet as she stood barefoot on the cold lab floor, staring out into the black eye . . . it consumed Siyona's vision. A black hole that was not a black hole. An emptiness that did not suck in all matter. There was something inside that abyss. Something stuck in that pit like a bone in a glutton's throat. Something that wreaked havoc with their calculations, that made their computers moan in protest. Something invisible. Something that lost its light into the darkness behind it. But what could survive gravity that sucked in light itself, yet remain on the rim of the emptiness?

A soul, Siyona thought, eyes stinging. *A god. A cruel god.*

She shuddered. Foolish thoughts. She was not some superstitious girl. She was an esteemed scientist--young perhaps, yes, and new at Kaperosa, yet a scientist nonetheless. She had not come here to fear the darkness but to study it, to--

You will worship us.

Siyona grimaced and doubled over.

You will weep for our glory.

Siyona's breath trembled. Her heart pounded against her ribs. Arms wrapped around her stomach, she stared up, stared through the window, stared into the dark eye of the black hole. No, not a black hole. A being. A presence. A god.

A god I must worship.

She should not have come here. Not to this lab at night, alone and afraid. Not to this rocky planet. She should have remained on Earth, safe in the light, yet now she was here, light-years from home, afraid, alone. She could not look away from something that was there, something staring at her, something she could not see.

Yet it could see her.

She wept.

When she finally tore her gaze away, it felt like ripping duct tape off her eyeballs. She screamed. At least, she tried to scream--what left her mouth was more of a moan, hoarse, weak, shuddering.

I can't do this anymore.

Tears streamed down her cheeks.

I can't stay in this place of silent halls, of windows, of the darkness outside. I can't stay on this rocky world orbiting this shadow.

She forced in a shaky breath. Tomorrow she would resign. She would summon a starship, even if it drained her life's savings. She would fly out, leave this place, fly back home. Back to safety. Back to where science made sense, where equations did not break, where a black hole did not stare into your eyes and whisper into your mind.

She had taken one step toward the door when she saw the ghost in the corner.

This time Siyona truly screamed.

It stared at her, a shadow, a shard of darkness, a piece of the god Yurei here within the observatory. A thing of writhing emptiness. Of two red, glaring eyes. Of a shadowy hand that rose, reached to her, grabbed her.

I never saw the beaches of Kitika, she thought. *I never felt sand beneath my bare feet or blue water around me. It's too soon. Too soon.*

He embraced her, a spirit, a torturer, a lover. His darkness spread around her, his red eyes tore into her, and then there was only one eye. Black. Laughing. All-consuming. Siyona's own eyes closed as she vanished into its welcoming emptiness.

* * * * *

"That's ridiculous." Lenora leaned back in her chair. "There's no such thing as ghosts."

"Something grabbed her." Dr. Harris stared at the monitor, clasping his hands on the tabletop. "Something made her vanish. Something we don't understand." The old man turned back toward Lenora, and his voice dropped to a whisper. "Are we so arrogant that we think we understand all forms of consciousness? Are we so confident in our knowledge that we think other types of life cannot exist--even an afterlife?"

Lenora didn't want to shudder. She wanted to laugh, to dismiss these words, to call them a mere ghost story, a tale best told around a campfire on Earth, not in a scientific facility on the rocky planet Kaperosa, orbiting a black hole. Yet she shuddered nonetheless. And she did not laugh.

Because a scientist is dead. One of my scientists. Her eyes stung. *One of my friends.*

"The soul is nothing but atoms," she whispered. "All we are--thoughts, emotions, memories--only atoms arranged into molecules arranged into our brains. When part of the brain is injured, memories can be lost, personalities can change. When the brain dies, so does the soul. Only atoms. So how can there be an afterlife? How can ghosts be real?"

Dr. Harris reached across the table and patted her arm. His eyes were mahogany, soft and kind. "I'm sorry, Lenora. I'm sorry you lost your friend. I know no words of comfort for this loss. But I know what I see in this video."

Lenora turned to look at the monitor. The video was playing in a loop. Again Lenora watched the scene--that scene that shot pain through her, that she could not stop watching.

Siyona, a young scientist with round glasses and bushy dark hair, stepped into the laboratory. For a moment the woman stared out the window into the darkness, observing the black hole that forever gaped outside. Then--a shadow in the corner. A blur. A black smudge shaped as a man. Red eyes blazed, and a hand reached out, and Siyona seemed to be screaming.

Then . . . nothing.

Both of them gone.

The shadow dispersed, and so did Siyona.

Lenora closed her eyes. The pain was too real, too great.

I know all too well what it's like, she thought. *To be young, ambitious, a woman seeking to understand the cosmos.*

Lenora was only thirty-four years old, yet already she led Kaperosa Observatory and the seventy-odd souls who lived and worked here. She had begun in darkness--the daughter of a Knight of Sol, a stodgy old man who mistrusted science, who had told her the stars were but a myth. Growing up in Cog City back on Earth, Lenora would look up at the smoggy sky, telling herself that the stars were real, that they truly did shine beyond the muck. At age eighteen, Lenora had escaped her father. She had blasted off Earth, traveled to the Mars Academy, and had finally seen the stars. Finally traveled to the stars themselves--to here, to Kaperosa, to the frontier of the unknown.

I took Siyona under my wing, Lenora thought. *An ambitious girl from a poor family, a girl much like I was. I groomed her, I brought her here . . . and I lost her. I'm so sorry, Siyona.*

The video was replaying again. A scientist in an empty dark lab. A ghost. A silent scream. Then . . .

"Wait." Lenora paused the video. "Look, Dr. Harris."

They stared together.

"What am I looking at?" the elderly scientist said, peering at the monitor. The video had paused just as the ghost was reaching toward Siyona.

Lenora tapped the monitor. A thin, trembling smile tugged at her lips. "Since when do ghosts have shadows?" She turned toward Harris. "That's not a spirit. That's a life form. That's . . . an alien."

She rose to her feet so fast her head spun. She took a shuddering breath, and her heart raced.

"An alien?" Dr. Harris said, frowning at the video.

"Planet Kaperosa is not empty like we thought." Lenora turned toward the window and stared outside. The rocky planes of this barren world spread outside the observatory. The stars shone above, everywhere but for one dark, gaping pit--the black hole Yurei, the anomaly that broke all their calculations. "We found life here. Life in the shadow of a black hole, no sunlight to warm it, no water or plants to sustain it. Yet life nonetheless." She spun back toward her colleague. "Hostile life."

Dr. Harris rose to his feet too. The old man's fingers trembled. "We must evacuate. Leave Kaperosa. Return to Earth."

Lenora shook her head. "No. I will not abandon years of research. I will not let Siyona's death be in vain."

She pulled her communicator out of her pocket. She stared at the small screen, and another pain filled her chest, another loss.

Her communicator's wallpaper displayed an old photograph, one taken almost half her life ago, when she had been only eighteen. A photograph of her with the man she loved, the only man she had ever loved. The man she had left.

Steel Starfire.

He had been only a youth then too, and joy had still filled him. Now he was older, somber, his smile gone. Now he was an exiled knight. Now he fought with the group of mercenaries who had saved the cosmos twice already--first from the skelkrin onslaught, then from the Singularity.

And now I need you, Steel, she thought, staring at the face from her past. *Now I need you to save me. To save a woman you once loved.*

Lenora began to dial.

"Who are you calling?" Dr. Harris asked.

She looked up at him. "The only people who can help us now. The galaxy's most professional, intelligent, and successful team of heroes. I'm calling the Alien Hunters."

CHAPTER TWO

TROUBLE WITH T-REX

As the mutated Tyrannosaurus rex roared, Riff raised his tranquilizer gun, only to discover that the syringe dart had been emptied.

Standing at his side, Romy hiccupped. "Tasty." The demon licked her lips, patted her belly . . . then crashed down onto the forest floor.

The dinosaur bellowed and burst into a run, trampling trees.

"Romy!" Riff shouted. "Romy, god damn it!" He grimaced and looked over his shoulder at the other Alien Hunters. "Hand me another tranquilizer dart."

His brother--Sir Steel Starfire, a knight in shining armor-- pointed at a pile of emptied syringes. The demon's tooth marks appeared on them all.

"Oh shenanigans," Riff muttered.

"Riff, damn it, the dinosaur's coming our way!" Nova shouted. The ashai gladiator pointed. The sunlight gleamed on her blond hair and golden catsuit, and she clutched her electric whip. Her green eyes widened with fear.

Riff glanced back toward the enraged, mutated beast racing toward him.

Oh bloody hell.

"Run!" Riff cried. "*Run!*"

He scooped the sleeping Romy into his arms and took off. Steel ran to his right, clanking in his armor. Nova raced to his left, her hair and whip fluttering like banners. Ferns bent around them, and the dinosaur roared behind, its feet shaking the earth with every step. Riff could barely run while holding Romy--the damn demon weighed a ton--but fear gave him the strength to keep going.

"This was supposed to be an easy job," Nova said. "Easy! Land on the planet. Tranquilize the mutant dinosaur. Airlift it back to the zoo. And you just had to let the demon come along, Riff."

He groaned, struggling to keep holding said demon as he ran. The dinosaur kept howling behind. Trees cracked. Leaves flew. When Riff glanced over his shoulder, he saw the beast gaining on them, baring fangs longer than his arms.

"I locked her up in the attic!" Riff shouted back at Nova. "It's not my fault she keeps sneaking out through the heating vents. God knows how she squeezes through. Damn demon weighs more than the dinosaur."

Romy moaned, held limply in his arms. Her eyes opened to slits, and she gave him a woozy grin. "You know, Riff, you really should try tranquilizing giant dinosaurs instead of running from them." She hiccupped, and then her eyes rolled back, and she drooled in her sleep.

Riff groaned.

"Brother, you're slowing down!" Steel cried, running ahead.

"Ditch the dead weight!" Nova shouted. "Toss the demon to the dinosaur."

"It'll only whet its appetite!" Riff shouted back.

The forest sloped toward the distant, misty valley where awaited the *HMS Dragon Huntress*, starship of the Alien Hunters. A few miles farther, past the mountains, lay the zoo the dinosaur had escaped from.

Damn fools cloning mutant dinosaurs! Riff thought. *Don't they watch old movies? Don't they know this always ends badly?*

Another roar pierced the forest, and foul reptilian breath washed over Riff. When he looked behind him again, the Tyrannosaurus was only a few meters behind.

The beast was massive. Riff had seen T-rex skeletons in museums--large animals, to be sure, but not much larger than a couple of elephants. But this creature, cloned in a lab and spliced with alien genes, dwarfed those old bones. It stood as large as the starship in the valley; all the Alien Hunters could easily fit in its belly. Shimmering green and purple feathers covered its hide, and its eyes burned with fury. Its arms perhaps were tiny, but its jaws opened wide, strings of saliva dangling between the teeth. Those were jaws large enough to swallow them all.

"Ooh look!" Romy's eyes fluttered open. "A baby dinosaur. Can I pat it, Mommy?" Her eyes closed again and she snored.

Riff was suddenly very, very tempted to see if dinosaurs liked eating demons.

The beast thrust down its neck and snapped its jaws.

Riff leaped.

The jaws slammed shut behind him, ripping his T-shirt.

Riff sailed through the air, still holding Romy in his arms, legs kicking.

Steel and Nova leaped at his side. They vaulted down the slope, hit the ground hard, and fell. As the dinosaur bellowed, the four Alien Hunters rolled downhill. Riff cried out as rocks and roots slammed into him. Nova cursed as she tumbled, a flash of gold. Steel clanked in his armor. Romy slid downhill while still snoring.

Dinosaur claws slammed down ahead of Riff.

He grimaced as he crashed into the scaly foot. At his side, Nova thudded into a tree, and Steel hit a boulder with a shower of sparks and denting metal.

Romy rose to her feet, stretched out her arms and wings, and yawned magnificently. A few dry leaves crackled in her hair of fire. "Oh my, I'm pooped." The demon blinked. "Hey, guys, look! That dinosaur you were searching for! I found it."

That dinosaur leaned down, opened its jaws wide, and prepared to swallow Romy whole.

"Damn it, Romy, fly!" Riff shouted.

The demon yelped, beat her wings, and rose with a wobble. The dinosaur's jaws snapped shut, narrowly missing Romy. The T-rex reared and opened its mouth again, attempting to catch the fleeing demon.

"Hey!" Riff shouted. He hurled a rock at the dinosaur. "Over here."

The feathered reptile spun toward him, drool spraying. The dinosaur's eyes narrowed with hatred, and it raced toward Riff.

"Down, boy, down!" Nova said. She leaped forward and cracked her whip. The dinosaur swung his own whip--a massive tail--driving it into Nova. The gladiator flew through the air, slammed into a tree, and fell down hard.

"By my honor, I will vanquish you, foul beast!" cried Steel. The knight charged forth, raising Solflare, his antique longsword. The dinosaur kicked Steel in the breastplate. The knight flew, tumbled downhill, and vanished between the trees.

Romy was snoring above in a treetop.

The dinosaur whipped its head from side to side, as if trying to decide which Alien Hunter to eat first.

I'm their leader, Riff thought. *I took this job. I brought them here. And I won't let them get eaten.*

"Hey, you giant chicken!" Riff placed his fists on his hips and flapped his elbows. "Yeah, you, you overgrown hen. Catch me!"

He spun around and began to run downhill again.

The dinosaur snorted and followed, feet shaking the forest, leaving the others behind.

Free of Romy's weight, Riff ran faster than ever. The trees blurred at his sides. The dinosaur's breath blasted his back, and the claws kept pounding down.

He slapped the communicator on his wrist.

"Giga!" he shouted. "Giga, do you hear me? Fire up the engines!"

18

The android, back on the *Dragon Huntress*, spoke through the speakers, voice chipper as always. "Happy to comply!"

In the distance, Riff heard the rumble of starship engines. The dinosaur roared in reply.

Riff jumped aside as the jaws snapped; they narrowly missed him. He ran on, following the sound of the *Dragon Huntress* rumbling ahead. He raced around a tree. The Tyrannosaurus's jaws closed around the trunk and snapped it in two. Branches rained onto Riff. He kept running downhill, reached a valley, and entered a sprawling meadow. Ahead, it rose from the mist: the *HMS Dragon Huntress*.

It was the most beautiful sight Riff had ever seen.

The ship wasn't particularly slick, elegant, or modern. Its hull was dented and scratched, its wings chipped. It could have been mistaken for a pile of scrap metal if not for its unique shape. The starship looked like a mechanical dragon, complete with a horned head that could spit out plasma like dragonfire.

"Giga, get ready to blast off!" Riff cried into his communicator.

"Happy to comply, Captain! Did you know there's a dinosaur chasing you?"

"Yes! Open the airlock! Now!"

"Happy to comply!"

Ahead in the meadow, the airlock door swung open on the starship's hull, and a staircase unfolded, stretching down toward the grass.

Riff ran across the misty field, arms pumping.

Only a few meters away from the starship, he realized that the ground was no longer shaking with footsteps, that the dinosaur was no longer roaring. Riff's heart sank. The Tyrannosaurus must have run back into the forest, eager to eat Romy, Steel, and Nova instead.

Riff turned away from the *Dragon Huntress*, prepared to reenter the forest and challenge the dinosaur again.

He nearly ran right into said dinosaur's foot.

The towering, mutated creature stood still in the grass, staring forward, a quizzical expression on its face. It seemed to have forgotten all about Riff. A choked sound left its maw.

"What the . . ." Riff muttered.

The dinosaur puffed out its chest and pawed the grass. It was staring at the *Dragon Huntress*. Ignoring Riff, it fluffed out its glimmering tail feathers.

"Oh boy," Riff said.

The dinosaur approached the idling starship, let out a beautiful bugle, and began to rub itself against the ship.

The trees rustled behind Riff, and he turned to see Nova, Steel, and Romy step out from the forest. All three were bruised and battered, and they limped across the meadow toward him.

Romy's eyes widened as she stared at the dinosaur. "I think he's a boy! And in love."

Nova covered the demon's eyes. "Don't look."

Steel grimaced and squared his shoulders. "This is ungodly."

Riff looked at the dinosaur defiling his starship, grimaced, and looked away. "Obviously, he thinks the *Dragon Huntress* is one of his kind. A lovely female of his kind, apparently."

The dinosaur bugled.

"Captain!" Giga's voice rose through his communicator. "Captain, the ship is rocking. Something is wrong."

"Very wrong," Nova muttered. "So wrong I don't think I'll ever want to fly in that ship again."

"We're flying in that ship right now." Riff walked toward the airlock; the staircase was still unfolded, leading into the ship. "Come on. Quickly. Before he's done."

"That won't be two minutes if he's anything like you," Nova muttered.

They raced into the *Dragon Huntress* one by one. Romy fell asleep halfway up the stairs, and Riff had to carry her again. Once everyone was safely inside, he shut the airlock, and they gathered on the main deck. The ship was still rocking and the dinosaur still trumpeted outside.

A trapdoor on the floor popped open. A broad, chestnut-colored head emerged, covered in fluffy white hair and a snowy beard.

"Gods of rock and metal!" rumbled Piston, chief engineer of the *Dragon Huntress*. "What is going on out there?"

Riff cringed. "I'm not sure how to describe it, but I'm pretty sure it's illegal in most star systems."

He left the main bridge, ran down the corridor, raced upstairs, and entered the command bridge. The chamber occupied the head of the mechanical dragon, its windshields affording a view of the misty valley and the mountains beyond.

Giga stood waiting here, the ship's Human Interface. The android wore a cobalt kimono embroidered with golden stars and moons. She smiled at Riff, pressed her hands together, and bowed. Her black bob cut dipped to brush her shoulders.

"Konnichiwa, sir! Welcome back to the *Dragon Huntress*. My sensors show that a giant dinosaur is busy performing a--"

"I know, now fly," Riff said.

The android tilted her head. "But sir, according to the Humanoid Alliance's wildlife conservation laws, the mating rituals of native species mustn't be disturbed, and--"

"Fly or I'm pulling out your battery."

"Happy to comply!"

The rumbling engines blasted out fire. The *HMS Dragon Huntress* soared.

The ship kept rocking.

Riff leaned sideways and stared at the mirror mounted outside the ship. He expected to see the dinosaur slide off the soaring starship, but the beast still clung on, even as the *Dragon Huntress* ascended. Its little arms clutched the hull, claws digging into the metal, and its thighs tightened like a vise. Its feathers ruffled as the ship flew.

"Sir!" Giga said. "We are currently breaking bylaw 7, section B, concerning the transportation of wild aliens without proper harnesses, and--"

"Blame Romy," Riff said. He could hear the demon snoring on the main deck even from here. "Gig, take us to the zoo. Gently. We'll land right in this big boy's pen and shake him off."

They flew over the mountains, the dinosaur still clinging on, and saw the zoo in the distance. It was filled with many extinct animals brought back to life: mammoths, dodos, pandas, and even a pen for pugs. One enclosure was empty. The *Dragon Huntress* glided down there now and thumped onto the dirt. The metal fence, which the dinosaur had mauled, was patched up, this time using reinforced steel that would take nuclear fission to break through. Riff doubted that a dinosaur that mistook a starship for his mate would be splitting the atom anytime soon.

As soon as the ship's engines were turned off, the dinosaur detached, fell onto the ground, curled up, and fell asleep.

"Definitely reminds me of you, Riff," Nova muttered.

Out the window, Riff saw the zoo director rushing into the enclosure, shouting and waving a bundle of papers. Riff left the bridge, passed through the main deck, and stepped over the slumbering Romy.

"Mommy," the demon mumbled in her sleep, "I hate Jimmy's guts. Can't we eat something else for dinner?"

Riff shuddered and quickly stepped outside.

"--and fifteen violations were broken!" the zoo director was shouting, brandishing his stack of papers. "Transportation of a wild animal without proper harnessing. Failure to sedate animal. Interference with animal's mating behavior." The zoo director flushed. "Not to mention landing a privately owned mercenary starship in zoo grounds. And--"

"We got your dinosaur back," Riff said. "Pay up, or I'm going to wake it up before I remove my starship. Your guests will get an eyeful."

Both men turned to look at the fence, where a group of school children were gaping in wonder at the sleeping dinosaur and dented metal dragon.

The zoo director flushed a deeper shade of crimson. He nodded and handed over a wad of cash.

"Excellent!" Riff patted the man on the shoulder. "Call us again anytime. That's Alien Hunters Inc. You have our number."

He returned to his starship, money in pocket. Their engines rumbled. They blasted off.

With fire, heat, and a roar that shook the sky, the *Dragon Huntress* burst through the atmosphere and emerged into the silent blackness of space.

"Captain," Romy asked over dinner that night, "is our spaceship going to have dinosaur babies?"

"What?" Riff frowned over his meal--takeout from a Happy Cow Shawarma stand orbiting the planet. "No, Romy."

The demon reached across the tabletop for a second shawarma. "Can you buy me a dinosaur baby?"

"No!"

Romy let out a huge whine. "But I want one! Buy me, buy me, buy me, buy--"

The demon's eyes rolled back, and she slumped forward, face hitting her plate. She snored into her shawarma.

"Found some leftover tranquilizer after all," Nova said, standing behind the demon, holding a syringe.

Riff sighed and stared at his fellow Alien Hunters--his crew, his friends and family, the people he cared most about in the cosmos. The snoring demon. Nova, his lover, an ashai gladiator in gold. Steel Starfire, an exiled knight still clad in plate armor, his brown mustache drooping down to his chin. Piston Bergelgruf, a burly gruffle with a long white beard, grumbling as he gnawed at his meal. Twiggle Jauntyfoot, a tiny halfling mechanic, nibbling her food. Even Giga the android sat with them, smiling sweetly, nuts and bolts on her plate.

We saved the cosmos twice, Riff thought. *First from bloodthirsty skelkrins, then from genocidal machines. And instead of living like heroes in mansions, we're trapping amorous dinosaurs and eating fast food.* He sighed, leaned back in his seat, and smiled. *And I wouldn't have it any other way.*

He was reaching for a cola when a communicator buzzed.

Instinctively, Riff looked at the communicator on his wrist-- it was the one clients normally messaged. But its screen was blank. He looked back up to see Steel staring at his own communicator, a small screen installed onto his vambrace.

The knight's gaunt cheeks paled. His lips tightened. His brown, hound dog eyes suddenly seemed more sad, more haunted than ever.

"Steel?" Riff asked, voice soft. "You all right?"

Everyone stared at the outcast knight. Steel sat stiffly, chin raised but face still pale. He turned to stare into Riff's eyes, and suddenly it seemed that Steel was no longer the grim, thirty-four-year-old knight but a mere youth. Afraid. Torn.

"It's Lenora," Steel said.

Riff's breath died in his chest. "Lenora . . ."

He remembered. Of course he did. The young woman who, years ago, had broken Steel's heart. The woman who had almost become Riff's sister-in-law. The woman who had gone on to become an esteemed scientist, whom they hadn't heard from in over a decade.

Steel nodded. "She needs our help."

CHAPTER THREE

STEEL'S LAMENT

The *HMS Dragon Huntress* flew through hyperspace, and Steel stood on the bridge, staring out into the distance.

It was past midnight, counting by Earth time, and the others all slept in their quarters. The lights were dimmed. Only Giga, the ship's interface, was here on the bridge with him. The android sat primly in one of the suede chairs, her eyes closed, asleep like the others. Outside, the lights of hyperspace streamed through the darkness: streaks of starlight, floating blue and purple orbs, and everywhere the lights of Steel's memories.

In his mind, Steel was back on Earth. No longer this haunted, haggard man but a youth. His eyes bright rather than sad. No mustache adorning his lip. No weight of armor or loss on his shoulders. A tall young man, eighteen years old, too thin, too much in love.

"I loved you more than the sun loves the sky," Steel whispered, staring into the darkness of space. "More than waves love the shore or thirsty roots love the rain. Perhaps I still do."

In the darkness, he seemed to see her face again. A girl with long brown hair, intelligent hazel eyes, and quizzical lips that loved to smile, that loved to kiss him. In those days, Steel would spend hours lying with her on the hill, watching the stars, listening to her speak of the wonders up there in the cosmos.

"And you flew off to those stars," he said softly. "You flew to shine among them, while I stayed behind. Serving your father. Choosing him over you." His throat tightened, he clenched his fists, and he lowered his head. "The man who banished me. So now I'm here, Lenora. Flying to the stars to find you."

The pain was too great, the regrets, the guilt, the thoughts of what could have been. All Steel could do was stand and struggle to breathe.

"Sir?"

The voice rose from behind him, gentle and high.

Steel turned to see Giga looking at him, her eyes soft with concern. The android had risen from her seat and stood a few paces away. As always, she wore a silken kimono, and her hair was just as silky. Yet now the delicate blossom sprouted a thorn. A katana hung across Giga's back, for the android was now more than a simple Human Interface. Piston had given her the ability to leave the *Dragon Huntress* on missions, and Giga now carried a blade just as deadly as Steel's heavy, antique longsword.

"I'm sorry I woke you, my lady." Steel bowed his head. "I will return to my quarters. And . . ." He looked back up at her. "You need not call me 'sir.' You know that."

She nodded. "And you need not call me 'my lady.'" A soft smile touched her lips. "You're no longer a knight, and I'm no longer a mere interface. We're both Alien Hunters now, nothing more or less. Yet we still speak like our old selves. Perhaps we still cling to our pasts." She stepped closer to him and put a hand against his chest. "The past can be hard to let go of."

Steel nodded, those memories always a pain inside him. Lenora's kisses, then her tears as she flew away. Her father's hard eyes, accusing, condemning Steel to exile. The long loneliness. The ridicule. The proud knight who had become an outcast in the countryside, a modern Don Quixote, the sigil of his order scratched off his armor.

"Do androids suffer from memories too?" He tucked an errant strand of Giga's hair behind her ear. "Do you too sometimes stare outside and remember?"

She nodded. Her voice was barely more than a whisper. "Androids remember. Androids dream. In my memories, I'm possessed by the Singularity again, flying through space to my master, calling upon him to destroy my body and claim my soul." She touched Steel's cheek, gazing into his eyes. "And in my memories, there is a man. A hero flying toward me through the darkness. A knight who saved me. Memories are like that, Steel. Some are full of pain, of shame, of loss, but others are joyous. Do not let your own demons possess you."

"My lady--I mean, Giga." He placed his hand over hers. "You are wise, Giga. That is a good memory for me too. Flying after you. Bringing you home to us."

"Home to you," she whispered.

For a moment, they stood staring into each other's eyes. A man of flesh in a metal shell. A woman of synthetic skin over a skeleton of metal. Two souls perhaps torn, perhaps lost. Giga's jasmine scent filled Steel's nostrils, and her eyes were soft, her hand warm against his cheek. Perhaps it was the shadows and lights, perhaps the memories of old love, but for the first time, Giga seemed to Steel not merely an android, not merely a fellow Alien Hunter, not merely a damsel to save, but a true woman. A woman who could love. A woman such as a young, bright-eyed man with no pain in his heart might have loved a long time ago.

"You lost someone," Giga whispered. "But you found us. You found me."

Her lips parted, and she leaned closer, and Steel wanted to embrace her, to kiss her, yet more confusion than ever filled him. He turned back toward the windshield. She turned with him. They stood together, holding hands, staring out at the shadows and streams of light.

* * * * *

Two Earth-weeks after setting out on their journey, the *Dragon Huntress* emerged from hyperspace to find a plane of existence even more surreal.

To Steel, all of space was strange. He had spent years of his life in a small, homemade castle in the countryside, riding a horse across the countryside, shunning technology. To him, the fields and forests of Old Earth were a cosmos entire. Yet in the past year, he had seen sights that still spun his mind: stars and galaxies that shone in the darkness, brighter than any lantern; massive, crablike warships of skelkrin predators; fleets battling over a planet-sized computer; and the eyes of an android, a machine built by man, that gazed at him with more warmth and love than most humans possessed.

Yet nothing in his journeys had prepared Steel for what he now saw--or rather, what he did not see.

A chunk of existence was missing before him.

"Yep," Riff said, standing at Steel's side on the bridge. "It's a black hole all right."

Steel kept staring out the windshield, unable to tear his eyes away. Calling this emptiness "black" seemed wrong. It made normal black objects seem bright as day. The hole in space wasn't just black, it was . . . almost alive. Almost a presence that drew his gaze, that tried to suck him in the way it sucked in all light.

"Specifically, the black hole Yurei," Giga said, sitting at the controls. "Several irregularities make it unique among black holes, drawing many physicists to study it. Would you like us to fly by the event horizon, Captain? I can take us just close enough that we'll have only a 6.8 percent chance of falling in."

Riff grimaced. "No thanks, Giga. We can barely land this ship without crashing. I don't trust us flying along a black hole's rim."

Clouds of luminous dust, several asteroids, and a rocky planet orbited the black hole. Steel pointed at the barren charcoal world.

"Is that planet Kaperosa?" he asked.

Giga nodded. "Yes, sir. A small planet, no larger than Earth's moon back home, and just as rocky and desolate. Current population: seventy-four, all scientists stationed in Kaperosa Observatory, studying Yurei. Well . . ." Giga tilted her head. "Following the news we received, seventy-three."

They flew closer to the planet. Steel stared, an iciness growing inside him. Even from this distance, he could see the observatory--a dim light--upon the rocky surface of Kaperosa. A small scientific outpost. Seventy-three souls. The woman he loved. And a dark presence, an evil Lenora would not explain in her message.

Steel tore his eyes away from the approaching planet, looked at his communicator, and read Lenora's words again.

Dearest Steel,

I wanted to open this letter with a conversational "Hello!" Or perhaps with an innocuous "How have you been? I've been well." I thought to ease into my words, to somehow break the ice with the small talk I know you've always thought useless. Truth is I don't know what to say, don't know how to make you believe that, for many years, I wanted to write to you but could not. That, for many years--for all these years--I've been thinking of you.

It's funny, isn't it? They say time heals all hurts. What a contemptible lie! Time loses all meaning in the darkness of space and the hidden burrows of the heart.

And now I've switched from small talk to bad poetry. I've always been better with numbers than with words, haven't I? I could speak to you for hours about the sky's equations, yet I could never properly tell you how much I loved you. How much it hurt when I left.

Yet now I need you, Steel. I need you here with me, among the stars whose tales I would endlessly regale you with. Because I've found something in the darkness. Something darker than space, darker than the innards of the black hole I now orbit. Something that invaded my observatory, that stole the life of a young woman, that still haunts us, stalks us, waits for us in the shadows.

My comrades call it a ghost. Yet what is a ghost if not a form of alien life? And so I'm writing to you, Steel Starfire, Alien Hunter. I need you. Now more than ever. Come back to me.

Always yours,

Lenora

As he read the letter, Steel could still imagine her, every detail: her brown tresses, her sparkling hazel eyes, the woolen skirts and sweaters she wore. He returned his eyes to the planet ahead. Would Lenora look different now, sixteen years later? Would he even recognize her?

I myself am almost unrecognizable, he thought. The tall, slender youth had become a haggard man. His brow was now lined, his temples graying, and a mustache drooped down to his chin. He was only thirty-four yet he looked a decade older. Lenora's father had taken him into the knighthood, the ancient order Steel had chosen over love, only to banish him, and those long years of exile had aged Steel. He had gone from carefree boy to somber knight to haunted outcast. Perhaps the question was: Would Lenora recognize *him*?

"Steel, you all right, buddy?" Riff came to stand beside him.

Steel stared ahead, jaw tight. "I am ready to do my duty, brother. Always. By my honor, we shall defeat whatever evil lurks on this observatory."

"That's not what I meant." Riff came to stand between Steel and the view. "I know this must be hard. When I had to go to Nova for help last year, it seemed to break something inside me, and--"

"A knight is always ready to defend the weak." Steel raised his chin. "Do not worry yourself, brother. My sword is ready. Always."

More words, Steel thought. Old words of old traditions. Perhaps his own version of "small talk." Perhaps another form of armor he wore to protect his soul, as surely as his metal plates protected his body.

Riff nodded. "If you want to talk about things, at any time, let me know." He slapped Steel's arm. "Until then, we go hunting."

As Riff wandered off to argue with Nova about something, Steel returned his eyes to the planet. The *Dragon Huntress* was growing near now. The rocky world covered Steel's field of vision, blessedly hiding that black hole. He could see Kaperosa Observatory below: a network of domes and walkways that clung to the planet like barnacles.

Lenora is in there. Lenora and whatever haunts her.

"Engaging thruster engines," Giga said. "Preparing to land."

With blasts of steam, the *Dragon Huntress* glided toward a small spaceport outside the observatory. A single ship was docked there--a large transport vessel, shaped like a dagger with wings as its crossguard. With screeches, clanks, and sputtering smoke, the mechanical dragon thumped down onto the surface.

Steel took a deep breath.

It's time.

For years, living alone in his castle, he had fantasized about this moment: of flying out to the stars, finding Lenora, trying to rekindle what they had lost. Now the moment was here, and he feared it--more than any ghosts that haunted distant halls.

Yet I'll do what I must. Your father might have stripped off my sigil, Lenora, but my heart is still the heart of a knight. I made a vow to protect those in need, and I will protect you too.

He turned to leave the bridge, hand clutching Solflare's hilt.

The others joined him: Nova with her whip, Giga with her katana, Twig with her wrench, Piston with his hammer, Riff with his gun, Romy with her pitchfork. They were his friends, his family, yet how could they understand the pain inside him?

As Steel walked toward the airlock, the others followed him, letting him take the lead. He was not the captain of this ship. He was not even second-in-command, a title Nova claimed. But on this mission, they knew to let him walk first. Perhaps they understood more than Steel knew.

Through the porthole, Steel saw a walkway stretch out from the observatory and attach to the *Dragon Huntress*'s airlock. Steel took a deep breath, opened that airlock, and stepped off his ship.

He entered the walkway and saw her there.

Steel froze, unable to walk any farther, unable to breathe.

"Lenora," he whispered.

* * * * *

"Steel." Tears flooded Lenora's eyes, and for a moment she stood still, hesitating. "I don't know what to say. Do I hug you?"

Steel stood before her in the walkway, his fellow Alien Hunters behind him, feeling so afraid, so awkward, even his armor not shielding him.

Lenora looked so much the same. Sixteen years had gone by, yet she looked like she had at eighteen--a beautiful woman of long brown hair and intelligent eyes. She still even wore her woolen vest and skirt. He had gone through hell and back, emerging a ruin of a man, yet she was still a flower of youth and innocence. And he still loved her. Steel realized that he'd never stopped loving her, and tears threatened to fill his eyes, and all his strength seemed to sap away.

He raised his chin. He had to cling to his strength, to his honor, the only armor that might still protect him.

"My lady, you've summoned me, and so I come. To serve. To protect. To defend the needy, to--"

"Yes. A hug." Lenora nodded, sniffing tears, and pulled him into her embrace. "Oh, Steel. Thank you for coming." She touched his mustache, laughing and blinking away her tears. "Look at you."

He smiled wryly, his arms awkwardly wrapped around her. "I aged for both of us. You look as beautiful as always."

More tears fell down her cheeks. "I heard what my father did to you, what happened, what--" She wiped her eyes, then smiled shakily. She caressed his cheek. "You look wonderful. Handsome as always. A hero."

He bowed his head. "Not a hero, Lenora. Only a man of honor."

She smiled, tears spiking her lashes, and looked across his shoulder. Her smile widened.

"Riff!" Lenora said. "Look at you. Same as always. Still wearing a *Space Galaxy* shirt."

Riff's grinned, stepped forward, and embraced her. "I'm pretty sure it's the exact same *Space Galaxy* shirt." He kissed her cheek. "Good to see you, Lenora. How's your little brother?"

Her face darkened. Her smile vanished. "Dee is . . . not well. He . . ." She wrung her hands. "A story for another time. Right now, we're in danger, and I'm being rude. Talking to you here in a walkway! Not even introducing myself to everyone." She waved to the other Alien Hunters. "My name is Lenora Rosetta, chief administrator of Kaperosa Observatory. Come with me, into the compound. Let me find you all something to drink and eat. You must be tired from the journey."

"Do you have any poodles?" Romy asked.

"No eating poodles!" Nova cracked her whip.

Lenora blinked, then shook her head and began to walk. The Alien Hunters followed, leaving their ship behind and entering the narrow halls of a haunted observatory.

CHAPTER FOUR

OBSERVING GHOSTS

Romy was bored.

Bored, bored, bored, *bored.*

Finally--*finally*--Captain Riff had let Romy off the ship in public, and it wasn't on any exciting planet full of crazy animals to eat. It was in a science station. Science! The boringest invention humans had ever come up with.

As the others sat in some *boring* lab, talking about *boring* numbers and calculations and other things that made Romy's brain hurt, she tiptoed away and sneaked into a corridor.

The devil may have invented algebra, Romy thought, *but that doesn't mean his demons have to understand it.*

She kept moving down the corridor, leaving the others behind. Dim lights shone overhead, and the walls were too close. Romy felt like she were walking back in Hell's tunnels.

"Romy!" rose Riff's voice from somewhere behind. "Damn it, Romy, where are you?"

"Let her wander off." It was Nova's voice speaking now. "Maybe she'll fly toward the black hole and fall in."

Ooh, fall into a black hole! That sounded splendid. Romy's tail wagged as she walked. She wondered if she could find a way out of the observatory, fly into space, and try falling into that black hole. She'd need to find a space suit and a jetpack, and she wasn't sure how she'd fly back here, but it would be interesting, and--

Two scientists came walking around a corner, saw Romy, and froze.

"Hiya." Romy waved a clawed hand, and her flaming hair crackled.

The pair screamed, spun around, and fled.

"Wait up!" Romy said. "I'm a demon, not a ghost! Wait! Hey, do you have any poodles around here? I'm famished."

She gave chase for a while, but the scientists vanished. Romy paused, panting, utterly lost. This whole observatory was more confusing than the network of heating vents back in the *Dragon Huntress*. Indeed, Romy felt as if she were exploring some coiling metal labyrinth. Corridors connected to cluttered labs full of dials, monitors, tubes, and telescopes. Ladders rose and fell. Lights flickered. Doorways whooshed open and thumped shut. The observatory hadn't looked too large from above, but now it seemed endless to Romy.

She remembered herself many eras ago, a young demon wandering the tunnels of Hell. This place was a little like Hell--too dark, too stifling, too dangerous. There was evil here. Romy could smell it.

Or maybe I'm just smelling myself, she thought. *I'm evil. I'm a demon after all.*

A glint of starlight caught her eye. Romy walked down a hallway and found herself in a round glass chamber. There were no solid walls here, just a transparent dome, revealing a view of space beyond. Romy felt as if she had entered the helmet of a giant astronaut.

A massive telescope stood here, larger than Romy, pointing toward space. Romy's tail wagged furiously, and she raced forward and hopped right onto the telescope.

"Onward, noble steed!" She kneed the telescope. "I am Sir Steel Starfire, a stuffy knight with crumbs in my mustache. I command you--gallop! Show me the meaning of haste." The telescope bobbed, and Romy beat her wings, spinning it around in circles. "Faster, loyal stallion! To battle, to--"

The telescope spun around to face the black hole outside, and Romy swallowed her words.

Yurei, the great black eye, seemed to fill her vision. She stared into the abyss. And it stared back into her.

It's alive, Romy thought. A shiver ran through her from her horns to her tail's tip. *It's looking at me.*

Suddenly she wasn't so sure she wanted to fall into that black hole after all.

She tried to look away but could not. Yurei seemed to be tugging her. Her hair crackled madly. She slid forward on the telescope--no, not slid but *pulled*, reeled in toward the blackness. She wrapped her thighs around the telescope, trying to hold on, to stay here, not to fall in, not to get sucked up, to vanish into that emptiness.

Red one . . . The voice spoke in her head. *Being of fire . . . come to me . . .*

"No," Romy whispered. "Please."

The black hole seemed to expand, to mock her, to laugh. *Come join the darkness.*

Romy couldn't tear her eyes away, no more than she could have torn off a part of her body. She sucked in air, struggling to breathe. Her legs were frozen, her head locked, but her tail still seemed to work. She gave a hard wag, and the telescope spun on its hinge.

The telescope swiveled away, and the black hole vanished from her line of sight. She found herself facing the shadowy back of the chamber.

There was no glass here--only a dark wall, a few instruments in the shadows, a bookshelf, a door. Romy exhaled shakily with relief.

Suddenly she no longer felt like exploring. She slid off the telescope, careful to keep looking at the wall, away from that great black eye she could still feel staring at her.

"I'm going to go back now," she said, speaking to the black hole behind her. "Back to my friends, to--"

A shadow stirred ahead.

Romy froze. Cold sweat washed her.

Shelves clattered. The door creaked. Red eyes opened in the darkness.

"Red one . . ." A presence spoke in the shadows, voice hoarse, deep, echoing--a voice from another world. "Come . . . to us . . ."

The shadows coalesced into a tall form, only half there. A ghostly hand reached out, woven of smoke, ending with black claws.

Romy screamed and thrust her pitchfork.

"A ghost!" she cried. "A ghost in the observatory!"

Swinging her pitchfork, she burst into a run.

She whipped around the shadowy being and barged out the doorway. Those claws lashed, and she screamed. Her arm blazed with pain. Her blood spurted. She kept racing down a corridor, leaving the lab behind.

"Ghost in the observatory! Ghost! Riff, where are you?"

That hoarse, echoing voice laughed behind her, and the darkness covered Romy's vision, and tendrils like a thousand clawed arms reached around her. Romy ran through the hallways as fast as she could, lost and trapped in the darkness.

* * * * *

"Ghosts?" Riff shook his head. "Nonsense. There's no such thing as ghosts."

"I'm pretty sure your underwear is haunted," Nova muttered, flicking her whip.

He groaned. "Must you talk about my underwear *every* time we meet a client?"

They all stood back in the domed chamber where Romy had claimed to see the ghost. Planet Kaperosa had since spun on its axis, and the observatory now faced away from the black hole;

the dome gazed upon a comforting starry sky. Riff and Nova stood side by side, while Steel examined the shadows. Romy sat in the corner, wrapped in a blanket, drinking from a mug of hot cocoa.

"I did see a ghost!" The demon shuddered. "A real ghost. A scary one."

Nova rolled her eyes. "You're a demon, for pity's sake. How could you be scared of ghosts?"

"Because they're scary!" Romy said. "Almost as scary as that time I opened the dryer and Riff's underwear flew onto me."

"Will everyone *please* stop talking about my underwear!" Riff turned toward Lenora, and his voice softened. "Does the demon's description sound familiar, Lenora?"

The young scientist stood by the glass wall, staring out into space. Her voice was low, so soft Riff barely heard. "Humans have always been frightened of the dark, yet drawn to it. Forever we've feared the unknown, yet sought to know it." She turned toward Riff, eyes damp. "Until now, our light could always banish the shadows. Here at last, in the endless darkness of space, we found a shadow that would not flee."

Somehow those words chilled Riff more than a thousand of Romy's ghost stories.

"What do you know about this ghost?" Riff said, hating that his voice sounded so thin.

"Ghost?" Lenora turned toward him and blinked. "No, Riff. I don't believe in ghosts either. I cannot. I will not. What we found here is alien life--a life not solid, liquid, or gas. A life we don't understand, a life from somewhere beyond. But life nonetheless. Life hostile. Cruel. Life that kills. These creatures-- and yes, we've spotted more than one here--have killed four of my scientists already. Their claws reach out, touch a living human . . . and that human vanishes."

Riff paced the chamber. With the planet facing away from the black hole, and with everyone around him, it was hard to imagine evil lurking in this place. Yet the scratches on Romy's arm were real.

"Play the footage, Lenora," Riff said, turning toward the monitor on the wall.

The young scientist nodded and pressed a button. The security video played on a wall-mounted monitor, showing Romy entering the observatory and riding the telescope.

"Are you pretending to be an amorous dinosaur?" Nova asked the demon.

Romy groaned. "I'm pretending to be Steel on a noble steed."

Nova tilted her head, staring at the footage. "It looks more like you're doing something unspeakable to it."

The demon began to object, and Nova scoffed, and Steel began to lecture Nova on her tongue, and the other Alien Hunters in the back of the room were laughing, and Lenora stared around in shock, and--

"Enough!" Riff roared. "Quiet, all of you. Just watch."

They all turned back toward the monitor. The footage now showed a shadowy figure materialize in the back of the room. Riff squinted, trying to make sense of it. The apparition flickered, swelled, shrunk, always changing shape, never quite turning solid. Red eyes kindled in its blobby head.

"Watch carefully, everyone." Romy pointed. "This is the part where I valiantly defeat the evil creature of shadows."

In the video, Romy wailed and made to flee, only to step on her tail and crash facedown. The demon beat her wings, soared, and slammed her head against the ceiling. Finally she stumbled out the doorway, fell again, and ended up hopping away with her hands on the floor, moving like an ape.

"Truly you are a valiant warrior," Nova said.

"The camera lies!" Romy bit her lip. "It also adds ten pounds."

"As does consuming entire boxes of donuts." Nova pointed at the floor where lay a cardboard box, crumbs and sparkles and demon drool inside it.

"I was hungry!" Romy pouted. "Ghost hunting makes you hungry. If you ever encountered a ghost, you . . ."

As everyone started bickering again, Riff tuned it out and turned toward Lenora.

"It seems we've found a pattern," he said. "Every time this ghost appeared, the witness was alone, facing the black hole." Riff frowned. "You told us this black hole is irregular. That scientists from across the galaxy flock here to study it. Why?"

Lenora was staring in wonder as Romy and Nova were slapping each other, with Steel, Twig, and Piston all trying to tug the combatants apart. The scientist blinked, shook her head in confusion, and returned her gaze to Riff.

"Yurei is unlike any black hole we've encountered," she said. "Black holes are, essentially, stars that collapsed under their own gravity. The forces of gravity are so strong, they suck in all four dimensions--the three physical dimensions as well as time. Even light cannot escape a black hole. But this black hole . . . our data shows that spacetime is sucked inside in a strange flow. It's as if there's . . . a chunk missing from the black hole. A piece in the middle, something we can't see, which causes our calculations to break. Almost as if there's something lodged in that black hole's throat. In fact, this black hole doesn't even seem to be round. More like . . . donut shaped."

"Donuts?" Romy perked up. "Where? Me want!" The demon salivated.

Nova dragged her away. "Shut it, or I'm going to shove you into our starship's engines and bake *you* into donuts."

Romy gasped. "Really? Can you put icing on me? Ooh, and sprinkles! Purple ones." She furrowed her brow. "Do you think I'd be able to eat myself forever?"

"Shut it!"

Riff closed his eyes, trying to ignore the noise. A black hole with a piece missing. Ghosts that appeared in the shadows, making people vanish. How could he fight something he didn't even understand, couldn't even touch?

"Captain, sir!" Rough hands tugged at his pants. "Captain! I've been going over the data, and I think I can trap one of them shady buggers."

Riff opened his eyes, looked down, and saw Piston rifling through a sheaf of papers. The gruffle stood a good foot shorter than Riff but twice as wide, his stocky body suited for the massive, rocky world he had come from. His white eyebrows bunched together, and his dark face screwed up in concentration. He tugged at his beard as he looked over a long string of equations on his papers.

"Trap one?" Riff said.

"Aye sir." Piston nodded emphatically. "I've been going over the numbers Lenora showed me, and well, sir . . . seems these are physical beings. Solid as you and me." Piston sucked his teeth. "Meaning we can trap them."

"Physical beings?" Riff tilted his head. "Piston, they look like ghosts. All smoky and . . . blobby."

Piston's bushy eyebrows rose. "Well, your eyes will deceive you, sir. Eyes do that. But numbers don't lie. These creatures have shadows, have a weight to them. I'm thinking a good, solid electromagnetic field, mounted between metal rods, should do the trick."

Riff sighed. "So long as we don't build a metal, female ghost for them to defile."

Piston nodded. "Aye, sir. I'll get right to building some traps. We'll set 'em across the observatory before the planet turns toward the black hole again." The gruffle looked over his shoulder. "Twig! Twig, you clod, where are you? Get down from that shelf! Go to the ship and fetch me our magnet poles."

Twig, no larger than a human child, was sitting atop a bookshelf, leafing through engineering books. She raised her eyes, blinked, and stared at Piston. "Magnets? You need to wipe another hard drive? Piston, I told you, nobody cares that you look at gruffle ladies on cyberspace. With their beards, they all look like men anyway, and--"

"Twig!" Piston roared, raced toward her, and began a doomed attempt to climb the bookshelf.

Riff winced as the shelves collapsed, raining books.

"I'm sorry," Riff said, turning toward Lenora. "I'm so sorry. I know we're not the most elegant pest controllers, but I promise you: We always get the job done. I--" Another crash sounded behind him, and Riff spun around. "Will you lot stop that! Show some respect, and--"

He frowned. The other Alien Hunters stared back at him, still and silent, the room untouched. The rumbling, crashing sound continued, and Riff realized it had come from the distance--from outside.

He stepped toward the round, glass wall and stared out at the spaceport. Alongside the *Dragon Huntress* stood the observatory's own starship: the silver, dagger-shaped *Drake*. Both ships' engines were rumbling. Smoke blasted out from their engines. They rose a few feet off the surface and hovered.

Riff looked around him. All the other Alien Hunters were here, even Giga.

"There are no scientists on the *Drake*," Lenora whispered.

"And nobody on the *Dragon Huntress*." Riff stared outside and his belly knotted. Through his ship's windshields, he thought he could see just the hint of swirling shadows.

"Ghost pilots," Romy whispered.

Riff spun away from the glass. He ran.

"What the hell's going on, Riff?" Nova shouted, running at his side.

"Our ships are being hijacked, that's what!" he said, racing through the halls.

Leaving us marooned here. His heart thudded. *Marooned on a dead, haunted planet orbiting a black hole.*

The ships' engines roared outside, and Riff cursed with every step.

CHAPTER FIVE

DRAGON RISING

Riff burst into the observatory's airlock, the last chamber between the laboratories and the rocky planet outside. Through the window, he could see both ships taking off, blasting down fire. The walkway, which had connected the *Dragon Huntress* to the observatory, lay in tatters on the planet's surface.

God damn it.

Riff whipped his head from side to side. Airlocks usually had a few spacesuits in them, and--there! He raced toward the wall where three suits hung, complete with jetpacks. He grabbed one and began to suit up.

"Steel! Nova!" he shouted.

They nodded, ran forward, and grabbed the last two space suits. None of them fit well, but they would have to serve. When Riff glanced out the window, he saw that both ships had already risen kilometers into the sky.

He pulled on his helmet and strapped on his jet pack.

"Everyone who's not in a suit, stay back in the corridor," he said. "Lenora, can you depressurize the airlock?"

The brown-haired scientist nodded, fear in her eyes. Standing in the corridor, she closed the airlock's inner door. Only

Riff, Steel, and Nova now stood in airlock, wearing suits and helmets.

The outer door opened. The air whooshed out.

Captain, knight, and gladiator ran onto the rocky surface of Kaperosa and kick-started their jet packs.

With roaring fire, they soared.

Riff clenched his jaw as his head rattled inside his helmet; it was too large. Steel soared to his right, and Nova to his left. Far above, Riff could see the two starships.

"Make for the *Dragon Huntress*!" Riff said into his helmet's communicator.

Nova's voice crackled to life, emerging from his helmet's speakers. "Really, Riff? I thought you wanted us to fly into the black hole!"

Riff curved his flight, rising toward the mechanical dragon above. Steel and Nova flew with him. If they could save only one ship, it would be the one they knew inside and out.

God damn it, faster!

Riff pressed the jet pack's throttle as far as it would go. The flames roared out, yet the *Dragon Huntress* was moving too fast, too far away.

We're not going to make it. Horror pounded through Riff. *It's going to fly away, and we'll be marooned here, a hundred light-years from civilization.*

He was cursing, the fear washing over him, when the *Dragon Huntress* turned to face him.

For just an instant, hope filled Riff. The ship was coming back!

Then he saw the cannon in the dragon's mouth heat up.

Fear flooded Riff, colder than the icy wastelands of the frozen planet Teelana.

"Scatter!" he shouted.

He tugged his jetpack's controls, shooting to his left. Steel flew to the right, and Nova blasted forward.

The *Dragon Huntress* spewed out her dragonfire.

The plasma showered down, a blazing jet, white and blue and flaring out to red.

Riff barely dodged the flames. The heat blazed against his boots' soles, melting them. He curved his flight and kept soaring. The fire slammed against the planet below, melting rocks.

"To the *Dragon*'s airlock!" Riff shouted. His jetpack thrummed.

"You think, Riff?" Nova said. "I thought we'd fly through the exhaust pipe!"

The gladiator soared beside him, her electric whip flailing. The *Dragon Huntress* blasted down more flame. The starship now spun in the sky, spraying dragonfire in a curtain. Riff cursed, whipping from side to side, barely dodging the flames. Steel shouted in the distance as fire splashed his arm, melting the space suit, but the knight kept soaring. The *Drake*, meanwhile, faded into the distance--now far beyond their reach.

Before the flames could rain again, Riff reached the *Dragon Huntress*, turned off his jetpack, and slammed into the hull.

He grunted with pain, clawing for purchase. With thuds, Steel and Nova slammed into the hull too, denting the metal, cursing.

The *Dragon Huntress* flew a good fifty kilometers above the surface now. The observatory was barely visible below, a mere glint on Kaperosa's rocky surface. In the distance, Riff could see it now, rising above the planet's horizon: the black hole.

Riff Starfire . . . spoke a voice in his head. *We will break you . . . We see your death . . . We see your death in pain . . .*

Riff tried to look away. He could not. The black hole tugged at his gaze. He felt as if somebody had driven wires into his eyeballs, forcing him to stare into the abyss.

And that abyss was staring back. Mocking him.

It's alive, he thought. *Yurei is a living being. A cruel entity. A dark queen.*

Her black soul bored into him, consuming him, driving through his innards.

You will worship me . . . You will call me Mistress . . .

Riff's eyes burned. His breath shook.

"Mi . . . Mis . . ."

"Riff, damn it!" Nova said. Clinging to the hull beside him, she yanked him toward her. Riff screamed as his gaze tore free from the black hole; it felt as if somebody had pulled scabs off his eyes. He shook his head wildly, banishing that unearthly voice. When he stared across the hull, he saw Steel open the airlock, exposing the staircase that led toward the main deck. The knight climbed in and Nova followed.

With a deep breath, Riff joined them, entering the *Dragon Huntress*.

They raced upstairs, barged into the main deck . . . and found the ghosts waiting for them.

Riff hissed. He couldn't fire his plasma gun in here, but he could still pistol-whip with the best of them. At his side, Steel raised his sword, and Nova cracked her whip.

The ghosts stared back at them with red eyes. For the first time, Riff got a good look at the creatures.

Yet, even staring directly at them, he could not decide what they looked like. The ghosts were constantly changing: bulging, shrinking, twisting. One moment the creatures were blobby, the next stick-thin. One moment they seemed to raise beefy arms, and the next, their limbs tapered into blades. They were shimmering black with just a hint of blue and purple, woven not of smoke as he had once thought. They were beings of flesh--solid flesh that reflected the light, that cast shadows--yet somehow . . . not fully here. Flickering in and out of existence, half in this world, half in some world beyond, unable to fully enter this plane of existence.

Even as their forms swayed, their eyes kept burning. Red. Cruel. Lusting for blood. Fanged mouths opened in their heads, and laughter rose from them. Ghostly laughter from another world.

"Welcome to your grave, ones of three," one of the ghosts said.

Riff looked around him. "This is Greenpine Cemetery, North Cog City?" He snorted. "I paid good money for a plot here, and the place looks like a dump. I was scammed."

"Not Greenpine," Nova said, "but just as haunted. What say you, Riff old boy, want to bust some ghosts? It's good exorcise."

He hefted Ethel, his heavy plasma gun. "Let's give these ghosts some boo-boos."

"Trick or treat time, baby," Nova said.

Riff nodded. "That's the spirit!"

Nova cracked her whip. "Whips are a ghoul's best friend, after all."

Steel groaned. "Will you two stop with the ghost puns and fight?"

With a sad shake of his head, the knight charged into battle, sword swinging. An instant later, Riff and Nova joined him.

One of the ghosts lunged toward Riff, bulging out, expanding to twice its previous size. With a hiss, Riff swung his gun, trying to slam the metal against the creature. But the ghostly alien contracted, a portion of its body pulling back to escape the gun. A clawed hand appeared out of nowhere to slam into Riff.

He cried out and fell back, blood dripping down his arm.

At his sides, his companions seemed to be faring no better. Steel swung his blade, but the apparitions kept changing form, bodies shrinking, growing, vanishing, reappearing, dodging the sword every time. Nova's whip swung, but the electric lash found no targets either. Whenever a weapon swung, the aliens changed their forms, then lunged with claws.

A dark hand slammed into Steel, cracking the knight's armor. A long digit whipped--perhaps a tail or a tentacle--slamming into Nova, then vanishing. The gladiator fell, her whip showering sparks.

A shadow drove toward Riff and grabbed his throat. Red eyes stared into him, burning with hatred.

Now, one of three . . . you scream.

And Riff screamed.

His skull unfolded.

His vision opened up.

And he saw it. He saw . . . full awareness. Shadows. Black fog in the air, a living thing, evil taken form. A hill that was a thousand hills. A rose upon its top, simultaneously wilting and blooming. A distant mountain that was a thousand distant mountains.

No. No. Riff wept. *It's too much.*

It was too wide, too much to see, too much to feel. All his life, his mind had viewed the world from within his skull--seeing, hearing, smelling, experiencing a flat reality. No more. Now the cosmos itself opened up, revealing . . . a child. Scared. An old man. Dying. A ship that was a thousand ships. And everywhere that red flower on that black hill, and beyond it . . . the mistress.

The Dark Queen.

Waiting for him.

It's Hell. I'm looking at Hell.

Riff ground his teeth.

"No!" he shouted. "No. No! Enough! I refuse! I will not join you there, I will not see this!"

He yanked his soul back into his body. His consciousness snapped back into his skull, sucked up like a noodle into a mouth.

He blinked, almost surprised to find himself back in a single starship. Where were the thousand--the millions--of *Dragon Huntresses* he had seen, the worlds folded into worlds? He was back in but a dream, a speck lost within a speck of a cosmos.

And the ghosts were still here.

Riff swung his gun, driving back the creature that had grabbed him.

"Nova, Steel, hold onto something!" he shouted.

The pair were still fighting the ghosts, with little success. Every thrust of their weapons missed, and both were cut and bleeding.

"Riff!" Nova shouted. "What are you--Riff, no!"

He nodded. "It's the only way. Now hold on!"

Nova groaned and grabbed onto the ladder that led to the attic. Steel's eyes darkened, and he grabbed on too.

"Time for an exorcism," Riff said . . . and hit the airlock controls.

Both doors swung open at once.

With a shriek, the air began fleeing the *Dragon Huntress*.

Riff was too far to grab the wall-mounted ladder, but he clung to the couch like a drowning man to a dolphin.

The ship roared, screeched, fluttered with fury. The board of counter-squares flew off the table. Pieces slammed into Riff like hail. Romy's crayon artwork tore off the walls and flew out the airlock. The goldfish was sucked right out of his bowl and flapped into space. Darts tore off the dartboard and flew like missiles; one scraped across Riff's shoulder. Dishes clattered. Toilet paper rolls flew like comets, leaving papery trails. The fleeing air was a typhoon, taking everything with it.

Including the ghosts.

The shadowy creatures streamed in the wind, stretching out into dark strands. They screamed, sounds like shattering glass, like snapping bones, like breaking minds. Their limbs fluttered, seeking purchase, finding none. One whooshed over Riff and blasted out of the airlock. Another followed. More streamed from deeper in the ship, draining from the corridors, the engine room, the attic, tumbling out into space.

The couch Riff clung to scraped across the floor, then lodged itself in the doorway. Riff held on, legs in the air, fingers nearly slipping.

"Are they all gone?" Nova shouted, clinging to the ladder on the wall.

"Yes, along with almost everything else."

Holding the ladder with one hand, Nova swung her whip. The lash hit the airlock controls, and the door slammed shut.

Riff fell to the floor, panting.

"Good thing we had these space suits on, isn't it?" he said into the vacuum.

Nova nodded. "Especially with us crashing."

"Yeah." Riff frowned. "Wait, what?"

"Crashing." Nova pointed out the porthole. "Crashing toward a massive rocky planet."

Riff ran.

The starship tilted around him.

He raced along the corridor, leaping over scattered plates, bed sheets, and clothes. He leaped onto the bridge and, through the windshield, beheld the planet racing up toward them.

Riff stumbled toward the controls and grabbed the joystick. He tugged back with all his might.

The *Dragon Huntress* reared in the sky, raising its nose away from the planet. But they were still moving too fast. The surface of Kaperosa approached at dizzying speed. The observatory lay below, its starship lot barren.

We're going to crash into the observatory.

Riff pressed the forward thrusters, desperate to slow the ship. He steadied its flight. He raised the nose a few degrees. He directed the *Dragon Huntress* toward the lot, prepared to guide it down.

A shadow stirred.

A dark figure rose before him.

Claws reached out.

Riff tried to leap back, and his hand slipped from the joystick. Shadows swirled. Nova and Steel cried out and leaped onto the bridge.

With a shower of fire and light, the *Dragon Huntress* slammed into the planet. Metal bent. Glass shattered. Then only the shadows remained.

CHAPTER SIX

MAROONED

Steel groaned.

Everything hurt.

It felt like an entire starship had fallen onto him. Which, he supposed, was not far off.

"Steel! Steel, can you hear me?"

The voice sounded miles away. A voice from another world. Were the ghosts calling him, summoning him back to that place? The memories filled Steel, and he shuddered. Again he saw that place--the place he had seen on the starship when the ghost had cut his armor and arm. The black hill, reflected countless times. The dark presence that filled the air, the sky, the soil. The rose, and him crawling, trying to reach the flower, to save it, knowing that the Dark Queen lurked beyond, and--

"Steel!"

The voice pulled him into the present. Steel blinked and moaned in pain. He looked up. He lay in ruins, pinned down under metal and glass. Flashlight beams waved back and forth, and a distant strobe light flickered. A figure stood above, small and dark, a silhouette.

Steel stiffened and reached for his sword, sure it was another ghost. But then the shadow spoke again, and he recognized that voice.

"Steel, can you hear me?"

"Giga!" he said, voice hoarse.

The android needed no space suit or helmet. She wore nothing but her kimono, and her katana hung across her back. She grabbed the metal beam that pinned Steel down and lifted it off him. It was a beam the strongest men would crumble under, but the android tossed it aside like a twig.

She knelt beside him. "Oh, Steel. You're hurt."

He did not spare himself a glance. He pushed himself onto his elbows. He still lay inside the *Dragon Huntress*, he saw. The ship had crashed and lay shattered, the hull dented, the windows broken.

"Are you hurt, Giga?" Steel struggled to rise, ignoring the dizziness in his head. "Did we hurt anyone when we crashed? How can I help? How . . ."

His words trailed off as his head spun. He blinked and swayed, then found himself leaning against Giga. The little android stood a foot shorter and weighed half as much, but she supported him--the tall knight in his armor.

"Let me help you," she said. "Lean on me. Let me get you inside."

Steel looked around. Hazily, he saw Riff and Nova climb out of the wreckage, both still in their space suits. Scientists of Kaperosa Observatory were rushing over to help.

"I must help them," Steel said. "I--"

"Now I help you," Giga said. "Not long ago, you pulled me out of a rough spot. Let me do the same for you."

She began to walk, holding him. Leaning against her, Steel walked too, steps shuffling. He was worried his weight would break her--she was so small--but the android was not as fragile as she looked. She was, Steel knew, stronger than him.

"Thank you, my lady," he whispered.

"Happy to comply, sir," she whispered back, smiling softly.

Cables sparked around them. Scattered fires burned, reflecting in shards of broken glass. They walked through the ruins, knight and android, as ash rained from the sky.

* * * * *

They sat together in the observatory cafeteria--a young scientist and a group of battered Alien Hunters.

"So we're marooned here," Lenora said softly. "The *Drake* is gone."

Riff nodded. "I'm sorry, Lenora. We could only save one ship, and, well . . . we didn't do a very good job of saving that one either. Piston and Twig are out there, working on it now, but it'll be days before the *Dragon Huntress* flies again."

Lenora lowered her head. "And whatever alien attacked you on the bridge, the creature that made you crash the ship . . . it's still out there." She shivered. "They might all still be out there. Or in here."

They all nervously looked across the cafeteria, seeking ghosts. Nova growled and clutched her whip. Steel tightened his grip on Solflare's hilt. Romy whimpered, hid under the table, and sucked her thumb. Only Giga seemed calm; the android sat primly in her chair, hands folded in her lap. Thankfully, no ghosts could be found, unless you counted the ghosts of old meals that clung to the plastic trays and plates.

Riff took a long, deep breath. "We have to get you off this planet, Lenora. You and all the other scientists here. We need you in a safe place while we stay and fight. Send out a signal! Call the nearest station for a ship. We need to evacuate anyone who's not an Alien Hunter."

Lenora bit her lip. "That would be a good idea, Riff, if the *Dragon Huntress* hadn't crashed into our communications antennae." She sighed. "We can receive signals from space. We can send out nothing."

A chill ran down Riff's spine like a ghostly finger. Marooned. No way to call for aid. Trapped on a dead planet haunted by the undead.

I need to get a job walking dogs, he thought. *Or maybe open a little hummus house.*

"All right." Riff rose to his feet. "Here's the plan. For the next couple weeks, Piston and Twig are going to work round the clock fixing the *Dragon Huntress*. Meanwhile, Lenora, I don't want any scientist walking alone. Groups of threes. Piston said these creatures might be sensitive to electromagnetic signals, so he built us these." He lifted the rod he carried. The tip thrummed, casting out a powerful electromagnetic field. "I want your people armed too, Lenora. Piston said he can teach them how to build more of these rods."

Lenora smiled thinly. "Believe it or not, Riff, I have an engineer or two on my team as well. They'll manage."

He nodded. "Good. We need weapons--for everyone here, not just us Alien Hunters. And traps. Magnetic traps to catch one of these bastards and interrogate it. I'm going to offer you security too--two guards at the observatory's airlock and a regular patrol through the halls. Wherever those ghosts are sneaking in from, we're going to stop them."

"Not ghosts, Riff." Lenora patted his hand. "Alien life. A new type of life form such as we've never encountered."

Riff cringed in sudden memory. Again he saw it before him: that dark land he did not understand, a land that expanded beyond his normal awareness. The charcoal hill. The flower atop it. The evil lurking unseen, a dark queen, mistress of the creatures. Life? Or something beyond life, beings from another dimension, from a hellish nightmare they could not hope to understand?

"I'll take the first patrol," Riff said. "Nova, will you join me?"

The gladiator nodded and hefted her own rod. "I'm up for round two. Let's see if we find some ghosts again." She glanced over at Lenora. "I mean--ancient, mysterious life forms such as we've never encountered . . . for me to kill."

Steel stood up and raised his chin. "I'll take first watch in the airlock."

"I'll join you," said Lenora, rising to her feet too.

Giga also rose from her seat. "And I'll help construct electromagnetic traps. Piston gave me the specs." The android leaned down to look at Romy, who was sucking her thumb under the table. "Romy, would you like to help me? You're good at calibrating the field distribution of electromagnetic quantum photon particles, aren't you?"

"Um . . ." Romy blinked. "Yes?"

"Excellent!" Giga smiled.

They all left the cafeteria, heading toward their tasks. As Riff walked down the dark hallway, he tried to curb the chill inside him. True, they were marooned here, stuck in a labyrinth on a distant planet, no way to call for help, ghosts lurking in the darkness . . . but he had his friends. He had a plan. He was ready to fight back.

So why did his heart keep pounding, and why, when he gazed out the window at that black hole, did visions of dark nightmares shake his bones?

* * * * *

Steel stood in the observatory's airlock, Solflare drawn, guarding the door. He stood with squared shoulders, chin raised, lips tight.

I'm ready to defend this observatory with my life, he thought. *For honor. For chivalry. For the people I love. My guard will not end until the evil here is vanquished.*

Yet somehow those old vows felt hollow. He was not truly a knight, was he? No. Sir Kerish Rosetta, Lenora's father, had stripped him of his sigil. He was an Alien Hunter now--a cheap mercenary, muscle for hire. Was there still honor in his profession? In his life?

He hefted Solflare, his knightly sword, modeled after the weapons the knights of ancient history had wielded. A battery thrummed deep within this blade, able to cast out beams of searing light. And now a new weapon had been added to the sword. Piston had patched magnets onto the blade's base. When activated, they would cast out a powerful electromagnetic field. Powerful enough, the stocky gruffle had claimed, to disperse any ghost flying his way.

"Would you like some coffee?" Lenora stood by a percolator, pouring a mug. An electromagnetic rod--a makeshift weapon fashioned from pipes and magnets--hung from her belt. As always, she wore a woolen skirt and a sweater vest. Her long brown hair was gathered into a bun, and her glasses perched on her nose.

Steel shook his head. "I don't consume drugs."

Lenora snorted. "I'll brew a second pot. Decaf." She sipped from her mug and sighed. "Lovely hot caffeine. You don't know what you're missing."

"There are many things I chose to miss when I swore my oaths." Steel raised his chin higher. "Coffee. Alcohol. And . . ."

And love, he thought. *Your love. A love whose loss I mourn. Even now. Even after all these years.*

Yet how could he say those things to her? How could he tell her that his vows too were an armor, protecting him from that old pain? How could he tell Lenora that whenever she looked at him, bittersweet pain stabbed him? How whenever he gazed into her hazel eyes, he felt like a boy in love again? She stared at him now, eyes eager, lips parted, waiting to hear the rest of his words.

". . . and material possessions," he finished lamely.

Lenora lowered her head and nodded. "You are a different man now. No longer the careless boy I once loved." She grinned suddenly and stepped closer to him. "Steel, do you remember that time back on Earth when we sneaked into a petting zoo at night?"

He grimaced. "That llama could spit."

She laughed. "I love llamas. I remember how I patted them, how fluffy the babies were, and how you stood watch over the entrance--like you stand watch here now. Only . . ." She touched his cheek. "There was less pain on your face then. Less weariness in your eyes."

Her touch shot warmth through Steel. Inside him, something hot and sad seemed to melt. And he was there again--a boy of eighteen, sneaking into the petting zoo with the girl he loved.

"I've grown up," he said softly.

"That's not always a good thing." Tears dampened her eyes, and she stroked his hair. "Your temples are gray."

"While your hair is still chestnut brown like the day we parted." Stiffly, he caressed that hair, wondering if he was stepping out of bounds, if she'd recoil . . . but she let him stroke it. It was soft, smooth, full of old memories.

"Do you remember what we did later that night?" she whispered.

Of course he did. Steel had never forgotten. It had been sixteen years, and he still thought of that night, still dreamed of it. It was still his favorite memory--better than the memory of taking his knightly vows. They had sneaked deeper into the petting zoo, found a grove of pines, and lain upon a park bench. For a long time, they had stared up at the stars, and Lenora had spoken in wonder of them. She had been able to name all the constellations, to point out distant worlds and speak of their secrets, vowing to visit them someday.

A comet had streaked across the sky, then another one, and then a great fireball of blue and red fire, gone as soon as it had appeared. Lenora gasped at its beauty, then turned toward Steel, eyes bright. He kissed her. He had never kissed a girl, yet it felt so natural, so right, and she kissed him back. They made love on that park bench under the stars, the trees rustling around them, then slept together until dawn, holding each other, and watched the sunset rise between the trees.

Perhaps it was the only time I felt true joy, Steel thought.

"I remember," he whispered.

Lenora blinked tears out of her eyes and turned away. "Decaf." She nodded, awkwardly smoothing her skirt, perhaps also overcome with memories. "I'll brew you a pot."

She returned to the percolator and spent a moment grinding beans, replacing filters, and adding water, her fingers trembling all the while.

"Lenora." Steel approached her. He spoke in a soft voice. "Lenora, I'm sorry. I'm deeply, deeply sorry." His voice choked. "I know that I hurt you then. I know that . . . that you wanted me to fly to those stars with you. I know that when I chose the knighthood, I broke your heart, and please believe me . . . my heart was broken too. For many years, I--"

She spun around. "Don't." She placed a finger against his lips. "It's all right. I understand. I didn't then, but I had many years here, in the darkness, to understand." She shook her head, hair swaying. "Funny, isn't it? We can use numbers to explore the secrets of the cosmos, yet matters of the heart? There's no logic to them."

"Perhaps that's why I chose the knighthood," Steel said. "To follow a simple code of ethics. To have matters of the heart reduced to a creed."

Lenora snorted, eyes still damp. "That's my father speaking. It's all I heard growing up. Can you imagine what it's like, being the daughter of a knight? Always our home was full of . . . unyielding honor. Discipline. Chivalry. Tradition." Tears streamed down her cheeks. "It's why my mother left. It's why I wept when you chose to follow my father, to join his order. I wanted us to fly to those stars we used to look at. To have adventures together. To see the cosmos. And you . . . you wouldn't join me." Her voice was hoarse. "You were so impressed with my father's armor, his sword, his stiff moral code, that you chose him. You chose him over me!"

She froze. Her voice echoed. Her face paled.

"Lenora," he whispered.

She turned away again. "I'm sorry. I shouldn't have yelled." She laughed bitterly. "Funny how old pain can lurk for so long, then emerge like this. With tears. With shouts."

Steel embraced her. He was bulky in his armor, creaking, no longer the youth who could make love on a bench but a stiff relic. Yet still he embraced her, and she wrapped her arms around him. He kissed the top of her head.

"It's all right," he whispered.

She wiped her eyes. "Except none of this is all right. Nothing here is. Not that black hole outside that breaks my equations and breaks the minds of those who look upon it. Not one missing starship, one broken on the ground. Not being marooned here, our communicators dead, and hostile life we don't understand haunting our halls. None of this is right, Steel."

"We'll make it right." He looked into her eyes, still holding her. "I'm no longer a knight, Lenora. Yes, I chose your father's path. I joined the Knights of Sol, the ancient order he spoke so proudly of. I served him. Yet I found corruption in the ranks of that order I thought so pure. I spoke out. I tried to cleanse the knighthood of its ills. And so he banished me, Lenora. With his own dagger, he scratched the sigil off my breastplate." He touched the mark on his chest, still showing those old scratches. "For many years, I was lost. An outcast. Just as lonely as you are here on Kaperosa. And so no, I'm no longer a knight, but I still have honor. And when I make a vow, I still defend it with my life. And I vow to you, Lenora. Not as a knight, not as an Alien Hunter, but as a man who loved you. Who loves you still. I will make this right."

She nodded and held him, resting her head against his shoulder. They stood like this for a long time, silent in the airlock. The coffee percolated. Outside, the black hole rose over the horizon, an emptiness in the cosmos filling the observatory with its all-seeing gaze.

CHAPTER SEVEN

CROSSING LINES

"I should never have let you try to land the ship," Nova said, marching down the corridor. "I swear, Riff, every time you try to fly, you end up crashing, and--"

"Nova!" Riff groaned. "For pity's sake. A ghost attacked me while I was landing."

The ashai rolled her eyes. Her golden catsuit, woven of bulletproof fabric, whispered as she marched. "Sure, Riff. Ghosts did it. Ghosts this, ghosts that. I bet it was also a ghost that made you gawp at the black hole while I was opening the ship's airlock."

"It was!" Riff bristled.

"See? You blame them for everything." She glared at Riff, her green eyes flashing. "I thought you were going to start taking responsibility for your life, Raphael Starfire. I thought you were going--"

"Nova." He grabbed her arms. "Listen to me. These ghosts--or whatever the hell they are--pop out of nowhere all the time. You saw them on the main deck. And if I hadn't been there to blast the airlock open, they'd have killed you, Steel, and me, then stolen our starship."

Nova snorted. "I had them."

"You had nothing! You and Steel were flapping your weapons around uselessly, causing no more damage than kids with foam swords." He hefted his electromagnetic rod. "Maybe these bad boys will finally do some damage. Until we kill these creatures, we need to stop bickering, and we need to work together. All right? We didn't defeat the skelkrins and the Singularity by bickering all day long."

Nova tilted her head. "We didn't?"

"Well . . . not *all* day long." Riff sighed. "In any case, let's keep patrolling. And keep your eyes peeled for ghosts. Oh, and Nova . . . don't look out the windows. At least not when the black hole's out there."

He shuddered to remember what he had seen when gazing into Yurei. The memory had been haunting him since. It had felt like . . . consciousness unfolding. As a child, Riff had once scratched his eye, and he had worn a patch for a month. When the bandage was finally removed, he suddenly remembered how much deeper the three-dimensional world seemed, how flat everything had looked with one eye. When gazing into Yurei, Riff had felt the same realization: how flat and muted his reality was. Inside that black hole, he had seemed to gaze upon true reality. Upon a black land woven of evil itself.

Grimacing, he thought of the rose on the black hill. Somehow he knew that he had to save that rose. To stop the evil in the dark sky from crushing it. Yet the hill soared up eternally, a distance he could not climb, and the Dark Queen lurked everywhere, watching, mocking him.

He looked at Nova, forcing his mind away from that memory. He gazed at her pale, freckled skin; her pointy ears thrusting out from her golden hair; the whip crackling in her left hand, her rod in the right. The warrior-princess often scolded him, mocked him, sometimes infuriated him, but Riff knew that Nova loved him. He knew that she would always fight at his side. He loved her more than anything in this cosmos, and gazing at her soothed his soul, and the goodness he saw in her melted his anxiety like rain melting snow, like--

"Riff!" She groaned. "Now stop gawping at me, or I'm going to whip your eyeballs off."

He sighed and kept walking, staring ahead this time. Maybe Nova was herself just as dangerous as a black hole.

Their patrol took them through the labyrinth of Kaperosa Observatory. The observatory had not seemed large from above-- a small complex of domes and walkways. Yet walking within it, the place seemed endless. Neon lights flickered. Staircases rose and fell. Tunnels connected to small, glass chambers, only to lead to more narrow burrows. During times of stress, Riff would sometimes dream that he was trapped, trying to reach a spaceport or exam on time, only to get lost, and the more he tried to find his way, the more lost he became. Walking here felt like one of those bad dreams.

I feel like an ant trapped in a glass ant farm. Perhaps that's all we are to Yurei. Ants in a box.

Humans had come here to study the black hole. Riff suddenly had the uncomfortable feeling that the black hole was studying them.

They found themselves walking down an outer corridor, the windows exposing the rocky surface and dark sky outside. The black hole was rising. Riff forced himself to stare forward, refusing to look out the window. But he could still feel Yurei outside, feel its black eye staring at him.

"It's too quiet," he muttered. "Where are all the scientists who normally work here?" He glanced into the labs to his left; the small, crowded chambers were empty.

"Hiding in their quarters," Nova said. "Scared. They're not warriors like me."

But there was a hint of fear to Nova's voice, and when Riff glanced over, he saw that her hands were tight around her weapons.

"It's not entirely quiet," Riff said. "I hear . . . something."

He cocked his head, listening, not even daring to breathe. A soft murmur like distant wind. A rumble, almost too low to hear, that sounded almost like a voice, the words too muffled to understand. White noise, that was all. Dark noise. Sound felt more than heard.

"Riff, you idiot!" whispered an echoing voice.

Riff started and spun around. A flash of gold caught his eye, then vanished.

"Did you hear that?" His heart banged against his ribs. "A voice? And did you see a . . . a golden flash?"

He stared down the hallway. Nothing. Only the dark tunnel stretching into shadows. Only the empty labs on one side, the windows on the other, gazing out into space. No ghosts. No more voices.

Nova frowned. "I heard nothing. Calm down, Riff. You're making me jumpy."

He nodded and lowered his rod. "I thought I heard . . . a familiar voice." He shook his head. "Never mind. Let's keep going."

Blessedly, the corridor with those dark windows ended. A doorway led them into a hot, humid greenhouse. Bright lights shone overhead, their glare hiding the view out the windows. Boxes of soil covered the floor, sprouting thousands of plants. Many of the plants were as large as trees. Their leaves reached toward the light, creating oxygen for the observatory, and the branches gave forth fruit. Herbs and lettuce grew from small gardens.

Riff inhaled deeply. Under the bright lights, surrounded by greenery, he almost felt at peace. Whatever evil presence he had felt in the corridor was gone. Here was a place too warm, too bright, too full of life for the undead to haunt.

Nova frowned down at a garden. "Carrots? Celery?" She glanced up at a tree. "Apples? That's rabbit food. Where do they grow the steak?"

"There's synthetic meat in the lab down the hall." Riff passed his hands through a tree's foliage.

Nova snorted. "Synthetic meat. So human. We ashais *hunt*. We eat real meat, raw, bleeding, fresh off the bone." She licked her lips.

"Is that why you scarf down so many hot dogs from the *Dragon Huntress*'s fridge?" He fluffed up a head of lettuce. "There's more meat in this than those, and--"

With a crackle, the lights died.

Riff froze.

Darkness filled the greenhouse.

With the glare of neon gone, the black hole loomed outside the windows, casting its gaze into the chamber.

"What did you do?" Nova whispered.

Riff raised his electromagnetic rod. Nova switched on her whip, and the lash crackled with electricity, emitting dim light. Shadows scurried. The trees creaked and the leaves swayed.

"Could be a power failure," Riff said.

Nova shook her head. "I still hear the generators humming."

Riff heard them too . . . and he heard other sounds. Scuttling feet. Heavy breathing behind him. Hot breath fluttered the hairs on the back of his head. He spun around, heart bursting into a gallop, but nothing was there.

He glanced back at Nova. "Let's get out of here."

She was only a shadow; he could see little more than glints on her golden armor and hair. The plants swayed around her like looming aliens, tilting forward. A shadowy arm reached out, tipped with claws, reaching to her shoulder.

"Nova!" He raised his rod and blasted out an electromagnetic wave.

A creature screeched, a sound louder than starship engines, high-pitched like steam fleeing a kettle. Riff's ears rang. Nova spun around too, flailing her own rod. Shadows danced madly. Feet pattered behind Riff, and he spun around again but saw nothing.

He froze, pulse beating in his ears.

He stepped closer to Nova, and they stood back to back, weapons raised.

"See anything?" she whispered.

"Thousands of shadows."

Just thousands of plants, he hoped.

"Listen to me, whoever you are!" Riff called out. "We're not here to hurt you. We don't want to fight you. We're humans--"

"Speak for yourself," Nova muttered.

Riff ignored her. "--we're humans and have come here in peace. Will you reveal yourself to me? Will you speak with me and--"

Again, he could not finish his sentence. With screeches, the shadows jumped toward him.

Riff swung his rod, blasting out his electromagnetic field. The waves pounded against the ghosts. The creatures howled, scattered, reformed, and drove toward him again.

Nova fought at his side. She swung her electric whip in one hand, her rod in the other. Her glowing lash lit the darkness, casting out sparks. The light fell upon blobby creatures and reflected in their crimson eyes. The beasts' claws glinted, and Riff screamed as they tore across his thigh. His blood spurted.

"Back!" he shouted. "You will leave this place! Back!"

He lashed his rod again. The electromagnetic wave crashed into ghosts. They fell back.

I'm hurting them. He snarled. *They can be hurt.*

One of the creatures swooped from the ceiling. Riff raised his rod, casting it back. It tore apart, dispersing into blobs of shadow. More creatures lurched from ahead, and one knocked Riff down, and he screamed in pain.

The rose.

The hill.

His consciousness fleeing his body, expanding into the other place, into the nightmare, mingling with the living shadows that floated over the mountains.

I have to climb the hill. I have to save the rose. I have to climb. To get there. But she's watching. She--

"No!" He roared. "I will not go there again."

He swung his rod in an arc. It felt like swinging it through jelly. The ghosts squealed and fell back, changing form, shrinking, growing, vanishing. The electromagnetic field pulsed, throbbing up Riff's arm, but he kept swinging.

The rod clanged into something hard.

A creature screamed, then vanished.

I hit it. It's made of flesh. It's solid.

He rose to his feet, swinging the rod again, driving forward, pushing the ghosts back.

No. They're not ghosts. They're solid. I felt one.

Hope rose in him, and he lashed his rod at another ghost, dispersing it into shards. He had beaten back two more ghosts when he saw Nova, and his hope crashed.

A towering beast, ten feet tall, loomed over her. Nova was a proud warrior, tall and strong, yet beside this creature she seemed small as a halfling. This creature seemed more solid than the others, woven of the same black substance that had filled his nightmarish vision. Its eyes blazed red, and the black hole swirled behind it, haloing the creature's head. Nova was screaming, her voice muted, barely in this world. She tried to lash her rod, but the creature grabbed it, and the weapon vanished.

Riff howled wordlessly and thrust his own rod.

Black tendrils appeared, swatting him aside. He crashed into plants, snapping their stalks. Blackness fell upon him, pinning him down, crushing him, constricting him.

The towering creature reached out its claws and grabbed Nova.

"Nova!" Riff shouted and fired his plasma gun.

The blaze stormed forth, tore through the creature, and slammed into the window behind it. The glass shattered. Air shrieked out from the greenhouse, flowing out in a typhoon as if draining into the black hole outside.

"Remember the tesseract, stupid," Nova whispered, meeting his gaze . . . and vanished.

The towering creature broke apart, shattering into ten thousand fluttering pieces like crows leaving a tree, each demonic bird dissolving into nothingness.

"Nova!" Riff shouted. "Oh gods, Nova!"

He fought in a fury, howling, swinging his rod, soon unable to scream as the air drained out. The ghosts mobbed him, laughing, mocking him.

"Captain!" cried a voice, and Giga raced into the chamber. The android swung her katana. Batteries were placed onto its blade, casting out an electromagnetic field. The android's hair and kimono fluttered as she fought, driving back the ghosts.

"Captain!" cried another voice, and Romy raced into the chamber, her pitchfork equipped with its own magnets. She too fought, driving the creatures back.

Riff fell to his knees, unable to breathe. The air kept draining out. Blackness spread before his eyes. Vaguely, he was aware of Giga sealing the broken window, and engineers of Lenora's team rushing inside, and Romy driving off the last ghosts.

"Nova," he whispered, and all he could see were her eyes again--green eyes staring into his, then vanishing, gone into shadows.

CHAPTER EIGHT

GHOST HUNTERS

"What do you mean, just . . . vanished?" Steel asked.

"I told you." Riff rose to his feet, knocking back his chair. He paced the cafeteria. "Just vanished. The claws grabbed her and she just goddamn vanished."

His heart thudded as he paced. His chest felt too tight, and he could barely breathe. When he passed by a window, he grabbed the blinds and roughly tugged them shut.

"Riff," Steel said, voice softer now. "Did you see them drag her away, or--"

"Why don't you keep the damn blinds shut?" Riff marched toward another window and tugged the blinds down, nearly shattering them. "I told you all to keep the blinds shut, the curtains dawn, the observatory closed off. I don't want anyone looking at that black hole, and I don't want it looking at anyone. Do you understand?" His voice rose to a shout, hoarse, torn with pain. "When will you imbeciles ever listen to me?"

He stared at them, panting, eyes stinging. Romy whimpered and sneaked under the table to suck her thumb. Steel stared back, eyes soft with pity. Giga lowered her head. Piston and Twig awkwardly twiddled their thumbs.

"Sir," Piston ventured, "I think I could take a look at the footage again, maybe--"

"No. I don't want you looking at any damn footage, Piston." Riff pointed at the door. "Back to the *Dragon Huntress*. I want you fixing our ship around the clock. You want to eat lunch? You eat while you work. Twig, damn it! Stop sniffling and go with him. Now! That's an order. You're not to leave the *Dragon Huntress* until she's spaceworthy again."

Twig nodded, rubbing out her tears. "I'll just finish my pudding and--"

"Now!" Riff roared.

The halfling all but fled the cafeteria, and Piston lolloped in pursuit. Soon Riff heard the sound of their power tools working on the ship outside.

A red, clawed hand reached from under the tabletop. Romy peered up. "I'll just grab Twig's pudding, if she's not going to eat it, and--"

"Romy, you too." Riff pointed at the door. "Get out of here."

"But--but--!" The demon's lips wobbled. "Piston said I just get in the way, and--"

"Go!"

The demon sniffed. "I'll just go look for Nova. Maybe I can still find her hiding somewhere . . ." Romy's eyes welled with tears. She turned toward the door, spun back, grabbed the pudding, then fled the hall.

Riff remained alone in the cafeteria with Steel and Giga. The knight stood, clutching his sword. The android sat at the table, head lowered.

Riff stared at them. His eyes threatened to leak tears again. He was their captain, their leader, yet now he felt himself losing control.

Have I brought them here to die? Have I led my family, my best friends, to death on a rocky world orbiting an evil goddess?

"With the greenhouse destroyed, we're almost out of food, almost out of oxygen," he said. "We have enough to last three days, and Piston and Twig said they'll need another two weeks to fix the ship."

"They'll work faster," Steel said. "And we'll tighten our belts. And the *Dragon Huntress* still has oxygen tanks."

"Enough for all seventy-three scientists on this observatory?" Riff asked. "That buys us another two days at most."

Steel took a step closer. His eyes darkened. "Then what would you have us do, brother? Give up hope? That I will not do. I will keep fighting. I am a warrior, I--"

"So was Nova!" Riff couldn't curb his shout, his tears. "She was like you. Proud. Arrogant. A warrior. And now . . . now she's gone, and--"

"Nova is still alive." Steel grabbed Riff's arms. "I will not believe that she's dead."

For the first time in years, Riff saw his brother mad. The knight snarled, baring his teeth. His brown eyes, normally so sad, burned with rage.

"I saw her die," Riff whispered. "Oh gods, Steel, I saw her die."

"You saw nothing of the sort." Steel glared at him. "Listen to me, brother. We have no body. No ashes. No sign of Nova. To me, that means that she still lives. Kidnapped perhaps. A prisoner of these creatures. But alive. We saw how these ghosts appear and disappear, popping out of corners, shadows, ceilings. If they can travel like that, they could have taken Nova with them."

Riff barked out a mirthless laugh. "You talk to me like I'm a child. Like I need to be comforted. I was there, Steel! I was there. She looked into my eyes as they killed her."

"We don't know that--"

"You don't know anything!" Riff shouted. "What do you know of what happened? What do you know of loss?"

Now Steel raised his voice to a roar. "Everything!"

Riff froze and stared. Giga started and covered her mouth. It was the first time either of them had heard Steel shout.

"Everything," the knight repeated, eyes red, mustache twitching. "I have known more loss than you can imagine, brother. The loss of a woman I love. The loss of my knighthood. The loss of all contact with others. The loss of everything I ever loved, ever cared for. All my life, I have lost, so do not lecture me, brother, about what I know or don't know. Yet no matter what I've lost, I always fought on. Calmly. With quiet dignity. No matter how many times I was knocked down, I got back up and I kept walking. And I expect no less from you, Riff. From my captain. From my older brother."

Giga rushed forth and embraced the knight, her hair falling down to hide her face.

Riff stared into his brother's eyes, then lowered his head. "I'm sorry, Steel. I'm sorry. And . . . I'm scared."

Steel's eyes softened, and his grip on Riff's arms loosened, turning into an embrace. "As am I. As is everyone here. You are not alone, Riff. I fight with you. Always."

Nova would say the same, Riff thought. Again he saw it-- her eyes staring into his. Her last words: *Remember the tesseract, stupid.* Then the shadow dispersing into a thousand crows, fluttering away, taking Nova with them. If Nova was still alive, was she screaming in that nightmarish land, the realm the black hole had shown him--perhaps the realm inside the black hole itself?

"Remember the tesseract, stupid," Riff whispered.

Steel frowned. "You call me a fool?"

Riff shook his head. "It's something Nova said." He began to pace the cafeteria again. "Tesseract, tesseract . . . an impossible cube."

He stared around him, peering into the corners, the shadows, the corridor beyond. What had Nova meant?

Giga approached him and spoke for the first time. "What do we do now, sir?"

Riff turned toward the android. He held her hands, looked over her shoulder, and met Steel's eyes. The knight held his gaze.

"The ghosts grabbed one of us," Riff said softly. "By god, I say we grab one of them."

* * * * *

Riff stood in the laboratory, a pale chamber with a tiled floor and harsh neon lights. The tables had been pushed aside. The windows' blinds were open, exposing rocky plains and black sky. The stars shone, and the galaxy's spiral arm spread like a trail of milk. Yurei still lay below the horizon.

"How are we doing, Gig?" he asked.

The android placed down her last metal rod, forming a square around Riff. "Final rod in place, sir. We're ready to go."

Riff nodded and looked around him. Several of the rods had been raised, reminding Riff of poles that formed lines in banks or theaters. Only in this case, it was not velvet ropes that connected the posts. Once turned on, an electromagnetic field would flare between them, strong enough to power a small town.

Giga glanced out the window. "It's almost time, sir."

Riff nodded. *Remember the tesseract, stupid.* He swallowed a lump in his throat. What had Nova meant?

Tesseract, tesseract, he thought. He knew that word. He conjured to mind a trip to a sideshow long ago, a hologram of an impossible cube. What did that have to do with ghosts? He didn't know.

All he knew was that the ghosts came from Yurei, the black hole. Until now, every time the ghosts had struck, they had struck under Yurei's watchful gaze. That black hole was releasing them like a hive releasing hornets. Riff would bet his life on it.

Perhaps I am.

Riff wished the others were with him. But Piston and Twig were working on the wreckage of the *Dragon Huntress*. Steel was guarding the observatory's airlock, and Romy was patrolling the corridors; Riff couldn't abandon the scientists, wanted to make sure at least two Alien Hunters were always on the beat. With Nova gone, that left just him and Giga here . . . hunting a ghost.

He stared out the window again, waiting for it--the black eye.

"It's a funny thing, fear," Riff said. "It must seem so strange to you, Giga. How humans are afraid of the dark. Of shadows stirring. Of the unknown. How we leak cold sweat, shiver, how our heart rate increases. How we act like fools. An evolutionary tool, meant to keep us out of the dark forests where tigers lurked." He laughed--a bitter, hollow sound. "Wasn't enough to keep us out of the true darkness, though. The darkness of space. And there are far worse things than tigers lurking in these shadows."

Giga looked at him. "I'm scared too, sir."

"I didn't know androids felt fear."

"We do." Her voice was barely a whisper. "I don't fear the darkness; it's only the lack of photon radiation within a slice of a spectrum. I don't fear the unknown; what I don't know inspires only curiosity. But . . . I fear loss. I fear losing my friends. The people I love." She lowered her head. Her chin-length, black hair rustled. "I'm so afraid for Nova. And I'm so afraid that the same can happen to you, to Steel, to everyone else." She looked at him again. "Is that wrong, sir? Is that not what fear is?"

"I think, Giga, that's exactly it."

She looked out the window. She shivered. "It's here."

Riff followed her gaze, and his innards clenched. A shadow was rising above the horizon, hiding the stars, bloating, emerging like a creature from a midnight swamp. Perhaps it *was* a creature. Yurei, vengeful Queen of Darkness, was awakening.

Starfire . . . we have her, Starfire . . . would you like to hear her scream?

He forced his gaze away before the rest of the black hole could emerge. Even this single motion, the flick of his eyes, blasted pain through his skull.

He gave Giga the signal. She nodded and left the chamber, staring from the doorway. In her hand she held the remote control.

Riff stood within the square of posts, staring away from the window, but he could *feel* the black hole behind him, staring at him, a presence in this chamber. Cruel. Evil. The same entity he had felt in the nightmarish landscape, or perhaps the landscape itself, an entire conscious world.

"I'm here," he said softly. "The one who saw your true form."

You saw nothing, one of three. A hum rose in the chamber, becoming a cackle. Desks rattled. Shadows swirled. *If you truly saw our faces, you would collapse screaming, your puny mind broken.*

"I don't know," Riff said. "I once walked into the bathroom without knocking and saw Piston naked. I don't think anything can scare me now."

Humor . . . a human failing. Soon your jokes will end, one of three. Soon all you will do is weep and beg and scream.

Riff lifted his plasma gun. He loaded a charge, letting the gun hum, click, and glow.

"Come then," he said. "Let's go another round."

With a screech, the shadows swarmed.

Riff spun around, gritting his teeth, to see the creatures descend from the shadowy corners. Their eyes blazed. Their mouths opened, revealing black fangs. Their claws reached out.

"Come at me!" Riff opened his arms wide. "Here I am!"

With the power of a storm, the creatures slammed into him.

Claws slashed at him. Eyes bored into him. The shadows engulfed him, tugging at him, pulling him toward the waiting black land.

"Now, Giga!" he shouted.

The rods around Riff crackled to life.

The ghosts screamed.

The magnets yanked Riff's gun from his hand, and his wristwatch tore off and flew. The electromagnetic field filled the space between the rods, forming an invisible cage.

The ghosts wailed and tried to flee. They flew toward the fields, shattering, breaking apart, screaming. One creature rose toward the ceiling, only to be knocked back down, slam against the floor, and disintegrate. They swelled, shrunk, twisted around.

"You like that, don't you?" Riff said. "You--"

He screamed as one of the creatures crashed into him, slamming him against the floor. More of the beasts piled up, scratching, biting.

Riff swung his electromagnetic rod, slamming the metal into them. The creatures changed form, contracting to avoid the blows. He hit one, heard it scream. He knocked another creature back and crawled, trying to escape the square of rods.

He made it past the border.

Claws grabbed his leg and tugged him back.

"Giga!" Riff shouted. "Giga, help me out of here!"

The android peered from behind the door. "I can't, sir! I'm a robot. This powerful an electromagnetic field would erase my memory banks." She cringed. "Oops! I just forgot the lower bound on the complexity of fast Fourier transform algorithms to convert a finite list of equally spaced samples of a function into the list of coefficients of a finite combination of complex sinusoids. Damn." She vanished behind the doorway again.

The ghosts tugged Riff back into the ring, lifted him into the air, and slammed him down. His shoulder hit the floor--hard. More ghosts piled up atop him, yanking at his hair, pounding his flesh like butchers tenderizing meat. Riff felt like a scrawny accountant who'd wandered into a wrestling ring to face a heavyweight tag team.

Brilliant plan, he thought. *Trapping myself with alien ghosts. Brilliant.*

The creatures grabbed him again, maws opening to bite.

Riff thrust up his rod.

The magnetic field repulsed one ghost, and Riff swung the rod again, slamming it against another. With his other hand, he fired his plasma gun. The blaze stormed across one creature, shattering it into a thousand shards that vanished like fleeing birds.

"Don't kill them, sir!" Giga cried. "We need them."

He groaned. More of the ghosts still fluttered around him, banging against the invisible walls of the cage. Riff tried to leave the trap--all he had to do was step between the poles!--but the ghosts kept swarming around him, spinning in a maelstrom.

Riff cursed, kicked, and knocked down one of the pegs.

The field broke. Ghosts began to flee like smoke from an opened oven.

Riff scurried with them. He scampered along the floor, exiting the broken cage. The creatures fluttered all around, knocking into him, fleeing toward the shadowy corners, the ceiling, the laboratory desks, and the corridor. Riff grimaced, struggling to push through them, feeling like a man shoving through waves of tar.

He grabbed the fallen rod. He howled with effort. It felt like trying to lift a fallen tree. Standing outside the cage, he pressed against the ground, grinded his teeth, and managed to lift the pulsing rod back into place.

Silence fell.

The creatures vanished.

Riff fell to the floor, battered and bleeding.

He looked around him, panting. Whatever ghosts had escaped the trap had also fled the lab. Desks, lamps, and computers lay smashed on the floor. Claw marks covered the walls. Black stains lay everywhere. After the roar of the battle, Riff's ears rang.

Slowly, clutching his weapons, Riff turned his head toward the trap.

Within the square of pulsing rods, fluttering back and forth between the invisible shields, was a ghost.

A savage smile tugged Riff's lips. "Got one."

Daniel Arenson

CHAPTER NINE

GHOST IN THE MACHINE

"Damn it, Twig, the quarter screws! Quarter!"

Piston growled and shook his fist at her. The gruffle stood on a ladder, clad in a space suit, a helmet the size of a pumpkin encasing his massive head.

"You said five-eights!" Twig cried back from her perch on the ship's wing.

The gruffle groaned. "Why would I want a five-eights screw to patch up the thruster engine coils? Think, you clod! Now go get them."

The *Dragon Huntress* still lay upon the rocky surface of Kaperosa, one wing shattered, the engines smashed, the nose crushed, the hull punched full of holes. Scaffolding covered the wreckage, and toolboxes lay everywhere. The stars shone above, and blessedly, the black hole now lurked below the horizon. A hundred meters away, the observatory lights beckoned through the domes and windows. There was real food in there, hot coffee and tea, companionship, warmth. But so long as the *Dragon Huntress* lay in ruins, that place--so near yet so far--was forbidden to Twig. On captain's orders, she was stuck out here, working on

94

the wreckage with nothing but that infuriating old gruffle for company.

"Now, you clod!" Piston rumbled, clinging to the ladder with one hand.

Twig grinded her teeth, anger rising in her. She was tired of that grumpy gruffle bossing her around. She wanted to kick her toolbox off the wing, storm back into the observatory, and watch a few episodes of *Space Galaxy* to cool down--and let Piston fix the damn spaceship on his own.

She sighed. But Riff had ordered her and the gruffle to remain out here, on the cold surface of Kaperosa, until the *Dragon Huntress* was spaceworthy again. And so Twig remained, nerves fraying, living off tablets and juice boxes and a healthy dose of gruffle curses.

"Here's your damn quarter screws!" She grabbed a handful of them from a box, scampered across the wing, and all but tossed them at Piston. "Happy?"

"No!" Piston's helmet fogged up. "Of course I'm not happy. We've been out here for three days with no rest, and there's nobody but a clod to help me, and--" He frowned at the thruster coils. "Well, I'll be damned. Needs five-eights screws after all."

Twig groaned. "Great, Piston. Genius engineer you are."

He blustered. "Exactly! I'm the *engineer*, not the mechanic. You're the mechanic, you clod, and you should know these things."

"I do know them!" she shouted. "That's why I gave you the right screws in the first place, you . . . you . . . you burly, bearded, bubble-brained . . . barnacle!"

Very slowly, Piston climbed from the ladder onto the wing. The gruffle stood a foot shorter than most humans, but he towered over Twig, a diminutive halfling, and weighed several times as much. Inside his helmet, his beard wrapped around his face like a pale python constricting its prey. His eyes burned with fury.

"Take that back," he said.

Twig might have been a fraction of his size, but she crossed her arms and glared up at him. "No! I'm sick of your name-calling, of your grumbles, of your mistakes. Yes, Piston! You make mistakes too. Now you will start behaving yourself, or--"

Piston roared and leaped toward her. Twig squealed and jumped back. She tilted, fell off the wing, and crashed down onto the rocky surface. Piston tilted on the wing too. Twig scampered aside a second before the gruffle slammed onto the ground, cracking rocks.

For a long moment, they lay still, moaning. The wrecked starship loomed above them, blocking the stars.

"You all right, Piston?" Twig finally said, voice hoarse.

He groaned. "I think I fell on your wrench." He reached under his backside and pulled out the dented tool. "I broke it."

Twig took her beloved wrench from him. The steel was now curved like a boomerang. "Only a gruffle can dent solid metal." She sighed. "I'm sorry, Piston." She rose to her feet and reached down a hand.

He grabbed her palm and nearly yanked her down as he stood up. "It's I who am sorry, little one." Tears filled his eyes, and his helmet fogged up. "I'm just a grumpy old gruffle, too old for this nonsense. You're the best damn mechanic I know, you clod. And my best friend. It's just . . . just this damn place." Piston shook his fist at nothing in particular. "This whole damn planet, the observatory, the smashed ship, and that black hole that's just waiting to rise. And those ghosts, Twig. Those bastard ghosts what's been snatching up people. I suppose . . . I'm scared."

"Me too." She shuddered. "Fighting skelkrins and robots was one thing. But how can we fight ghosts, an enemy we don't understand, an enemy from another world?"

Piston tightened his lips. "We'll leave that to the Big Folks to figure out. Riff and Steel are going to figure out how to fight 'em. They're the warriors of the group. We're the little crafty ones. Our job is to be here, fixing this hunk of junk starship." He returned to his ladder. "Twig, there's a loose connection on the inner side of the engines. Would you climb into the engine room and see if you can weld it together?"

She nodded. "Will do. Let's fix this damn dragon, evacuate everyone, and then blast this whole planet to bits."

She climbed the dented staircase into the airlock and the *Dragon Huntress*'s innards. Vacuum still filled the broken ship, and Twig kept her space suit and helmet on, and her jet pack hung across her back. The main deck, once a cozy living area, lay in ruins. The goldfish, the dart board, the cushions, the board games--all had blasted out of the starship when the ghosts had hijacked it. The chamber seemed so sad to Twig now, all its good memories like ghosts themselves, mere echoes in her mind.

Curbing her tears, Twig opened the hatch on the floor and climbed down into her own domain, the realm that had been her kingdom for over a year now--the *Dragon Huntress*'s engine room.

Yet here too she found a different place.

The towering hyperspace engines, once gleaming turbines of polished steel, now lay tilted and cracked. One thruster turbine now lay on the floor like a broken drum. Cables had torn off the wall, sticking out like weeds from a ruined castle. The heart of the *Dragon Huntress* was broken, and it felt to Twig like seeing the injuries of a loved one.

This ship is one of us, Twig thought, running her palm across a cracked cooling pipe. *The eighth Alien Hunter.*

"I'm going to fix you, *Huntress*," she whispered. "I promise."

A hand grazed her shoulder.

"Piston?" Twig spun around, frowning. But she saw nothing. Only the dangling cables, the shadows, the cracked engines.

A ghost, she thought, tensing.

Then she barked a laugh. She was just on edge. Just nervous, imagining things.

"Twig, you found the loose connection?" rose Piston's voice from outside.

Twig nodded and turned toward the back of the room. She had a task to do. She had taken another step when something grabbed her arm from behind.

She spun around again. She raised her dented, electric wrench. It was shaped like a boomerang now, since Piston had fallen onto it. When she tossed it into the shadows, the wrench flew in an arc, sprayed out sparks, then boomeranged back into her grasp.

A shadow scurried and vanished into the darkness. A toolbox fell over. A lightbulb swung, then exploded. Nearly all light vanished from the engine room.

"Who . . . who's there?" Twig whispered. Her knees knocked. "Romy, is that you? This isn't funny."

Something scuttled in the darkness. Red eyes opened to slits.

"Romy!" Twig said, voice shaking. "Stop that."

She pressed a button on her wrench, and electricity crackled between the prongs. She began to tiptoe toward the shadows. She could hear the creature now--its hissing breath. She could smell its stench--a stench of rotten meat. Jaws opened in the darkness, revealing gleaming fangs.

Twig ran toward the airlock.

The shadow pounced.

Heavy blackness slammed into Twig, engulfing her, smothering her scream. Those red eyes burned, and a nightmarish land unfolded around her, a realm of endless sky and a dark, mocking queen.

CHAPTER TEN

DARK WORLD

When Nova woke up, she looked around her and didn't understand what she saw.

Years ago, she had seen a story on the news about a blind old man who ran a soup kitchen. Had never seen a damn thing. Finally his community had gathered together, raised money, and paid for prosthetic eyeballs. When the old man had opened his new eyes, had seen the world for the first time, he had been utterly confused. Colors, shapes, movements--it was all totally new, totally incomprehensible.

Right now, wherever she was, Nova felt the same. It was as if a new sense, a new part of her brain, had turned on for the first time.

She seemed to be trapped inside a cage, but she could not grasp how the bars were arranged. They flared out at odd angles, and when Nova tried to grab them, she kept missing. It seemed like the cage was reflected in mirrors, repeating itself and twisting in on itself. Nova had once owned a book of drawings by MC Escher, a human artist who had designed impossible structures. This cage, she thought, would confound even him.

The cage swung from a massive black tree, and the land beyond seemed even stranger. Wherever Nova was, it was no longer the planet Kaperosa. That much was certain. The sky was black, the ground rocky. But that ground was not flat, not even curved. It flared up, sank, rose all around her, twisting at every imaginable angle. The ground was both above Nova and below her simultaneously. The sky was both stormy and calm, both dark and clear and showing the stars.

Nova felt sick.

A hill rose below, fractured into several hills like a beam of light through a crystal, and upon its crest grew a red rose. Nova stared at the flower, her breath catching. She could see a single rose, yet . . . she could see it in multiple states. She saw the seed being planted. She saw the rose bloom. She saw it wither and die. Yet it never changed, frozen in time, its lifespan spreading ahead of her.

But strangest of all--more than the rose, the hill, the sky-- were the visions of herself.

Nova could see a stream of gold stretch across the landscape--a million reflections of Nova Tashei, like the frames of animation spread out side by side. To her left, she saw herself manhandled into this very cage. Towering, angular creatures were dragging her by the arms, similar to the ghosts that had invaded the observatory but larger, solid and gleaming. At first Nova started, ready to fight, but these creatures too were mere slides, mere memories that floated in the air. To her right, Nova saw reflections of herself fleeing the cage, racing toward a starship on the land below. She recognized the *Drake*, the dagger-shaped ship stolen from the observatory, and she saw that starship in a million reflections flying into the distance. The farther these slides were, the more blurred they became.

"I'm looking through time," Nova whispered. "I can see my past. My future." Her breath shuddered. "Where am I?"

A voice answered behind her. "In the great darkness of Yurei."

Nova spun around, reaching for her whip.

She froze and let her hand drop.

Nova's eyes widened, and a gasp shook her chest.

"Twig!" she cried.

The mechanic stood in the cage a few feet away from Nova. The halfling had been easy to miss. Twig stood only about half as tall as Nova, and her body--even clad in a space suit--was thin as a sapling. A jet pack hung across her back, and she held her helmet under her arm. Twig's black hair hung down to her shoulders, and her blue eyes stared at Nova with sadness.

"They got both of us," Twig said. "They kidnapped you first, Nova. I was still in the observatory when it happened. Yet I've been trapped here for days, and you've only now arrived. Time acts strangely inside Yurei."

Nova was a proud warrior, a great gladiator. Back on the *Dragon Huntress*, she had spent most of her time with Steel--the only other Alien Hunter who knew how to fight. In her service upon the *Dragon Huntress*, Nova had gone down into the engine room only once, finding little in common with its short denizens.

Now, however, the sight of Twig's round, pale face shot hope and love through Nova. She leaped forward, knelt, and pulled the tiny mechanic into an embrace.

"Twiggle Jauntyfoot!" Nova laughed and mussed the halfling's hair. "Yes, they got me too." She narrowed her eyes, scrutinizing Twig. "Are you hurt, little one?"

Twig shook her head. "I don't think so. They didn't hurt me. Just . . . took me here."

"Took you? Who?"

The halfling shuddered. "The ones of four. The *shades*. That's what they called themselves."

Nova turned around, looking from side to side, seeking the creatures. Her head spun, and she nearly lost her lunch. Whenever she moved, Nova left reflections behind her, filling the cage with them. When she moved her arm before her, she left a trail of gold.

Though she saw crisp images of herself, she saw only blurry reflections of the enemy. The "shades" had left this place, and already their afterimages were fading.

"They're the ghosts from Kaperosa," Nova whispered.

Only in this place, they were different. Much larger, flaring out, creatures of many limbs and eyes. Fully formed. Gone was their blobby smokiness; here they took solid form, at least judging by their reflections.

"I'm looking through time," her reflection said to her left. "I can see my past. My future. Where am I?"

"In the great darkness of Yurei," Twig said behind her.

Nova spun back toward the halfling. "You already said that."

"They got both of us," one of the halfling's reflections said.

Nova clutched her head. She fell to her knees. She shuffled closer to Twig, trying to block out the blabbering reflections, and grabbed the young mechanic's arms.

"Where are we?" she said.

"Inside the black hole," said Twig--the real Twig, Nova thought. "On the Dark Planet, a world that floats within the blackness of Yurei. Look behind you. Look at the sky."

Nova looked behind her, peering between her reflections and the cage bars. Far in the distance, a rocky world floated in the sky. It was Kaperosa, she surmised, but no longer the round planet it had always been. It too was refracted, spreading out, stretching into rocky rings. If not for the distant glint of the observatory upon it, she might not have recognized it.

"I'm looking through time," said a reflection.

"They got both of us."

"Where am I?"

"Took you? Who?"

"I'm looking through time."

"Where am I?"

The damn reflections kept prattling on, repeating the same words over and over. Nova groaned. A moment later, her reflection groaned too.

Thank goodness Romy isn't here, Nova thought. *The demon's echoes would crack the whole cosmos.*

"Why is this happening?" she whispered to Twig, daring not speak louder to add to the incessant patter. "Why these reflections, why is the ground all around us, why does the cage coil and curve? You're smarter than me, Twig. What's going on?"

Why am I so afraid? Nova wanted to ask too, but dared not. An ashai warrior must never know fear. Yet now cold sweat washed Nova, and her fingers trembled, and her heart beat too fast. She could fight in worlds she understood. How could she fight something she couldn't even comprehend?

Twig leaned closer, holding Nova, and whispered, "We're in a higher dimension."

Nova blinked. "You mean a parallel universe?"

"No." Twig shook her head. "We're in a four-dimensional reality."

Nova tilted her head. "Twig, I can name every type of sword across the galaxy, and I can recite the creeds of a hundred martial arts, but you'll have to dumb down science for me."

Twig nodded. "All right. A single dimension forms a line. Two dimensions can form a square. Three dimensions can form a cube. Four dimensions form . . . well, what we see around us. We're three-dimensional beings caught in a four-dimensional world, like a flat paper square floating through a room."

Nova looked around her at the chattering reflections. She stared far to her left, where her faded reflections were being dragged across the landscape and into the cage.

"So why can I see through time?"

"I'm not sure," Twig whispered. "But I think that what you and I have always thought of as 'time' is simply the fourth dimension. A dimension we've always been marching along at a steady pace, like a train moving on a track. But now that we're *in* a four-dimensional world, well . . . time is just another direction we can take. Same as walking side to side or jumping up and down."

Nova looked to her right. More of her reflections spread out there in a stream like cards spread across a table. She watched the reflections jumping out of the cage, leaping toward the rocky earth, and racing toward the *Drake* which stood below. Smudged reflections of Twig seemed to be running with her. Farther out, the reflections were hazy, but it looked as if the starship was flying out of the black hole.

"There it is," Nova said softly. "My future." She turned back toward Twig. "We're going to escape this place. And we're going to fly back. I know it. The reflections don't lie."

Nova smiled thinly, drew her whip, and began lashing at the cage bars.

CHAPTER ELEVEN
DEMON'S WRATH

They stood in the media room, dozens of scientists and a handful of Alien Hunters, watching the monitor.

Watching the tragedy of Earth.

"By the stars," Giga whispered and turned away.

Steel embraced the android, staring over her shoulder, his jaw clenched.

Many here had tears in their eyes, but Steel would not cry. He had to be strong. For Lenora. For Nova and Twig--both vanished, perhaps still alive somewhere. For the rest of them. His insides roiled, and his teeth gnashed, but he forced himself to keep staring at the monitor.

The footage showed Earth . . . an Earth falling.

The ghosts swarmed across the streets, toppling cars, smashing buildings, clawing people. Whoever they touched screamed, flickered, and vanished from reality. News reporters raced with the crowds. Steel's chest clenched as the footage showed Cog City, his hometown. Highways were collapsing and buildings falling. Thousands of aerocars filled the sky, fleeing the city. And everywhere the ghosts swarmed, covering the planet in a shadowy miasma.

"The creatures' ships seem to have traveled here from Yurei, a black hole a hundred light years away," a news reporter was saying, running down the street. "There is no word from the human observatory studying the black hole, and all we know is that our guns have no effect on the ghosts, that--"

The monitor showed a swarm of the blobby creatures leaping down into the crowd. The reporter screamed, then shattered into a thousand black shards. The cameraman fell, and the footage showed nothing but feet pounding down the street.

"I should be there," Steel whispered. "I should never have left. I'm a Knight of Sol, sworn to defend the Earth." His fists tightened. "Yet now I can only watch, helpless to stop the slaughter."

Romy stood nearby, tears rolling down her cheeks. Riff stared with dark eyes, fists clenching and unclenching at his sides. Lenora huddled with her fellow scientists, embracing them. All stared together, eyes damp.

"We need to fly there," Steel said, voice hoarse. "We need to fix the starship. We need to be there. We--"

"No," Giga said.

Steel stared at her. The android was still embracing him, but her tears had dried, and she stared up into his eyes. Giga was barely taller than his shoulder, slender as a sapling, but a deep strength filled her eyes. The others turned to look too, tearing their eyes away from the footage of destruction.

"No?" Steel asked.

"No," Giga repeated. "No, we do not need to be on Earth."

"Giga!" Steel said, holding her at arm's length. "Don't you care that people are dying? That these ghosts are destroying the planet, that--"

"They are not ghosts," Giga said. "And of course I care. I might be an android, but I'm not a pitiless machine. I want to save the Earth. It's my planet as much as it's yours, Steel. And we would not serve it by dying there. This--right here--is exactly where we need to be." The android looked around her at the others. "Those creatures come from Yurei. This black hole we're orbiting. We cannot defeat them with conventional weapons, but we can study them. We will not win this war with swords, guns, hammers, or whips . . . but with wisdom. We must stay, and we must study them. We must understand who they are."

As always, whenever he gazed into the android's eyes, whenever he felt her soft touch, Steel's anxiety and pain melted. She was ever like a mug of warm, mulled wine, offering comfort in the cold.

"As always, you are wiser than I am, Giga." He kissed the top of her head, then turned to look at his brother. "I believe it's time, Riff, that we ask your trapped ghost some questions."

* * * * *

The brothers stood in the lab, staring at the ghost in the trap.

The creature screeched, fluttering inside the invisible electromagnetic shield. It grew to grotesque size, filling the entire square, then shrank. It howled. It snapped teeth. Its head contracted to a pinpoint, then swelled, then screamed again. For an instant the creature nearly vanished, shrinking into a mere speck, then expanded with rage, exploding in a big bang, crashing into the shield and falling back down.

"Release me!" it cried, voice rising from another world, emerging from the floor, the walls, from inside Riff's own skull. "Release me or you will scream for eternity."

Riff tapped his cheek. "I think . . . no."

The alien screamed again. It thrust toward Riff, jaws opening to an obscene size, large enough to swallow a man whole. Riff stood calmly. Centimeters away from him, the ghost slammed into the force field, then crumpled and fell back.

"Enough of these games," Steel said. The knight stepped forward and raised his sword. Battery packs were strapped onto the blade, pulsing out their own magnetic wave. "You will answer our questions, shadowy one, or I will hurt you."

The ghost spun toward the knight and hissed. Its body twitched like some rabid octopus squeezing between stones.

"Ah, the outcast knight," hissed the creature. "The man who swore to defend Earth, yet abandoned it during its hour of need." The ghost cackled, a horrible sound like snapping bones. "The man who abandoned his lover to join an ancient order, only to be banished from that order like an errant cull. Tell me, Steel Starfire . . . as my brethren slay your fellow humans on Earth, how will you justify your failure to the one you love? What will you tell your sweet Lenora as the Earth burns and you cower here? Or perhaps you will abandon her again, like you did all those years ago, as I crush her bones and suck her blood and--"

Steel thrust his sword.

The blade drove through the trap's force field and pumped out electromagnetic force of its own.

The creature within screamed in pain.

The ghost parted along the blade, fluttering outward. It tried to lash its claws but cut only air. It fell back, shrank, and bunched up in the corner. From there it glared with burning eyes. Steel thrust Solflare again, casting more waves against the creature. It writhed and wailed.

"Enough," Riff said. He guided his brother's sword down. "He's had enough pain for now."

The creature curled up, hissing, teeth gnashing before vanishing into shadows.

"What are you?" Riff said. "Tell me everything and we won't hurt you again."

The ghost leaped up, flew across its square cell, and slammed into the force field. "I will tell you nothing, one of three. But you will tell me everything. All your secrets. All your shame. You will scream of them as you beg me to let you die. Perhaps you will tell me how you let your mother die, how the cyborg slew her while you cowered in your bed. Or perhaps you will tell me how you let your precious Nova and Twig vanish. Oh yes, Starfire. I know about the ashai and the halfling. My brethren break them as we speak. They too are screaming and begging. How they weep! How much pain they take!"

Riff grabbed the sword from his brother and thrust the blade.

The ghost screamed.

As Riff kept the sword pointed forward, both terror and relief filled him. Terror that Nova and Twig were being hurt. Relief that they still lived.

"You will talk!" Riff said, finally pulling the sword back. "Do you hear me, creature? You will tell me your name. You will identify your race. You will answer everything I ask, or we'll keep hurting you. If you tell me everything I need to know, I will contact your masters and swap you for Nova and Twig. Until then you will cooperate."

The ghost flowed closer like smoke. It stared at Riff, and in its eyes, Riff saw visions of that nightmarish land, of a red rose upon a black hill.

"Hurt me all you like, one of three," the creature whispered. "My tolerance for pain knows no bounds, much like my cruelty. Stab me with your blade. Crush me with your invisible fields. Do to me as you like, but I will not tell you what you want to hear. I will say only this: my mistress, Dark Queen Yurei, is coming. On the day of her arrival, you will all die in agony. Every soul here will be hers to torment."

Riff glanced at Steel. The knight stared back, eyes hard. Wordlessly, they stepped to the back of the room. They stood by a wall lined with shelves topped with handheld computers.

"What do we do?" Riff whispered.

Steel's eyes darkened. "I do not relish the idea of hurting it some more. It angered me. I lashed out. But I do not wish to cause it more pain."

Riff glanced at the creature, then back at Steel. "We might have to. It has Nova and Twig. And maybe the scientists who vanished from this observatory before we got here. And . . . oh gods, Steel, these creatures are attacking Earth. Killing thousands, maybe millions. We need information fast about how to defeat them. Every moment we wait, more people are dying."

Steel's teeth gnashed. "So we become torturers? We abandon all honor?"

"I don't know." Riff lowered his head. "I don't like the idea of hurting a living being any more than you do. Even a cruel being like this one. But what if it's the only way to save the Earth? To save Nova and Twig?" He grimaced. "God, Steel . . . they might be torturing Nova and Twig right now."

Steel stared at the creature at the back of the room. His eyes narrowed, and his eyebrows bunched together. "Yet even if we proceed to hurt it, will it speak? So far it's tolerating the pain. We could find ourselves hurting it for hours, staining our souls, only for it to continue to mock us."

Riff stared at the creature too. It glared from its pen, panting, hissing, eyes burning, mocking them. Riff had the uncomfortable feeling that it had heard everything they had whispered here.

Remember the tesseract, stupid, Nova had said. Riff lowered his head. He missed her.

"Uhm . . . sirs? Can I help?"

Riff turned to see Romy tiptoe into the lab. The demon had snagged a lab coat from somewhere and cut holes in the back for her wings. Horn-rimmed glasses perched upon her nose, and she held a telescope under her arm.

"No!" Riff said. "Get back to guarding the airlock. And take off that ridiculous getup. You're a demon, not an astronomer."

"But I *am* an astrony mare!" Romy said. "I have a diploma!"

She raised a framed diploma. Below the words *Doctorate in Astronomy*, somebody had crossed out the name *Lenora Rosetta* with a crayon, replacing it with a scribbled and misspelled *ROMI*.

Riff pointed at the door. "Out."

"But I can help!" The demon stamped her feet. "I'm not only a scientician. I'm also a torturer, Riff. A real torturer. From Hell!" Her tail wagged. "I used to torture the souls of sinners. I was good at it. Real good. How they screamed!"

Riff and Steel stared at the demon. Romy waved back. It was hard to imagine Romy torturing anyone. With her goofy grin, slipping glasses, and wagging tail, Romy looked no more intimidating than a shih tzu. Yet she *did* have sharp claws. Her hair *was* woven of fire. And her mouth *did* sprout fangs that could tear through metal; Riff had seen the marks they left in the *Dragon Huntress*'s engines. Could the demon be speaking truth?

"Romy, Hell doesn't even exist," Riff said. "You're talking rubbish."

"Oh yeah? If Hell doesn't exist, then how am I a demon? Huh? Huh? I ain't no alien. I torture aliens!" She growled. "Oh please, sir. Please let me torture him. I promise I'll be really good at it, just like I tortured sinners in Hell. I'll get you all the information you need. Please please please please please--"

"Fine!" Riff said.

"Please please please please--"

"I said fine!"

Steel frowned. "Brother, are you sure?"

"No." Riff sighed. "But we're not having any luck on our own. And if we don't let Romy try, she'll just keep begging. Maybe if we're lucky, she'll annoy the demon to death."

Romy nodded. "Good. Now out, both of you! Go outside. This will get ugly."

The demon removed her glasses and doffed her lab coat. Suddenly she changed. Her smile turned wicked, and she licked her lips. Her burning hair crackled, and more fire burned in her eyes. She twisted her claws, and tongues of flame raced across her body. She raised her pitchfork, and the prongs spurted out fire.

Riff felt the blood drain from his face. For the first time since he'd known her, Romy seemed like a true demon from Hell--delighting in her wickedness and utterly evil.

Steel and Riff stepped out of the lab into the hallway and closed the door behind them. Red firelight beamed under the door . . . and the screams began.

* * * * *

Riff and Steel waited outside, pacing the hall. The ghost's screams, curses, and howls filled the observatory. Riff could barely stand the sound.

Finally the screams died.

The lab door opened, releasing puffs of smoke.

Romy stepped out, tail wagging.

"Done," she said.

Riff and Steel glanced at each other, then back at the demon.

"And?" Riff asked.

Romy yawned. "And I'm tired. Think I'll have a nap. And a bath. Any baths around here? Oh, and do they have poodles in this observatory?"

"Romy!" Riff grabbed her. "Damn it, did the creature talk?"

She frowned. "What creature? Piston? Now now, Riff, he might be a gruffle after all, but calling him a *creature* is--"

"The ghost!" Riff shook her. "For pity's sake."

"Oh . . . that creature." Romy frowned. "He's not a ghost, Riff. He's a *shade*. He told me!"

"So he talked," Steel said, eyes dark. "The torture broke him."

Romy nodded. "I told you I'm good. He talked. Told me lots and lots of interesting things. Oh, those crazy things he said! So many marvelous things. Things you--"

"Tell us!" Riff said.

The demon poked his chest. "So impatient! Fine. I'll have a bath *later*. Anyway, they're shades. Aliens! You know why they look like ghosts? Because they're *four dimensional* aliens. He explained it. See, some creatures are like snakes. Just a line. One dimensional. Other creatures are like flatfish, those flat little things that lie on the ocean floor. Two dimensional. Most creatures are like me. Three dimensional. Sometimes too three dimensional, especially after too many donuts." The demon glanced over her shoulder at her backside, then back at Riff. "Anyway, these creatures are *four* dimensional. But we can't see their four dimensional side. We only see what three dimensions let us see."

Riff frowned. "What does the fourth dimension even look like?"

Romy shrugged. "I dunno. Never saw it. But imagine you met a flatfish. And the flatfish always lived in a very flat world, and all he could see was flat slices. If you suddenly appeared in two dimensions, the people in flatfish-land would only see bits and pieces of you. Sort of like if I chopped you up like a ham, slice by slice. The flatfish would never see the full you, just the two dimensional slices, one at a time as you passed through their world. That's why the shades keep changing shapes and looking all weird. We're always losing that fourth dimensional bit of them. We're just seeing three-dimensional slices. If you visited their world, you'd finally see what they really look like. Which I don't think is very pleasant at all." Romy licked her lips. "I'm suddenly hungry for ham. Anyone got a ham around?"

Riff thought back to Nova's words. *Remember the tesseract, stupid.*

"Nova tried to tell me," he said. "A tesseract is a four-dimensional cube. She knew somehow." He grabbed the demon. "Romy, did the shade say anything about Nova and Twig?"

"Oh yes, he did. Said he's got them in a cage. And a few other people too. And that they'll never, ever release the prisoners, not ever. Not even if I kept torturing him."

Steel tilted his head. "Romy, I don't see blood on your claws or pitchfork." The knight squinted. "How did you get this information? How did you torture it?"

Romy grinned. "The usual way! I played my accordion." The demon reached behind her back and whipped out a large, red accordion. "Want to hear?"

"No!" the brothers said.

But the demon was already playing. Riff cringed and Steel covered his ears. The sounds were horrible. It sounded like an army of dying cats, or perhaps mating cats, or perhaps cats dying while mating.

"Enough, foul demon!" Steel said.

"See?" Romy lowered her accordion. "It works every time. I always tortured prisoners in Hell this way. For starters. Oh, it got worse, Starfires. Much worse. After I played the accordion, I made the shade smell my stinky socks. And I gave it a good, solid wet willy. Oh, and an Indian burn. That really did the trick. But it wasn't until I showed him photos of our vacation to planet Kitika that he really spilled the beans. Nothing like a good reel of holiday slides to get people talking."

Riff groaned, not sure that he believed the demon, not sure that he cared.

"All right," he said. "Good. We know more. We know a little about them. And . . ." His voice choked. "We know that Nova and Twig are alive. Did the shade say anything else, Romy?"

The demon shook her head. "Nah. Nothing else interesting. Just that . . . well, something about a thousand of his friends on the way over here."

Steel hissed and drew his sword. Riff grabbed his gun.

"And you didn't think that interesting?"

Romy yawned. "Boring! They won't be here for another full hour. Well . . . probably more like half an hour now, what with us all talking here." She stretched. "I'm going to look for that bath. And a ham to eat while bathing. Call me when the ghost army is here!"

The demon wandered off. Riff and Steel looked at each other, then burst into a run.

CHAPTER TWELVE

REMEMBER THE TESSERACT

Nova's whip slammed into the bars, again and again, leaving trails
of light. The cage flared out around her, cubes attached to cubes,
a tesseract in four dimensions. It spun Nova's head, and her mind
refused to comprehend what she saw, but she still knew how to
lash her whip, and she kept slamming it against the bars.

Finally the metal shattered.

Nova snarled. She turned toward Twig and grinned
savagely.

"Ready to fly with me, little one?"

The halfling nodded and doffed her jet pack. "We have only
one of these. You take it and hold me." She smiled tremulously.
"I'm only half your size, after all."

Nova nodded, slung the jet pack across her back, and lifted
Twig. She held the halfling under her left arm, and she gripped
her whip with her right hand.

"Ready?" Nova asked.

Twig nodded. "Let's rock and/or roll."

"For fire and venom!" Nova cried, the ancient words of her
people . . . and leaped out of the cage.

Her jet pack roared out fire. Ashai and halfling blasted out into the sky.

The four dimensions of Yurei roiled around them. Nova's head spun. The land swirled. The ground wasn't flat but rose in endless spheres. The sky folded in onto itself countless times. When Nova glanced behind her, she saw fresh reflections spread out like cards--herself jumping out of the cage, whipping the cage, being dragged into the cage. She stared ahead and saw her future there . . . saw the shades attacking.

"Twig!" Nova cried.

"I see them!"

The towering, shadowy creatures loomed ahead. Each was thrice Nova's size, flying through the air. Black robes fluttered across them, their hems burnt. Their eyes blazed red, and their claws reached out, bone-white. In four dimensions, she could see their wrath, their terror. Her mind still could not fully grasp them--they flared out into the fourth dimension, a shape that spun her mind, a mind used to a three-dimensional world. But she saw their malice. She saw their bloodlust.

Jetpack roaring, Nova screamed and flashed her whip.

"For fire and venom!"

Ahead of her, her reflections exploded, flaring out into a hundred directions. In some paths, translucent slides showed Nova torn apart, the shades clawing her, feasting upon her flesh, tossing her bones down to the ground. In other directions, the beasts caught her, dragged her into her cage. In yet another path, she slew them, but Twig died with showering blood and screams.

Even here, the fourth dimensions could be bent, Nova realized. Even here, destiny was not written in stone. Whatever they were doing here was shaking time itself.

Then the shades reached her, and all Nova knew was the fire of war.

"For Ashmar!" she cried, whip lashing, casting out sparks of electricity.

"For the Alien Hunters!" Twig cried out and tossed her wrench.

The shades screamed. Nova's whip slammed into one, burning its charcoal flesh. Twig's electric wrench crashed into another beast, then boomeranged back into the halfling's hand. The flames roared and spread, soon engulfing the alien.

The aliens shrieked and thrust forward. Nova screamed as claws lashed against her, raising sparks along her armor. Twig howled as claws tore at her arm. One shade clawed at the jet pack, and the fire died. Nova plummeted down, tugged the cord again, and blasted out more flame. They shot forward.

"Keep flying, Nova!" Twig shouted, held in her grip. "Make to the starship! To the *Drake*!"

More shades flew toward them. The creatures were massive, large as black mares, but they flew with the lightness and speed of wasps. Nova swung her whip, forcing them back, casting out her sparks. Twig kept tossing her wrench. The electric weapon slammed into shades, then flew back into Twig's waiting grasp, leaving a trail of reflections.

We might be stuck inside a black hole, our past and future spreading around us like a deck of tarots, Nova thought. *But damn it, we can still hunt aliens.*

Her whip lashed again, cutting the creatures down, and Nova laughed as she fought. With a shower of electricity, the ashai and halfling tore through the enemies, gliding toward the *Drake.*

The dagger-shaped starship lay on the rocky surface of the Dark Planet. Several shades floated around it, robed and hooded. The aliens stared up, eyes burning like red lanterns, and raised black hilts. Crimson fire blazed out, forming crackling blades.

"Come to die, ones of three," they hissed.

Twig cried out, her voice high-pitched but full of rage. The halfling fired lightning from her wrench. Holding Twig under one arm, Nova blasted down toward the enemy. Her whip lashed, casting a lightning bolt into another creature. Ashai and halfling landed on the rocky surface before the starship, snarling.

The shades charged toward them, fiery blades crackling through the air, showering sparks.

"For the Alien Hunters," Nova whispered.

One fireblade swung toward Nova. She lashed her whip and cut through the fire. As the alien leaped toward her, she ducked, ran, and leaped up. Her whip swung again, slicing through the creatures, scattering chunks of their flesh. The aliens roiled all around her. She fought within an endless stream of them, a sea of burning eyes, lashing claws, snapping teeth, creatures that spread all around, behind her, above her, in her past, in her future. She cried in rage and kept tearing them down.

Twig fought at her side. The mini-mechanic leaped through the air, somersaulted, and tossed her wrench. Her eyes burned like blue fires. Her electricity crackled, kindling the enemy's robes. A fireblade grazed the halfling, burning strands of her hair and leaving a line on her cheek, but still Twig fought, carving a path toward the *Drake*.

The ship was the only thing here that still made sense to Nova's mind, a three-dimensional object in a world of four dimensions. She leaped toward it, cut another shade down, and yanked the door open.

"Twig, with me!"

The halfling tossed her wrench. It flew, knocked down a shade, and boomeranged back into Twig's hand. She leaped into the starship with Nova. The two landed inside the airlock and slammed the door shut behind them.

The door rattled. The hull dented. The ship rocked. The shades were slamming against it, biting, clawing.

"With me, Twig! Help me find the bridge."

They ran together through the ship. The *Drake* was long, narrow, and dark, a blade with wings. The ship rocked madly as they ran. Dents kept appearing on the hull. Through the portholes, Nova saw fireblades slamming against the metal, chipping it away. She and Twig kept running toward the nose of the ship.

"Nova, watch out!" Twig cried.

Nova hissed. A round creature leaped up, a massive mouth that flared out into multiple jaws, a rolling ball of teeth connected by black tendons. Nova swung her whip, tearing through it, scattering teeth and jawbones. They kept running. Another creature rolled through the fuselage, leaped up, and flew toward them. It was vaguely canine, sprouting a dozen drooling heads. Twig blasted forth lightning, knocking it down.

"Shade pets," Twig muttered. "Ugly bastards."

"Not too ugly," Nova said, cutting down another beast. "You should see Earth's Chihuahuas."

"I like Chihuahuas!" Twig said.

Nova groaned. "You would."

The ship shook madly as a fireblade tore into the hull before them. Nova lashed her whip through the rent, cutting down the alien outside. Twig whipped out duct tape and sealed the breach, and the two kept running. They burst through a doorway and onto the bridge.

A windshield afforded a view of swirling, four-dimensional rocks and hills. Between them, in the distance, Nova could see planet Kaperosa floating in space, stretched across time, its reflections forming a ring. Two leather seats faced control panels.

Between the seats lurked a massive, smoky serpent.

The python rose, fractured into many coiling creatures, a four-dimensional hydra with multiple heads. All those heads now hissed and thrust toward Nova and Twig.

Behind them, the ship screeched as fireblades kept cutting at the hull.

"Twig, know how to fly?" Nova shouted, leaping back as a serpent's head thrust toward her.

Twig ducked beneath another striking snake head. "In theory."

"Good enough! Fly us! Now! I'll take care of the snakes."

Twig spurted electricity from her wrench, roasting one serpent head, and nodded. The halfling somersaulted through the air, landed in a seat, and pushed down on the throttle.

The *Drake*'s engines roared.

The ship bolted forward.

The serpent's heads drove toward Nova, fangs dripping venom.

As the *Drake* rose into the sky, Nova swung her whip. Electricity filled the cabin. The lash tore through one serpent's head, cauterizing the wound. The ship rocked madly, spurting out flame, soaring and tilting. Through the windshield, Nova saw the four-dimensional Dark Planet spinning all around, a jumble of land, sky, and stars multiplied and spreading into all directions. It felt like flying through a funhouse full of mirrors.

"I can't see where I'm going!" Twig cried, tugging at a joystick.

"Focus on Kaperosa." Nova pointed at the planet ahead. "Keep staring at it and fly!"

The serpent heads screeched and thrust back toward her. Nova ducked and rolled. Her lash flew again, slicing off another head. Two severed heads now snapped their jaws on the floor, dragging themselves closer to her. Nova kicked one aside, cracked her whip, and severed a third head.

"Enemy ships ahead!" Twig said.

Nova glanced out the windshield to see black, impossible ships--they were shaped as tesseracts--flying toward them.

"Fire!" Nova shouted.

"How?"

"The red button! Do it! Shoot them down!"

Twig hit the controls. Photons blasted from the *Drake*'s starboard cannon, streamed through space, and slammed into the enemy ships.

With just as much force, the serpent slammed into Nova. She fell to the floor. The scaly creature coiled around her, constricting her. Nova's hand clutched the whip's hilt, but with her arms pinned to her sides, she could not lash it. She floundered, unable to free herself.

"Nova!" Twig cried, turning toward her.

"I'm fine, keep flying!"

Twig returned her gaze forward, and she fired more photons at the enemy ships. Nova writhed on the floor. The snake heads struck, and fangs slammed into her armor, unable to pierce it. The serpent wrapped tighter around her. It perhaps could not pierce Nova's armor, but it could crush her within it.

Nova could not lash her whip, but she could still switch it on.

She clicked the switch on the handle.

Electricity raced through her.

Nova flailed like a fish, screaming. The electricity bolted through her and into the serpent. The creature squealed and released her.

Shaking, Nova rose to her feet and swung the lash. In a single, fluid movement, she severed the serpent's final three heads.

"How we doing?" Nova asked, limping toward the second seat. Smoke rose from her armor.

"Could use some help," Twig said. "I can't fire both cannons at once. My arms are too short."

Enemy ships still flew ahead. The tesseracts screamed as they streaked through the sky, leaving trails behind them. With so many afterimages crowding her vision, Nova couldn't decide how many enemy vessels flew here. She didn't care. She didn't need to blast them all, just cut her way through.

She pressed her own controls, firing the *Drake*'s portside cannon.

Twin beams shot through the darkness, slamming into the ships ahead. The cosmos seemed to explode with spinning, shattering metal.

Leaking air, dented, and wobbling, the *Drake* shot between the enemies and out of the black hole.

They burst into open space.

Nova grabbed her own joystick, struggling to steady the swaying ship. Monitors mounted above showed her the rear view; the carcasses of enemy ships floated there, smoking and tilting. Hope rose in Nova for the first time since waking up inside this black hole.

"We can defeat them," she whispered. "We know their secrets now. We know where their home world is--a Dark Planet inside the black hole. We can win. We'll fly back with the *Dragon Huntress* and blast their whole damn world apart."

* * * * *

As the *Drake* flew out of the black hole, planet Kaperosa loomed ahead.

Nova had expected to see a spherical world, but even outside of Yurei, she was still stuck in four dimensions, it seemed. Kaperosa did not appear as a three-dimensional sphere but as a great tube that stretched across the sky. Nova frowned.

"Why is the planet stretched out into a ring around the black hole?"

"We're seeing the planet in four dimensions." Twig's eyes gleamed. "We're seeing it across time as well. We're seeing its orbit around the black hole--countless spheres spreading in rings around the darkness."

Nova pointed. "I see a light. The observatory." She frowned. "Actually, a line of light. Countless observatories."

Twig shook her head. "No. Only one observatory, but appearing as many to us."

Nova growled. "But we're out of the black hole! Why are we still stuck in four dimensions?"

Twig tilted her head. "I don't know."

Nova glared at the halfling. "Aren't you a scientist?"

"A mechanic! Not the same. And this is new, Nova. I didn't even think such a thing was possible. I don't know how this happened." Twig sighed. "I understand so little."

"And I understand nothing," Nova muttered. "All I know is my whip, my fists, the fire in my belly. New dimensions?" She snorted. "Give me an old-fashioned skelkrin to kill, and I'm a happy girl. This place makes my brain hurt."

The ring of countless planets--no, one planet stretched across time--grew closer, soon covering their field of vision. Nova directed the *Drake* toward one image of the observatory. The network of tunnels and domes clung to the rocky surface, smeared across the higher dimension. It was like seeing a speeding car smudged in an overexposed photograph. Beside the observatory rested the *Dragon Huntress*, still out of commission. A squat figure in a space suit stood here, welding the starship together.

Piston!

Twig engaged the thruster engines, and Nova managed to guide the *Drake* onto the lot. They thumped down beside the *Dragon Huntress*.

Piston didn't even turn around.

No scientists stretched out a walkway.

Nova glanced at Twig. The halfling stared back, her large blue eyes gleaming in the shadows.

"Doesn't he see us?" Nova said.

"I don't know," Twig said. "Let's suit up."

They grabbed helmets and oxygen tanks from the wall, then left the bridge. They walked through the dented fuselage of the *Drake*, over the corpses of dead shade pets, and out onto the surface of Kaperosa.

The *Dragon Huntress* loomed ahead on the lot, a towering metal dragon, its hull still smashed. Piston stood on a ladder, welding one of the ship's cracked wings.

"Hey, you bozo!" Nova said, marching up toward him. "I'm free. Free!" She jumped around. "Rude as a rhino, you are."

She froze and gasped.

Up on the ladder, Piston was crying softly. Tears streamed down his brown cheeks, dampened his white beard, and fogged up his helmet.

"Where are you, Twig?" the gruffle whispered, lips trembling. "Where are you, my friend?"

"I'm right here!" Twig shouted, jumping up and down.

The gruffle froze, then turned around. His eyes narrowed. Then he shook his head and let out a sob.

"I miss you so much, Twig, that I can almost hear your voice." He lowered his head. "Where are you, little one?"

Twig leaped around. "Over here!" She raced forward and tried to grab the gruffle, but somehow the halfling's small hands kept missing.

"Oh, Twig." Piston returned to his welding. "How can I fix this ship without you? How can I live without my little clod friend?"

Twig and Nova looked at each other.

"I don't like this," Nova whispered.

Twig shuddered. "Neither do I. Let's go inside."

Leaving the gruffle to his work, Nova and Twig approached the observatory's airlock. The door spread out into multiple reflections. Most were still closed, but in one reflection, the door was open, and they stepped through, entering the shadows of Kaperosa Observatory.

Nova blinked.

The insides of the observatory were a hodgepodge of dimensions. The walls kept turning around her. The stars streamed outside in streaks. Scientists walked through the corridors, leaving trails of reflections.

"Are we really here?" Nova whispered. "Are you sure we're not still in the black hole, and this is some illusion?"

Twig grimaced. "This is the place. But we're still stuck in the higher plane."

A scientist walked ahead of them, not seeming to see them, leaving a wake of himself.

"This place is full of ghosts," Nova muttered.

"Or maybe we're the ghosts now," said Twig.

They kept walking, heading deeper into the observatory. People bustled back and forth, a crowd of thousands. Nobody seemed to notice them. In the round, glass dome, the telescope appeared as a disk, pointing at once in all directions. In the cafeteria, ten thousand meals topped the table.

A scent of jasmine tickled her nostrils, and Nova turned to see Giga walking down a corridor. The android seemed to wear several kimonos at once, each a different color, each alternating, vanishing and reappearing.

"Giga!" Nova shouted and ran into the corridor after her. "Giga, can't you see me?"

The android turned toward her. Her dark eyes narrowed, and a furrow appeared on her brow. Clicking and humming sounds rose from her mechanical innards.

"Giga!" Nova said.

She tried to grab the android, but she couldn't seem to grasp her. Her fingers barely ruffled the android's kimono.

"Giga, can't you hear me?" Nova shouted.

The android stared at her, perplexed, then shrugged and turned around. She marched away.

Nova spun toward Twig. "Let's blow some fire."

"In the observatory?" Twig cringed.

Nova nodded, doffed her jet pack, pointed it forward . . . and blasted out a spurt of flame. The fire roared, a shrieking inferno. The jet pack tore free from Nova's grasp, whizzed across the chamber, and finally clunked down.

Two scientists walked by, passing right through the flames.

"Bit warm in here, isn't it?" one said.

His companion nodded. The pair walked on.

Nova groaned. This was ridiculous. She raced through the halls. Twig ran behind her. They burst into a laboratory.

"Romy!" Nova said. "Romy, can you see me?"

The demon held a purple crayon, drawing dinosaurs onto the wall. She froze and looked over her shoulder.

Nova breathed a sigh of relief. "You can see me, can't you, Romy?" She stepped closer and grabbed the demon. "Where's Riff? I--"

Romy gasped. "A ghost!" she whispered. "Oh god, a ghost!"

"Romy, I'm not--"

But the demon was already fleeing. She raced across the lab, managed to trip on her tail, then pushed herself up and ran down a hallway, wailing about golden ghosts in the lab.

Twig came to stand at Nova's side. "It's no use. We're stuck in the higher dimension."

"Why can't they see us?" Nova said, turning toward the halfling.

Twig lifted Romy's fallen crayon and drew a stick figure on the wall. "Imagine that this figure lives in Flatland, a two-dimensional world. Somebody three-dimensional, staring at the wall, will see our flat stick figure. But our flat gentlemen will have no idea that anything exists beyond the wall, beyond his flat realm. He can only see other flat figures drawn onto the wall."

Nova groaned and placed her hand against the wall. "There, I'm two-dimensional now."

"Your palm is." Twig nodded. "Now our flat figure can see the shape of your hand, but not the rest of you. A slice. A ghost." Her shoulders slumped. "That's how we appear now. Flutters of color. The hints of a voice. Four-dimensional beings barely able to communicate with the three-dimensional world. Ghosts."

Nova sighed, gazed out the doorway Romy had fled through, and frowned.

Out in the corridor, she saw herself.

An older reflection of her, no dents or scratches on her armor, was walking down the hall with Riff.

"I should never have let you try to land the ship," the reflection of Nova was saying, marching down the corridor. "I swear, Riff, every time you try to fly, you end up crashing, and . . ."

Nova--the real Nova, here and now--gasped.

"It's me the day they grabbed me." She turned toward Twig. "That was the day I walked with Riff to the greenhouse. The day we fought the ghosts there, and they snatched me." She made a beeline to the doorway. "I have to stop this from happening."

Twig ran in pursuit. "Nova, I don't know if that's wise! We don't know if we can change the past. And even if we can, we don't know the ramifications."

Nova ignored her. She burst out into the hall and saw her old self--Nova from a few days ago--walking toward the greenhouse with Riff. She followed.

"Riff!" she shouted. "Riff, you idiot!"

His reflection paused.

He turned around.

Nova shouted again and leaped up and down, but Riff only shook his head, turned away, and kept walking. Nova growled and followed.

"Nova, wait!" Twig said. "If you change time, you can create a paradox."

Nova snorted. "Paradoxes, schmaradoxes. I leave that to the scientists." She kept following the reflection of herself and Riff.

"Wait!" Twig's pockets jangled as she raced alongside. "If you stop yourself from being kidnapped, you'll have never met me inside the black hole, never escaped the tesseract cage, never come here . . . to stop yourself from being kidnapped. Which means that the kidnapping would still happen. Which means that you will escape, will come here, will stop it . . . and you'll create an impossible loop, Nova. A version of the Grandfather Paradox."

"So?" Nova kept marching down the corridor.

"Well, that could lock the entire cosmos into some kind of knot. It could undo the very fabric of our reality. I don't know what would happen." Twig blinked and tapped her chin. "To be honest, I'd be kind of curious to see it. But . . ." She shook her head wildly and grabbed Nova. "No. I can't let you do this."

Nova spun toward the halfling and hissed. "I don't care what you say. I don't need your permission to do anything." She shook off the grasping little hands. "Now help me or shut it."

Ahead, the younger Nova and Riff stepped into the greenhouse. The current Nova followed, Twig fast on her heel.

She found herself back in a hot, steaming room full of plants. Nova could now see the plants rise from seeds, grow taller, and finally wither, all at once. The younger Riff and Nova--the ones from a few days ago--were exploring the place, hunting for ghosts.

Nova froze and gasped.

"They're everywhere," she whispered.

The shades covered the ceiling, clung to the walls, crawled along the floor. The creatures hissed, stared down at Nova and Riff with blazing eyes, scuttled back and forth. These were not the ghostly creatures Nova had previously seen. From her current plane of existence, the shades appeared fully formed, four-dimensional, demons of charcoal flesh, claws, fangs, and burning eyes.

And the younger versions of Nova and Riff couldn't even see them.

"Riff!" she shouted. "Nova! Younger Nova!"

They couldn't hear her. They kept walking among the plants.

"Carrots? Celery? Apples?" said the younger Nova. "That's rabbit food. Where do they grow the steak?"

"There's synthetic meat in the lab down the hall." Riff passed his hands through a tree's foliage.

The younger Nova snorted. "Synthetic meat. So human. We ashais *hunt*."

As the reflections spoke, the shades grew closer, leaning down from the fourth dimension. Still the pair couldn't see the creatures.

"Why can't you see the enemy?" Nova shouted. "Damn it. Riff! Nova!"

Twig stepped closer to her. Her gleaming blue eyes looked so sad. "Because they're like the stick figure on the wall. They can't see what's in the higher dimension."

Nova clutched her head. Of course. Damn it! The shades weren't ghosts. They were *always* in the observatory. Always watching, hovering in the dimension the humanoids couldn't see. Their reflections scuttled around the younger Nova and Riff, always there, waiting to pounce.

"They're not really here," Twig said softly. "We're just watching reflections. Just memories. A thing that happened, that we can't change."

The lights went out. The shades swooped.

Just a memory, Nova told herself, watching helplessly.

"Riff, damn it!" she shouted. "Nova! Can't you hear me?"

She stood helplessly, watching the battle. The shades appeared as nothing but ghosts to the younger her, but standing here, a four-dimensional being herself, Nova could see their true forms. They kept backing away from every lash of the younger Nova's whip. In three-dimensions, their forms would appear to be contracting and morphing. From her new vantage point, they simply stepped aside from each lash, as easily as a three-dimensional being pulling back from an aggressive stick figure on a wall.

But I can hurt them.

"For fire and venom!" Nova cried and swung her whip. The lash arched through the air . . . and passed right through the shades, doing them no harm.

"They're just memories." Twig lowered her head. "We're just seeing the past. Come on, Nova, let's get out of here."

Nova stared, eyes damp. The shades were grabbing the younger her now, wrapping their arms around that naive woman, dragging her away from Riff.

I can't let them take me. Nova's heart fluttered. *I can't let this happen to me. To be trapped like this, able to see the man I love but unable to speak to him, to let him know I'm here.*

"Riff!" she cried, and now tears streamed from her eyes.

Because I love you, Riff, she thought. *I've loved you since I was a girl. And now I'm doomed to forever float above you as a ghost, watching you grow old without me, always there, never able to tell you.* It seemed to Nova a fate worse than death.

"Damn it, Riff!" she shouted. "I'm in the fourth dimension. The shades are too. They're everywhere, Riff! Always watching you. Like me. Like me . . ."

She thought that maybe he heard her. His eyes flicked toward her, then away again. Shades were pinning him down, cutting his skin.

Nova growled.

She raced forward.

I will stop this.

She barreled forward, shoved between the memories of shades, and grabbed the younger version of herself.

Her fingers passed through nothing . . . and then she snapped into place.

The two Novas, old and new, became one.

Gripped in the shades' claws, she turned to look at Riff. He lay on the ground, pinned down, and met her gaze.

"Remember the tesseract, stupid," she whispered.

And then the shades yanked out her younger half, ripping it away, and it felt like Nova's soul was torn free.

Her eyes rolled back. She fell to the floor.

"I've got you, Nova." Twig grabbed her. "Come with me. We're getting out of here."

Nova limped out of the greenhouse, leaning on the little halfling. They made their way down the corridor and into the glass dome. The telescope stood on its stand, facing the black hole above. The stars shone around the gaping pit.

Nova stared toward that dark eye, toward Yurei.

"It looks different now," she whispered.

Twig shuddered. "We can see the world within."

They stood together, holding each other, staring through the glass toward the hole in the sky. Inside the black hole, like a lurid Christmas ornament, hung the Dark Planet of the shades.

As they stood watching, countless starships shaped as tesseracts rose from that strange world. The warships streamed out of the black hole, heading toward Kaperosa.

"Enemy ships." Twig shivered. "Those aren't reflections."

"It's the shade armada." Nova clenched her fists. "And they're coming here."

CHAPTER THIRTEEN

HALLS OF SHADOW

Riff stared out the window and felt the blood drain from his face.

"There they are," he whispered. "All their might and fury."

Steel stood at his side in the airlock, chin raised, hands clasping the hilt of his massive sword. The knight's face remained hard, his eyes dark. "By my honor, I will fight them until my last breath."

"I'd rather you fought them until *their* last breath." Riff hefted his gun.

Steel said no more. Behind them, a score of scientists stood in the airlock. Each held a rod crackling with electromagnetic radiation, weapons to banish ghosts. Each stared out the window, waiting for the enemy fleet. They all wore space suits and helmets, the visors raised. Oxygen tanks hung across their backs. If the shades breached the observatory, they would need them.

Riff returned his eyes to the window. The ships were approaching rapidly, flickers in the darkness that blocked the stars. The ships changed form as they flew, contracting, flaring out, their angles forever morphing.

Remember the tesseract, Nova had said.

As Riff stared out the airlock window at the approaching vessels, the memory pounded through him.

"Remember the tesseract," he whispered.

Steel frowned. "Remember what?"

"That's what Nova told me. Before they grabbed her. Remember the tesseract." He stared out the window at the enemy vessels. "That's what they are. Tesseracts."

Riff barked out a laugh. Of course. He remembered that day. Nova and he had visited the Museum of the Strange in the asteroid belt, a floating sideshow of mutated calves in jars, the bones of medical mysteries, wax replicas of deformed circus performers . . . and a holographic projection purporting to show a tesseract.

"A tesseract!" Riff repeated. "A four-dimensional cube."

Steel narrowed his eyes. "You speak in riddles."

Riff shook his head. "A single dimension is a line. Two dimensions allow a square. In three dimensions you get a cube. In four dimensions . . . a tesseract." He pointed at the fast-approaching ships. "That's what they are . . . seen in our own three dimensions. Nova knew."

He stared at the black ships. Their shapes could only exist in their higher dimension. In his three-dimensional world, they looked convoluted, cubes cobbled together into impossible, mind-twisting constructions.

"I don't care what they are," said Steel, "only that they die at my blade." He inhaled deeply. "Fight well, my brother. I am with you. Always."

The ships landed outside, slamming onto the planet with a jolt that shook the observatory.

Riff looked behind him at the scientists who stood there, holding their rods.

"This is your last chance. Step down into the cellars now. Lock the doors. Be safe."

They stared back, eyes hard. Lenora hefted her magnetic rod and raised her chin. "If we cannot repel the enemy, there will be no safety anywhere. We fight with you, Starfire brothers."

Perhaps unconsciously, Steel took a step sideways, placing himself between Lenora and the airlock door.

Outside, coiling shapes were emerging from the tesseracts and bounding across the surface. Growing. Changing. Shrinking. Appearing and reappearing.

Remember the tesseract.

"Not ghosts," Riff whispered. "Beings from a higher dimension."

With shrieks and thuds and denting metal, the creatures slammed into the walls and doors of the observatory.

Riff snarled and aimed Ethel, his loyal plasma gun. Steel raised his blade. Behind them, the scientists hefted their rods.

The doors rattled. Dents appeared across them. Outside the fused silica windows, the shades stared with red eyes, opening maws thick with white teeth. Their swirling, shadowy forms hid the world beyond. Their laughter and screams filled the airlock. Deeper in the observatory, Riff could hear metal shatter and Romy scream.

He stared at the door. Waiting.

It shook. Again. Again.

A crack appeared in the wall.

A dent shoved into the doorway.

Riff and the others lowered the visors on their helmets.

With shrieking air and ethereal screams, the doorway shattered.

Riff fired his gun.

Plasma blasted forth, showering over the creatures. Steel thrust his blade, casting out a disk of light and a pulsing electromagnetic field.

The shades howled. Several of them fell back, shattering. The rest flowed forth, claws outstretched.

Riff fired again, blasting another creature, but the horde was too strong. The shades shoved into the doorway, mobbing him. Riff fell and swung his rod, trying to hold them back.

"For Sol!" Steel cried, swinging his blade, tearing through the creatures, scattering shreds of their black flesh.

"For . . . science!" Lenora cried, thrusting her electric rod. Her fellow scientists fought around her, casting out their electromagnetic fields.

Shades howled, a deafening sound, a sound so loud Riff thought it could split his skull. He struggled to his feet, fired his gun again, slew another creature. More slammed into him, knocking him down again. Jaws materialized around his leg and snapped shut, tearing into his skin. He pistol-whipped the shade, then fired upward into a swooping ghost. Claws lashed at him.

And more of the enemy kept pouring in.

They flowed through the door like polluted water. They smashed the windows. They scuttled across the ceiling, then rained as black tar.

"By my honor, by the light of Sol, you will not pass!" Steel cried, swinging his sword in circles. But the ghosts swarmed across him too. Their claws sparked against his armor. Their fangs drove into his breastplate, cracking the metal. Their shadowy, convulsing bodies knocked him down and they laughed, drooled, screeched.

"Now you die, ones of three. Die. Die. Die."

The room shook as more tesseract ships shrieked outside. Between the shades, Riff caught a glimpse of the sky outside. The enemy ships hid the stars, covered the surface of Kaperosa like a blanket, and still more flew. Still more shades emerged.

"Now you die. Die. Die."

Riff stared in horror, barely able to breathe.

Nova and Twig--gone. The *Dragon Huntress*--dead. All hope for aid--lost. The Earth--dying, maybe already gone.

Fear, colder than the grip of ten thousand ghosts, twisted Riff's heart.

If I die, I die fighting side by side with my brother.

He grabbed Steel and tugged him up.

"The airlock is lost!" he shouted. "We fall back. Back into the observatory. We'll fight them in the labyrinth of corridors."

One scientist fell beside them. The shades leaped onto the old man, tearing into his flesh. Blood spurted. The creatures howled as they fed upon him. To Riff's right, another man fell, the dark creatures tearing him apart.

"Fall back!" Riff shouted. "Back! Lenora, get them into the corridors."

Blood seeped from a gash on Lenora's head, and scratches covered her arms. But she nodded. Swinging her rod before her, knocking the shades aside, she herded scientists into the corridor. Every man or woman who left the airlock merely made room for more shades to stream in.

Riff and Steel stood side by side, firing their weapons. Plasma and electricity lit the airlock. A fog of the creatures hid the floor, the walls, the ceiling. Riff could see nothing but their inky flesh, their red eyes, their teeth, and beside him always, his brother.

"It's been an honor to fight with you, brother," Steel said.

"We ain't done yet." Riff fired his gun. "Back!"

The last scientist fled the airlock. Walking backward, weapons firing, Riff and Steel followed.

The corridor was narrow, closing in around them, trapping them here in a labyrinth of metal. Ahead, the airlock shattered. Its walls and ceiling collapsed, revealing an endless cloud of the creatures. With triumphant laughter, the enemy flowed into the corridor.

"Die, ones of three. Die!"

The labyrinth of Kaperosa Observatory shook and echoed with ghostly howls, with laughter, and with the screams of the dying.

* * * * *

The dark wave flowed through Kaperosa Observatory. Steel felt as if the network of corridors and chambers were the innards of some alien conch, tossed into a pit of tar, the sticky darkness invading its twisting halls.

So this is where I die, he thought. *So this is where I fall in glory.*

As Steel stood in the corridor, swinging his sword, a thin smile tingled his lips.

It was a good place to die.

The shades swarmed. Their fangs and claws dented and cracked his armor. Their bodies swirled around him, grabbing him, showing him visions of a nightmarish land of black hills, stormy skies, a laughing queen. Outside the window, the black hole loomed, laughing, a mouth waiting to engulf him, to take him to that shadowy realm. Yet Steel would not let them take him. With blade, with cold determination, he fought back.

For the Alien Hunters. For Lenora. For all life.

"Fall back!" Riff cried behind him. "To the inner chambers! Back!"

Scientists were rushing back, fleeing deeper into this labyrinth, but every step, they fell. The creatures emerged from the ceiling, from the walls, bubbled up from the floor, seeped through vents.

Riff fought at Steel's side, plasma gun filling the chambers with light and heat. Giga leaped through the air, katana swinging, cleaving the shades. But the creatures kept advancing, ten more appearing for every one that fell. A scientist swung a rod, driving two ghosts back, only for a third to leap from the ceiling, envelop him with blackness, and tear him apart.

"Steel, come, to the inner chambers!" Lenora said behind him. Blood splashed her space suit. Not all of it was her own.

Steel nodded. "I will hold back the evil. Go, take them deeper!"

Fear filled Lenora's eyes, but she nodded. She herded her people back. Steel stood his ground in the corridor, teeth bared, swinging his blade, refusing to fall, refusing to let the enemy reach Lenora.

I failed you once, Lenora, many years ago. I will not fail you again.

That old pain dug through him. None of this should have happened. How Steel wished he could turn back the years! To be young again, eighteen and in love!

If I could go back in time, I would never have left you, Lenora. I would have gone with you to the stars, not joined your father's order. We could have married, raised a family, not ended up here.

Steel roared, swung his blade, and cleaved a ghost. A wall shattered at his side, and more shades emerged, and he fought them, howling in his rage.

I'm sorry, Lenora.

His long years of servitude, of exile, had given him this strength. Made him a warrior. Perhaps now, with this strength beaten into him, he could at least save Lenora.

Yet could he truly save her? What awaited them in the innards of the observatory if not more battle, a death in a trap? Why did they still fight if no hope remained?

"Piston!" Riff shouted into his communicator. "Piston, we need the *Dragon Huntress* flying!"

The gruffle's voice rose through the speakers. "I'm doing all I can, sir! But . . . without Twig, I can't fix the turbines, and--"

"Fix them now!" Riff fired his gun, melting a shade. "Fix them and bring the ship to the observatory roof. Now! That's an order!"

Riff still clung to hope, Steel knew. His brother still believed the gruffle could save them, that the *Dragon Huntress* could swoop down with glory, pick them up, deliver them to safety.

Yet Steel knew: *I was always meant to come here, to die here. This is why I spent years in the knighthood, then years in exile, honing my blade, my inner strength.* He swung that blade now, slaying the enemies. *To come here. To die in darkness. With Lenora.*

"Steel, come on, hurry!" Lenora cried behind him, retreating into an inner lab.

You cannot flee me, knight, rose a voice in his head. Outside the window, the black hole seemed to laugh, to mock him, a swirling pit ready to swallow him. *You cannot save her. I will keep you both alive, knight. You and the woman you abandoned. You will both scream eternally in my darkness.*

Steel raised his head and stared directly into that black hole.

The Dark Queen laughed within, tugging at him, showing him visions of his body broken, of Lenora screaming at his feet, of a land of endless torment and devilry, a dark hell in the bowels of space.

Steel stared and smiled thinly.

"No," he whispered.

Behind him, Lenora retreated into the lab. Steel swung his blade in a great arc.

"No!" he roared, cutting down the enemy, and stepped back with the others into the innermost chambers.

Perhaps he could not win this fight. But they would never take him alive. He would slay the enemies with his sword until he could slay no more . . . and then he would fall upon it.

They fought in shadowed chambers, racing through the labyrinth of Kaperosa, trying to move upwards, to reach the roof, to reach Riff's hope of rescue.

I do not fear falling upon my sword, Steel thought as he fought up a staircase, holding the shades back as Lenora and the others climbed with him. *Yet do I have the courage to grant Lenora the same mercy?*

For the first time in the battle, Steel felt some of his courage wane.

Would he dare drive Solflare into Lenora's heart, grant her a quick death before the ghosts could grab her? Would he do the same to Riff, to Piston, to the others? His eyes stung, and his hands trembled, and he roared in pain as he fought. He would do what he must. A knight always did what he must. Yet the horror seemed too great to Steel, a weight too heavy to bear.

How can I find the strength for this? Whatever gods can hear me, grant me the courage.

A soft golden light flickered.

As Steel fought on the staircase, climbing ever upward, he gasped.

The golden light shone again.

A spirit! A spirit of gold fought with him! He could barely see the figure, but as he fought, it seemed to Steel that a woman of light, golden as dawn, was fighting ever at his side. A goddess from another world. A comforting presence. The others did not see her, but it seemed to Steel that the spirit met his gaze, offered him comfort, strength, an answer to his prayers. Her light flared out, casting back the enemy, guiding him onward.

"My lady," Steel whispered, tears in his eyes. "My lady of light."

He did not know what goddess this was, what benevolent presence had sent him this protector. But as the golden light shone at his side, new strength filled Steel. Perhaps not all hope was lost. Not all in the cosmos was visible to him. The darkness was full of evil, of devils he did not comprehend. Yet there was goodness too in the worlds beyond, goodness that watched over him.

They fought onward, holding back the enemy as they climbed the stairs. Alien Hunters. Scientists. And an angel of light, blessing him.

CHAPTER FOURTEEN
SWORDS AND SHADES

Twig tossed her wrench through the corridors, knocking down shades, but more kept flowing in, an endless ocean of the beasts. Nova fought at her side, sneering, terrible to behold, her electric whip a bringer of light and death. For every shade Twig killed, the ashai warrior slew twenty.

Yet there are thousands here, Twig thought. *Maybe millions. Too many.*

Still stuck in the higher plane, Twig no longer saw the shades as ghosts. They loomed, solid, ten feet tall, creatures of burnt robes and withered flesh. Twig wished she were back in three dimensions, fighting only shadows, fighting with her fellow Alien Hunters. Riff shouted at her side, firing his plasma gun. Giga somersaulted through the air, bouncing off the walls, swinging her katana. Romy wailed as she fought, lashing her pitchfork. But none could see Twig and Nova, two souls lost in the fourth dimension--ghosts themselves.

All but . . .

Twig frowned.

"I think Steel can see you, Nova!" she shouted, leaping into the air and thrusting her wrench.

Nova stood a few paces away in the corridor, lashing her whip. Riff and Giga were fighting a few steps back, herding the surviving scientists onto another staircase. Steel stood ahead, swinging his sword, fighting at the vanguard. While the others seemed oblivious to Twig and Nova's presence, Steel kept glancing toward Nova, smiling softly.

"Steel, can you see me?" Nova shouted, standing at his side, helping him hold back the enemy.

The knight glanced toward the ashai. "My golden lady," he whispered.

When Twig stared at Steel's armor, she could see flecks of gold reflected in the metal, a mere spirit of light, vaguely shaped as a woman. Nova's ghost--how her gleaming armor and flowing hair appeared in three-dimensions.

"He can see your golden armor!" Twig cried. "A rough image, at least."

A shade leaped toward her, and Twig lashed her wrench, electrocuting it. Another one of the creatures slammed into her, tearing at her flesh. Twig's blood spurted and she screamed.

"Twig, get to the *Dragon Huntress*!" Nova cried. "You're no more use here. You have to help Piston fix the ship."

Twig groaned. "I can't! I can barely touch anything in three dimensions anymore, and Piston can't see me. I'm just a ghost to him."

"Then go and haunt him!" Nova shouted. "Get out of here, Twig. Do what you can. I don't care how. Get the ship flying!"

Tears stung Twig's eyes as she fought. How could she help? She had tried to grab ahold of objects in three dimensions, only to see them slip between her fingers. She had tried to speak to the other Alien Hunters, but so far, only Romy and Steel seemed to have noticed their presence at all, and--

Twig's breath caught.

Romy!

Of course!

Back when Nova and I first entered the observatory, Romy saw us. She thought us ghosts. She fled. She too can see us.

The battle moved upstairs into an attic. Twig pulled down the visor of her helmet. The observatory scientists, clad in space suits, did the same. A hatch opened, and the battle moved onto the rooftop of Kaperosa Observatory.

Twig could see the black hole directly above. It seemed to have grown tenfold, nearly covering the entire sky. A sea of shades surrounded the observatory, climbing the walls, flowing through the corridors, an endless tidal wave. More shades kept charging up the stairs from deeper in the observatory, trying to push through the defenders.

"Twig, we're dead if the *Dragon Huntress* doesn't pick us up now." Nova pointed. "Go!"

Twig tightened her lips. She nodded. She jumped, lashed her wrench at a shade, and landed before Romy.

"Romy!" she shouted.

Twig stood barely taller than Romy's bellybutton. It was hard enough to get the demon to notice her even in three dimensions, let alone with Twig stuck in the higher plane.

"Romy, can you hear me?" Twig grabbed Romy's hips, surprised that her hands could feel the demon, not pass through her. "It's me, Twig."

The demon looked down and gasped. "A tiny ghost!"

"It's me! It's Twig. Twiggle Jauntyfoot." She grabbed Romy's clawed hand. "I need your help."

Romy's wings and tail stuck out from holes in her space suit; the latter wagged furiously. "You turned into a ghost! You look all funny and smudged. How did this happen?"

"No time to explain. Come on!" She tugged Romy. "Beat your wings and fly."

How could Romy see her? Why could Twig touch the demon? Perhaps demons had a strong connection to the astral world, to the realm of spirits and ghosts in the higher plane.

Whatever the case, Romy heard and obeyed. The demon took flight, beating her bat wings. Twig clung to her.

"Fly to the *Dragon Huntress*, Romy. We have to help Piston fix the ship."

Romy flew, leaving the roof behind.

Shades flowed up toward them, black robes fluttering.

Twig tossed her wrench. The metal flew, slammed into the beasts, cast out lightning, then snapped back into Twig's hand. Romy thrust her pitchfork, shooting flames out from its prongs, knocking the enemy aside. They kept flying.

The *Drake* stood in the yard, still trapped in the fourth dimension; Twig could see the ship, but it would not be able to ferry her friends. Beside it rose the *Dragon Huntress*, still in the three-dimensional world. Both starships stood in shadows, all but forgotten. The shades kept their attention on the base, clawing to reach the fleshy prizes within, leaving the starships to rust.

"Into the *Dragon*!" Twig shouted.

Romy beat her wings. "Okay, friendly little ghost."

They glided down, landed, and raced into the *Dragon Huntress*'s airlock. Twig led the way, dragging Romy down into the engine room.

Piston was bustling through the shadows, grumbling and stumbling over tools, pipes, screws, coils, and a thousand other loose pieces.

Twig stared in horror. The engines were a mess--their pieces scattered across the floor, nowhere near operational.

"Piston!" Riff shouted through the communicator mounted on the wall. "Hurry!"

"I'm trying, Captain!" Piston cried out, eyes damp, lips shaking. He returned to the disassembled engines. "Fingers too thick. Too many parts. I can't do this without Twig, I--" Piston finally noticed Romy and scowled. "Get out, demon! I'm a very busy gruffle. Out!"

Romy wagged her tail. "I'm here to help. Did you know that the engines are all over the floor?"

"Yes!" Piston shook his fist at her. "Now get out and let me fix it. No! Put that down, Romy, stop chewing on the tension coils!"

Romy pouted. "But they're tasty!"

Twig knelt and tried to lift some loose screws, but her fingers passed through them. She was still nothing but a wisp here, invisible to Piston, unable to do her work.

"Romy, can you hear me?" Twig said.

Romy looked down at her. "Yes, little ghost!"

"Good." Twig grabbed the demon. "Let me climb onto your shoulders and guide you."

Romy knelt, and Twig scurried up and straddled the demon's shoulders. Romy's flaming hair rose in a pyre before her, but the flames were soft and warm, not burning like true fire.

"Now, Romy, I need to lift those screws over there." Twig pointed. "No, the ones beside those. And that big, round piece of metal that looks like a hubcap."

"Okay!" Romy lifted the pieces.

"What--put those down!" Piston said.

Twig whispered into Romy's ears, and the demon repeated her words. "But Piston, somebody needs to align the generator rings or the turbines won't reach sufficient velocity to ignite the fuel charges. Can you pass me that three-quarters wrench and some bronze-alloy wiring?"

Piston froze and blinked. "What--?"

Romy groaned, still repeating Twig's whispers. "Piston, now! Quickly. And for pity's sake, get back to calibrating the generators. We won't be able to route power to the thruster engines unless you can ensure alternating currents through the circuit panels. Now let me plug in the intake pipes, or the turbines will be banging against iron. Unless you want more fried spark plugs and ripped thruster valves?"

Piston rubbed his eyes. "How do you--?"

Romy placed her hands on her hips, repeating Twig's words. "Oh, and don't forget to turn the turbocharger three times left. Three times! And let's line up that intercooler, but wait till the fuel rails are installed. Then we can install the fan butts."

"Fan *belts*," Twig whispered into her ear.

"Fan *belts*." Romy nodded. "Now let's get to work."

Piston shook his head in wonder. "Romy, yesterday you were drinking from the toilet bowl, and thank goodness Riff stopped you before you could foul the water cooler. I have no idea how you know all this, but . . . damn it, yes, let's get to work. Let's get this ship flying!"

They got busy. Twig kept tugging on Romy's arms, directing her hands to the right places. The demon worked in a fury, sometimes pausing to gnaw on a bolt or rod before Twig could knock it free. Piston worked alongside. The pair moved so quickly they appeared almost as ghosts themselves. Bit by bit, the engines came together.

"Piston, I need you!" Riff called through the communicator. "Now, now, now!"

Twig guided Romy's hand, connecting the last valve and snapping the turbines into place.

"Done!" Romy said. "I'm a genius monkey."

"You mean *mechanic*," Twig said.

Romy pouted. "I'd rather be a monkey."

Piston raced across the engine room, flicking switches. "Damn it! Spark plug's fried. Romy, over here! Stick your head into that engine there."

"No!" Romy gasped. "I'll get soot all over me."

"I need your flaming hair. Go! Now!"

"My hair isn't even that hot, and--"

"Do it!"

Romy wailed but ran forward, knelt, and thrust her head into the engines. Her hair of fire crackled. Twig watched, invisible, holding her breath.

For a long moment--silence.

Then, with a roar, the engines ignited. Great turbines spun. Smoke filled the engine room. Romy wailed and pulled her head out; soot covered her face.

"Uhm, Piston?" Romy said. "Is there anyone on the bridge to actually steer?"

The gruffle froze and his eyes widened. "Romy, go! Fly us!"

The demon nodded and beat her wings. She rose to the ceiling, emerged into the main deck, and ran. Twig ran behind her. They raced down the hall, leaped upstairs, and burst onto the bridge. A plethora of control panels spread ahead. Through the windshield, Twig could see Kaperosa Observatory. The last survivors stood on the roof, swinging their weapons, trying to keep the host of shades at bay. The creatures covered the landscape, thousands of them, a sea of claws and fangs and inky flesh.

"Romy, the joystick!" Twig shouted, still unable to grasp anything.

Romy nodded, leaped forward, and grabbed the reverse throttle. The ship lurched backward, spinning, nearly crashing down.

Twig wailed, leaped onto Romy's back, and yanked her arm downward. "This one!"

Romy nodded, grabbed the right controls, and began to raise the ship. The *Dragon Huntress* roared, engines spewing fire. Ahead upon the landscape, the shades turned toward the starship, hissing. Several tesseract vessels began to rise.

"Romy, dragonfire!" Twig cried. "The red button!"

Romy's lips trembled. "I don't like this job. Can we play counter-squares instead?"

"Do it! Do it now!"

Romy moaned and pressed the red button.

The *Dragon Huntress* roared out her dragonfire. The jet of plasma streamed forth, spinning and crackling, and tore into a tesseract ship. It shattered into jagged metallic cubes. Romy tugged the joystick, lowering the *Dragon*'s head. Her fire rained upon the shades climbing the observatory walls.

Twig jumped for joy. "You're doing it, Romy! You're doing it! Now fly over the roof. We have to evacuate everyone."

Romy wagged her tail. "I'm a parrot!"

"Pilot, Romy."

Her wings drooped. "But I want to be a parrot."

Twig wrapped her small hands around Romy's long, clawed fingers, guiding the joystick. The *Dragon Huntress* flew forward, blasting out flame, and hovered above the last survivors. Above loomed the black hole, its swirling eye gazing down with rage.

* * * * *

Giga stood on the roof, leaping, sliding through the air, somersaulting. Her katana swung so quickly it appeared like a disk of light. Her feet slammed into one ghost, knocking it down. She flipped backward, kimono fluttering, and thrust her sword into another beast's throat. She leaped ten feet into the air and spun in a ring, legs kicking, knocking the enemy back.

She landed on the ground, stretched out one leg, and spun, knocking creatures down. Her blade flashed, sticky with the black blood of the ghosts. She glanced up to see the *Dragon Huntress* hovering down, thruster engines blasting. The ship's dragonfire raged, knocking back enemy vessels. The airlock popped open, and Piston stood within, lowering cables.

"Come on, you clods!" the gruffle shouted. "All aboard!"

Giga glanced around her. What had started as a hunt would become a rescue operation--if they were lucky. Thousands of shades were still climbing the walls and bounding across the roof.

We might not all have time to flee, Giga realized.

She let out a shriek, bounded into the air, and swung her katana down into a shade.

"Lenora, into the ship!" Steel shouted. "Climb!"

The scientist shook her head. "Not until the others are safe." Lenora ran toward the cable and began helping one of her men--an old scientist with white hair--climb the cable into the waiting *Dragon Huntress.*

A scream sounded to Giga's left. She spun to see the ghosts grab another scientist--an elderly woman--and rip into her flesh. The scientist's screams died as the ghosts dragged her corpse away.

Giga leaped into the air and kept fighting.

I learned how to fight when the Singularity possessed me, she thought. *I fought my friends then. Now I fight to save them.*

She cried out wordlessly, leaped into the air, and kicked. She bounced from ghost to ghost, feet slamming against them, blade cutting through their limbs. She was still an android of three dimensions; there was no parameter for a fourth dimension in her algorithms. She could only see projections of these beings from a higher plane, only their shadows in this world. But it was enough. Enough to kill them. Enough to give the others time.

The last of the surviving scientists climbed the cables. Riff followed.

"Come on, Steel and Giga!" the captain said when he reached the airlock. "Into the ship."

With only Steel and Giga now on the roof, the ghosts swarmed with new vigor. The two fought back to back, swinging their blades in semicircles.

"Climb, my lady," Steel said. "I'll hold back the enemy."

Giga thrust her blade, impaling an alien. She had begun this journey a meek, frightened android, barely capable of more than parroting a few preprogrammed phrases. She had grown. She had fought in battles. She had seen the cosmos. She had become a great warrior, perhaps even deadlier than Steel. But she also knew that he was still a knight at heart, that his honor would not let him climb into the ship before her.

Giga nodded. "Hold them back for me, sir."

She leaped, grabbed the cable, and scurried up to the *Dragon Huntress*.

Below, Steel stood alone on the roof. Thousands of the enemy spirits surrounded him, a tarry sea. The knight still swung his blade, and Giga frowned. At his side flickered a golden light, a dancing flame shaped like a woman, appearing and vanishing, cracking a whip of lightning. But when Giga blinked, the image was gone.

Steel gave a few last swipes of his blade, then grabbed the cable. The *Dragon Huntress* began to ascend at once, not even pausing to let Steel climb to the airlock. They rose higher, leaving the observatory below. Steel dangled off the cable, and for an instant, it seemed to Giga that the golden light clung to him, the spirit rising with him.

It's a spirit of goodness, Giga thought. She had no true human emotions, just whatever emotions her algorithms managed to conjure, but she could sense the goodness of that golden light, the blessings it bestowed upon them.

"An angel," Giga whispered.

An enemy tesseract flew toward them, and the *Dragon Huntress* roared out her fire, breaking the tesseract into cubes. Steel climbed and entered the airlock with Giga, and they pulled the door shut.

"Steel." Giga leaped onto him and embraced him, clinging so tightly she almost dented his armor.

"My lady." He kissed her forehead. "I would have gladly died to save you."

She looked up, tears in her eyes, and caressed his cheek. "Never, Steel. Never die for me. Promise. Promise me that."

"I promise," he whispered, then pulled her back into an embrace. They stood together in the airlock, holding each other close, never wanting to let go.

Below, the observatory grew smaller as the *Dragon Huntress* rose, and soon the entire planet was but a sphere in the distance, a world they had come to save, a world they had failed.

We leave behind ruins and death, Giga thought, her cheek pressed against Steel's breastplate. *We leave behind Nova and Twig.*

Her tears streamed down her cheeks, and despair clutched her mechanical heart.

CHAPTER FIFTEEN

LOST SOULS

Riff stood on the bridge of the *Dragon Huntress*, head lowered, eyes stinging.

How do I go on? How do I fly away like this . . . without them?

Steel stood at his side, armor cracked, a bandage wrapped around a gash on his head. Giga sat in one of the bridge's suede seats, head lowered. Scratches covered her synthetic skin, and her kimono hung in tatters. Piston stood in his armor of brown leather and iron bolts, staring from side to side helplessly, and tears ran down his cheeks and into his snowy beard.

"They're gone," the gruffle whispered. "That . . . that pea-brained clod. And that sweet lass with her whip and beautiful eyes." The old engineer pulled out a handkerchief and wept. "I should have died instead. I'm old. I'm old! Why do I linger on while those two precious girls are lost?"

"They're not lost!" Romy said. The demon had changed back into her dinosaur pajamas, and she held her teddy bear. "They're right here, Piston. God! Did you go blind in your old age?"

"Romy!" Riff reeled toward her, glaring at her. "Hush. We must show them respect." A lump grew in Riff's throat. "We'll have a ceremony. We'll . . ."

Romy rolled her eyes. "For pity's sake, sir. Nova and Twig are right here!" She pointed at the hula dancer and bulldog bobblehead on the dashboard. "Can't you see them?"

Piston stopped weeping long enough to roll his eyes. "It's finally happened. The demon's gone mad."

"That happened long ago," Riff muttered.

Giga rose from her seat, gently took Romy's arm, and guided her off the bridge. All the while, the demon kept blabbering. "Right there! Look at them. Look!"

"Hush, sweetness," Giga said, guiding Romy downstairs. "Let's go put you to bed."

"I'm not a baby! I'm five thousand years old. I'm telling you, I saw Nova and Twig!"

Giga patted her head. "I know, sweetness. I know. Let's tuck you in and you can tell me all about it."

The two vanished down into the main deck. Riff closed his eyes. The bridge felt so empty without Nova. A piece seemed to be missing from Riff's heart.

Where are you, Nova? What happened to you?

She was still alive. The ghosts still had her somewhere. Riff was sure of it. He clenched his fists, opened his eyes, and looked out into space. Planet Kaperosa was only a speck in the distance now, and the black hole but a faded patch.

"We retreat today," Riff said. "But we do not give up. We do not forget those we left behind. We'll be back. With more knowledge. With more strength." His lips peeled back in a snarl. "I swear this on my life. I'm coming back for you, Nova and Twig. Wherever you are."

Steel placed a hand on Riff's right shoulder. Piston lolloped up to his left and patted his arm.

"I better return to the engine room, laddie," said the gruffle. "Engines still making a strange sound. Gods of rock and metal know what Romy was doing to them. If she weren't a demon, I'd swear she were possessed. It's as if Twig's voice were speaking through her, and . . . oh that little clod."

Tears filled the engineer's eyes again. Dabbing them with his handkerchief, Piston wobbled off the bridge.

"I need to leave the bridge too," Riff said. "Steel, will you hold down the fort? Lenora and her people need to see I'm here, need to talk to me, to know I'll look after them. They lost people too." Riff's heart gave a twist. "Twenty-three scientists . . . gone."

Steel nodded. "Go, brother. I'll steer us onward."

The knight sat by the controls and stared out into space. The ship turned, leaving Kaperosa far behind.

Riff stepped off the bridge.

The *Dragon Huntress* was a small starship, not much larger than a suburban home. Even with its old crew of seven Alien Hunters it had been crowded. Now two of those Alien Hunters were gone . . . and fifty refugees of Kaperosa Observatory filled the ship.

As Riff walked down the corridor, he saw them in the ship's chambers. Several of the wounded lay in crew quarters on cots, bandaged. Two scientists lay in Riff's own bedroom. One old man sat in the escape pod, and others huddled in the kitchen over bowls of soup. Riff nodded to every man and woman he passed, speaking comforting words.

Finally he reached the main deck. Scientists filled the place-- sitting on the couch, pacing the chamber, staring out the porthole. Lenora stood among them. Blood stained her woolen skirt.

At once everyone crowded him, asking countless questions.

"Why are the engines rattling?"

"Where are we flying to?"

"How long will the life support last?"

"Are we able to fly in hyperspace?"

Riff had to raise his hands and raise his voice. "Everyone! Please rest assured that we're going to get you home safely. We have enough supplies and air to last for days, and--"

"There is no more home!" one man cried out, his hair disheveled. "We all saw the reports from Earth. Those damn shades have been attacking Earth, killing countless of people. Earth might be gone by now."

A woman fell to her knees, tears in her eyes. "My family is on Earth. My husband. My children. My parents . . ."

"Where are you taking us, Starfire?" a man shouted, marched forth, and grabbed Riff. "We could have done some good on Kaperosa. We could have studied these beasts. Now we're floating in this rattling tin can of yours, light-years away from civilization, and--"

"Enough!" Riff said. "Listen to me, everyone. Earth has not yet fallen. It's under attack. So might be other planets. But we haven't lost this war yet. We're not floating through a desolate cosmos, no safe haven to be found. I promise you. We're sending out signals as we speak, trying to find the nearest Humanoid Alliance planet where it's safe to land. We know that the ghosts have been attacking Ashmar, Gruffstone, and other major worlds, but they haven't yet reached the outposts. The forest moon of Oranin looks like our most promising destination. We can fly there, find shelter, and--"

"No." Lenora stepped through the crowd toward Riff, and a cold hardness filled her eyes. "No, we will not waste even an hour flying to safety. Safety?" She tugged at her woolen skirt. "How can we hide when our base, our world, our entire civilization is overrun? When beings from a higher dimension slay all that our species has built? So no." Lenora shook her head. "I will not run. I'm no gunslinger like you, Riff. I don't have a sword like Steel or Giga, no pitchfork like Romy. I'm a scientist. And I will fight these creatures with science. With knowledge. I will continue to study them."

Riff took her hands in his. His voice softened. "Lenora, the base is overrun. The labs, the telescopes--the entire planet of Kaperosa--gone. My team and I are Alien Hunters. Pest controllers. Not an army. This is war on a cosmic scale, this is--"

"I don't mean we should return to Kaperosa." Lenora stared steadily into his eyes. "We made an error there, Riff. For years, we studied irregularities in the black hole. For years, we could not comprehend why our equations were failing. But I understand now. I know. Our equations failed because we were calculating them in three dimensions, while all along . . ." She shook her head in wonder. "These creatures were lurking in a dimension above our own, one we could not see. A Dark Planet floats inside the black hole, the homeworld of those creatures that attacked us. I've been so blind. I should have seen it. It took Nova's message to finally let me see." Tears flooded her eyes. "And now people are dead. Because of my failings."

"Lenora!" Riff pulled her into his arms. Her tears dampened his shoulder. "I've known you for many years, my friend. And I've never known you to fail at anything. This was not your fault. Do you understand that? It was nobody's fault. We're going to make this right."

Lenora nodded, rubbed her eyes, and stepped back. "We are. And not at Kaperosa. There's a man who can help us. The greatest expert in the universe on four-dimensional beings. A genius who can help us fight them . . . who can help us rise into their very plane of existence." She raised her chin. "My brother."

Riff blinked. "You mean . . . Dee?"

He remembered Dee Rosetta from years ago. A scrawny boy, a couple years younger than Riff, with huge glasses and messy hair. A boy the neighborhood bullies had loved to torment, tugging up his underwear, breaking his glasses, shoving him down.

Riff remembered a bumbling, awkward youth who had spent most of his days reading science fiction and playing *Damsels & Dragons*.

"But . . . Lenora." Riff lowered his voice. "I heard that, well . . . a few years ago, that . . ."

Lenora nodded. "That he was sent to an insane asylum. Yes. I'm not ashamed to say it. But did you know why he was committed?"

Riff thought back to the news reports. "The media reported that he invented a weapon that could wipe out the universe. That they had to lock him up."

"He invented a four-dimensional engine." Lenora placed her hands on Riff's shoulders. "He invented a way to rise into the higher plane. He came back speaking of ghosts, spirits, gods, and dark queens."

Riff shuddered to remember that land he had glimpsed--a higher plane of existence. A black realm. A swirling dark sky. A rose on a dark hill. An evil presence lurking in every shadow.

"And Dee visited that world . . ." Riff whispered. "It's enough to drive any man mad."

Lenora nodded. "Our father indeed thought him mad. When Dee returned, speaking of what he saw, our father locked him up. Dee still languishes in The Holy Knights of Sol Asylum, a prison for the mentally ill." She sighed. "The prison my father himself runs."

"Your father . . . is the warden?" Riff stared into her eyes with shock.

She lowered her gaze. "And this does shame me. Yes, Riff. My own father keeps my brother locked up. After he stripped off Steel's sigil, Lord Kerish Rosetta left Earth, opened a prison on the planet Athemes, and became the most notorious warden in our galaxy. But that is where hope lies." She raised her head again and stared into his eyes. "We must speak to Dee. We must free him from his prison. And then . . . then we must build his four-dimensional engine, fly into Yurei, and burn down the alien world."

* * * * *

Nova wandered the *Dragon Huntress* like a ghost, invisible to all, mute, unable to even touch the ones she loved.

"I can't even eat the damn food," she muttered.

She stepped into the kitchen. A few of Kaperosa's scientists sat at the table, eating cereal. Nova tried to grab a bowl of her own, but her fingers kept missing. She reached for a box of cereal, but it felt like trying to perform surgery while standing upside down and staring into a mirror. She succeeded only in knocking the box over, startling the scientists at the table.

"It's no use, Nova," Twig said. The halfling stood on the counter, trying to open a pack of hot dogs, but her fingers kept missing it. "We'll have to tighten our belts. We can come back when everyone's sleeping and try again."

Nova groaned. She felt as if walking through a hall of mirrors. Not only was everything distorted, the damn reflections were everywhere. She couldn't decide if there were fifty survivors on this ship or fifty thousand. Every time somebody moved, they left a stream of reflections like holograms.

They left the kitchen: an ashai warrior, clad in a golden catsuit, a whip in her hand, her pointed ears sticking out from her blond hair; and a halfling girl, screws and bolts jangling in the pockets of her cargo pants, wrenches hanging from her tool belt. Their own reflections stretched out all around them.

Twig yawned. "I want to sleep, but there are people in my bed. And on the couches. And all over the floors. And in the escape pod. And I think I saw somebody sleeping in the hallway closet on a pile of coats."

"We'll crowd into Riff's bed," Nova said. "I sleep there anyway and there's always room left on my side. You're small enough to squeeze in. Like a baby between her parents." Nova paused. "Wait, that's wrong. I'm sorry, Twig. I'm really sorry. I shouldn't have said that. You fought bravely, and you fixed this ship, and you saved our lives. I'm being an idiot."

Twig sighed. "I'm used to people thinking I'm a baby. When you're three-foot-five and sound like you're on helium, not everyone treats you seriously. It's all right, Nova."

"No, it's not." Nova shook her head and knelt before the halfling. She held Twig's shoulders and stared into her blue eyes. "I know that I never acknowledged you much. You or Piston. For so long on this ship, I stayed on the higher decks with Riff, with Steel, with Giga. And . . . I never even said hello when I passed you in the corridor, Twig. I never even realized what important work you were doing down in the engine room. I thought of you as a kid. But you're some kind of genius. And even braver than I am. I am a warrior, and you earned my respect, Twiggle Jauntyfoot. Forever. You aren't just my crewmate now. You are my sister."

Twig's eyes dampened. "Sisters," she whispered.

They walked down the hall and entered the captain's quarters. Riff was sleeping in his bed. Nova winced to see an old, faded reflection of herself lying in bed with him, wearing one of his old *Space Galaxy* T-shirts. She remembered that night, remembered snuggling up to him, whispering in his ear, kissing him, and falling asleep holding him.

But that's only a reflection, she thought. *Only a memory.* She watched Riff's chest rise and fall as he slept. *Will I never kiss him again?*

"Riff," Nova whispered. She leaned down and tried to touch his shoulder, to rouse him, but her fingers passed through him. "Riff, can you hear me? Wake up, Riff. It's me. It's Nova."

He stirred in his sleep. "Nova," he whispered.

Hope leaped in her. "Yes! It's me, Riff. Can you hear me?"

His eyes opened, but they were full of pain.

"I miss you, Nova," he whispered. "Come back to me."

"I'm here." Her voice choked, and her tears fell. She tried to touch his cheek but could not. "I'm right here. I love you."

"I miss you," Riff whispered, staring right through her, seeing nothing. "I'm going to find you, wherever you are."

His eyes closed and he slept. Nova lowered her head, tears stinging her eyes.

After a long moment, Twig padded up and patted Nova's arm. "I'm sorry, Nova. He'll see you again someday. I know it. We're going to find this scientist they're all talking about, this expert on dimensions. He's going to fix this."

Nova nodded. "I'm glad you're with me, Twiggle Jauntyfoot."

Twig climbed into the bed first, barely taking up any room. As soon as the halfling's head hit the pillow, she was asleep. Nova stood for a moment, staring down at the little mechanic.

Are you my last companion in the cosmos, Twig? Are we to remain like this forever, just the two of us--and that blasted demon who can see us?

Finally Nova climbed into bed too. Gently, she lay down right where her older reflection lay, so that the two Nova--past and present--overlay each other. Lying like this, Nova could almost imagine that she truly held Riff, that her breath truly tickled the back of his neck, and she thought that she could almost feel him against her.

"I love you, Riff," she whispered.

"I love you too," he whispered back, half-asleep.

Before she could say more, Nova slept.

* * * * *

As the *Dragon Huntress* floated through hyperspace, Steel knelt in the escape pod, gazing out at the lights and praying silently.

Please, light of Sol, guide my way. Let me find my strength. Let me be strong for Lenora, for my family, for my ship, for a cosmos drowning under shadow.

The round windows of the escape pod showed streaming lights, floating orbs of color, and coiling clouds of space dust. Here in hyperspace, with the fabric of spacetime warped around him, Steel could not point out Sol, the distant star of Earth, his beacon. Perhaps he would have to seek a light inside himself, a light inside his ship.

"A shadow falls," he whispered. "And Nova and Twig are gone. And I don't know if there's enough light inside me to fight back this darkness."

Steel thought back to the visions the shades had shown him. A nightmarish land. The Dark Queen. A realm with no light, no hope. A realm that would claim the cosmos, drown these lights outside, unless he could fight back.

Steel wanted to stand strong, to raise his chin, to cry out like a warrior, like Nova, to speak of victory and honor. Not to feel this fear, this doubt.

"Doubt has filled me since I lost you, Lenora," he said, speaking to the lights.

The door creaked open behind him. Steel turned to see Giga enter the escape pod. She held a mug of steaming soup.

"Sir?" she said. "There's food in the kitchen, sir, and I thought you might like some chicken soup. Piston cooked it." The android hesitated. "I'm sorry to have disturbed you. I know it's hard to find privacy in a ship full of survivors."

"It's all right, Giga." He reached out his hand. "Thank you. I would love some soup. Would you like to join me?"

She smiled, stepped forward, and handed him the mug. "I do not require sustenance, sir."

"Call me Steel," he said.

"Happy to comply, sir! I mean, Steel." She stood beside him in the escape pod and gazed outside into space. "They're pretty, the lights. I often like to stand and watch them."

The escape pod was small, barely large enough to contain both of them. Giga's lavender kimono brushed his hand, and her scent of jasmine filled his nostrils. He thought back to that day the Singularity had possessed her, driven her out of the *Dragon Huntress* and into battle. He had donned a space suit then, flew after her through the fire and light, grabbed her, and pulled her home. He remembered how her eyes had gazed into his, alternating between love and hatred, between the woman she was and the creature she had become.

I'm glad you're back with us, my lady. I'm glad to have you with me.

They stood together in silence for long moments, watching the streams of light. Finally Giga spoke softly.

"Do you wish she could stand here with you, Steel?" She lowered her head. "Lenora? Do you still love her? Do you think that . . . that you will marry her?"

Steel sighed, a deep sigh that ran through him, clanking his armor. "I still love her. I don't think a love such as this can ever die. But it's a love from my past, Giga. A love that will remain in memory." He shook his head. "My duty is here, on the *Dragon*

Huntress, fighting with my friends, defending the stars. Hers is with her people, studying the secrets of those stars." He turned to look at Giga. "Our relationship ended for a reason, one that we cannot mend. Too much time has passed. Too much pain. We have both moved on."

Giga gazed up at him, her dark eyes large and damp. Her hand reached out to clasp his.

"But I still see love in you," she whispered.

He nodded. "There is still love."

Giga lowered her eyes, then looked back up at him, and now tears flowed down her cheeks. "I once loved a man. I once had my heart broken. I do not have a heart of flesh and blood. It's a heart of metal, yet it too feels pain. A pain I cannot forget. How do you move on, Steel? How do you heal?"

"With my friends," he said. "With new meaning to life. With new people to love."

Giga embraced him, pressing her cheek against his breastplate, and closed her eyes. He kissed the top of her head, marveling at how soft her hair was.

"I'm scared, Steel," she whispered. "I'm scared for Nova and Twig. For all of us. For the cosmos. For you." She held him close. "But I love my friends. I love you, Steel. That will give us strength."

They stood together in the escape pod, holding each other as the lights streamed outside.

CHAPTER SIXTEEN

DUNES

Overflowing with survivors, the *Dragon Huntress* limped toward the planet of Athemes.

Riff sat on the bridge, staring at the distant world. The planet was mostly desert, beige and lifeless. A single river wrapped around the equator, halving the planet, and lush rainforests spread along its banks. It looked like somebody had taken a golden ball and encircled it with a green and blue ribbon.

"So here it is," Riff said. "The penal planet of Athemes. The most infamous rock in the Milky Way. Every criminal's nightmare."

Giga sat beside him. She tilted her head. "Planet Athemes has a rich history, sir, going back a hundred thousand of years-- long before humans opened a prison here. It was fifteen thousand, four hundred and seven years ago that the Kafra dynasty first built a system of irrigation along the Ereef river. The eighteenth dynasty currently reigns in the rainforest, sir, and they worship a rich pantheon of gods. The sun god, Tarach, is the current dynasty's house god, though many other deities still fulfill roles in the natives' daily lives, guiding everything from beer making to funerals. Of special note is the goddess Mikana, the hawk goddess, who--"

"Gig." Riff placed a hand on her arm, silencing her. "It's all right. We're not here to spend time with the natives. We're here to visit The Holy Knights of Sol Asylum, speak to Lenora's father, and see if we can talk to Dee."

Giga's eyes widened. "But . . . sir! The Knights of Sol did not build the prison. They only rule over it. The native taweret race built a complex labyrinth in the style of their most ancient temples. You see, sir, the natives believe that the Knights of Sol are themselves deities. They are an Iron Age society, sir. The Knights of Sol, who flew here from Earth on great starships, are seen as sky gods. In fact, it was King Dahatek of the seventeenth dynasty--he was the son of Queen Zia, whom many believed a goddess herself, daughter of Mikana--who first wrote that--"

"Giga, it's all right." Riff knew that the android, when excited about a topic, could speak for hours and even days about it. "Just stay near me and give me nuggets of information on the fly, not all at once."

As he watched the planet grow nearer, sadness welled in Riff. Until now, on every new world they reached, Nova always walked at his side, whip ready to fly. For the first time, Riff would visit a planet without her--without her strength, her love.

He thought back to last night. Not long after falling asleep, he had woken for only a moment, and lingering in half-slumber, he had almost thought that Nova lay beside him. He had almost felt her breath on his neck, almost heard her whisper, "I love you." Perhaps he was like Romy, imagining things in his grief.

The *Dragon Huntress* kept flying toward the planet. The atmosphere was rich and warm here, similar to Earth's. As they plunged through it, fire flared around the *Dragon Huntress*'s hull. The hula dancer swayed on the dashboard, nearly dislocating her hips. The plastic bulldog bobbed his head. Riff clung to his seat. A piece tore off the ship's nose and flew through the air. The hull clanked, loud as gunfire. Riff winced, sure that Piston's quick repairs would collapse, scattering them into countless pieces.

He exhaled in relief once they were past the stratosphere. Giga brought the ship to a gentle glide. Riff wiped sweat off his brow.

They were still high above the surface. Riff stared down at the land. The desert spread below, endless dunes and rocky mountains. Through it spread the Ereef river, gleaming blue, the planet's single artery of life, circling the equator. The rainforest spread along its banks for several kilometers, two green ribbons encircling a blue thread.

As the starship kept descending, Riff saw that cities rose from the greenery. At first, he noticed pyramids soaring into the sky, a kilometer high. Among them rose columned temples, obelisks, and palaces of sandstone capped with gold. Statues rose among them, large as skyscrapers, depicting men and women with the heads of animals.

"It looks like . . ." Riff whispered.

"Like Earth's Ancient Egypt." Giga nodded. "The Egypt you're familiar with, sir, was founded by ancient astronauts from planet Athemes. Aliens from here traveled to Earth fifteen thousand years ago on magnificent ships--great clockwork galleys built of wood, complete with oars and sails, that floated across space. They crashed onto Egypt, where the local humans worshipped them as gods and built great cities, modeled after the cities of Athemes."

Riff tilted his head. "Giga! Egypt--founded by ancient aliens? You sound like one of those conspiracy theorists from cyberspace."

"But it's true, sir!" Giga nodded. "You know the gods from Egyptian mythology--Anubis with the head of a jackal, Horus with the falcon head, and so on? All aliens from Athemes. It's quite sad, really." Giga lowered her head. "The Athemians have since lost the ability to space travel. Once humans worshipped them. Today they worship humans."

Riff wasn't sure he believed any of it. Ancient Egypt's gods--aliens? It sounded like a bad TV show.

"Just find the prison and land us by it," he said.

"Happy to comply!"

As the ship glided down, the door creaked open behind them, and Lenora stepped onto the bridge. She had washed her woolen vest and skirt, and she had braided her brown hair. Her glasses perched upon her nose, magnifying her hazel eyes. The bloody, bruised survivor was gone, yet more fear than ever seemed to fill Lenora. Her cheeks were pale, her lips tight, and her fingers clutched at her skirt.

"I can see it below," Lenora whispered. "My father's prison. The place where my brother languishes."

He looked at her. "You said your father can be reasoned with. That he'll let us speak to Dee. Yet you seem nervous."

She gulped. "My father . . . has always been strict. He treated our own house like a prison, himself the warden. The Knights of Sol taught him harsh discipline, unforgiving justice. If you think Steel hard, you ain't seen nothing." She shuddered. "It's funny. I'm halfway through my thirties, Riff. As old as he was when I was a child. Yet I'm still scared of him."

Riff thought about his own father, the traveling magician, crazy old Aminor. He wondered where the old man was now. He missed him. Aminor was always off on some mysterious quest saving the galaxy . . . somehow always leaving Riff to fight his own cosmic threats.

I miss you, Dad, he thought.

"Which building is your father's prison?" Riff asked.

Lenora pointed. "The tall pyramid with the cap of iron."

"Taking us there, ma'am!" said Giga.

Soon the *Dragon Huntress* was gliding directly over a lush, sprawling city. Ziggurats rose here, coiling buildings of sandstone, their facades painted with hieroglyphs. Columned temples rose among them, their staircases lined with statues of men with heads of jackals, hawks, and hippopotamuses. Obelisks rose from cobbled squares, their tips capped with platinum. Everywhere swayed palm trees, fig trees, and rushes. The river flowed through the city, and on it sailed countless ships, their sails white, their decks overflowing with baskets of fish, perfumes, exotic birds in cages, and gleaming gemstones.

Past swaying rushes, vineyards, and palm groves spread the desert. As lush as the riverbanks were, the desert was barren. The dunes rolled into the horizons, and yellow mountains rose in the distance toward a pale sky. The pyramids of Athemes rose from the desert, a kilometer high, dwarfing any pyramid back on Earth. Six among them were polished to a sheen, and gold capped their tips. The seventh, farther back, was built of craggy bricks, and its tip was forged of dark iron.

"There it is." Lenora pointed. "The last pyramid. The Holy Knights of Sol Asylum. My father's prison for the insane."

Giga nodded. "The Knights of Sol first came here from Earth a thousand years ago. They hired the tawerets, an endemic race of aliens with hippopotamus heads, to construct the most complex prison they could. The knights imprison most of their enemies on the moons of Jupiter, but some enemies--the most ruthless, psychotic ones--are deemed too dangerous to be held within our solar system. Those ones are brought here. The tawerets believe the Knights of Sol to be sky gods, their prisoners to be demons of the underworld. Of course, the knights are only humans, but in the ancient Scroll of Taweret Mah, it is written that--"

"Thank you, Gig." Riff patted her shoulder. "Remember, less infodump. Just give us snippets of information on the fly. Can you land us by the prison?"

Giga smiled. "Happy to comply!"

The *Dragon Huntress*'s thruster engines roared, and the ship slowed to a hover, then clanked down in the sand outside the towering, craggy pyramid. Palm trees bent. Camels fled. With a puff of smoke and a rattle, the engines turned off.

The door creaked open, and Romy stepped onto the bridge. The demon was dressed as an ancient pharaoh, complete with a snake tiara, and an Eye of Ra pendant hung around her neck. She held out her arms like an Egyptian.

"It is I, Pharaoh Romy!" she announced. "I'm ready to enter my domain."

"I hope you mean the ship's attic," Riff said. "Cuz that's where you're staying."

Romy moaned, tossed off her snake tiara, and grabbed a bullwhip and fedora. "Can I go as an archaeologist?"

"No! Attic."

"A mummy?" She began wrapping herself with toilet paper.

"Attic!"

The demon whined and stormed off, mumbling about how Riff was going to get hit with an ancient curse, and she was not going to be there to save him.

Riff turned back toward Lenora. "I'll let you do the talking. Whatever happens, I'm here with you. And so is my crew."

I only wish you were here with us, Nova and Twig, Riff thought.

Lenora kissed his cheek. "Thank you."

They left the bridge and stepped onto the main deck. The scientists rescued from Kaperosa still crowded here. Steel stood among them, clad in his full plate armor. The old sigil on his breastplate, the sun of Sol, had been scratched off; a badge with the words "Alien Hunters" appeared there instead. The knight's face was hard and cold.

"All right, Steel?" Riff said, approaching his brother. He knew what this meant to the knight. Here, in this pyramid, waited the lord who had knighted him . . . then banished him.

"I am ready," Steel said, chin raised, but Riff saw the ghosts in his eyes. "Always."

Lenora wrapped her arms around Steel and leaned against him. Riff turned toward the airlock and opened the door. The light and heat of the planet Athemes flowed in, hitting them like a wave. Riff stepped out onto the sand of a new world.

* * * * *

Steel stood in the sand, staring ahead at The Holy Knights of Sol Asylum.

The pyramid loomed above him, a kilometer high. Each of its bricks was the size of the *Dragon Huntress*, craggy, roughly hewn by alien hands. The triangle soared toward a tip coated with iron. An engraving of an eye shone there, reflecting the sunlight, glaring at the desert, the river, and Steel. He narrowed his eyes, staring back.

"You cast me aside, Lord Kerish," he said softly. "As you cast aside your daughter. But we're back. You will not cast me aside so easily again."

Steel spoke to himself alone, yet Lenora seemed to hear him. She slipped her small, pale hand into his large, callused one. He looked at her, and she gazed back with soft eyes. In them, he saw the same love that had shone years ago. The same eyes he used to spend hours gazing into.

"We need not fear him," she said.

Steel nodded and returned his eyes to the pyramid. "And we do not."

Yet both were lying, Steel knew. They did need to fear Lord Kerish Rosetta. Lenora's father ranked high among the Knights of Sol, a close companion to the Supreme Leader who reigned on Earth. While the Supreme Leader mostly concerned himself with prayer and ceremony, it was Lord Rosetta who meted out the Knights' justice. He was judge, jury, and executioner of this ancient knightly order, ruling not only sworn knights . . . but the knighthood's enemies.

A man who committed his own son to prison, Steel thought. *A man who once considered me a son as well.*

"Camel ride, sir? Ma'am? Camel ride?" A camel lolloped forth, bearing a tasseled saddle.

Steel narrowed his eyes, searching for a camel handler. Then he realized the camel himself had spoken.

"Ride for two credits, sirs!" the animal said.

Steel shook his head. "We're heading to the prison. That's only a hundred meters away. We can walk."

The camel turned to look at Giga, bells jangling across his saddlebags. "Ride for the android? Sand is very dangerous for androids, ma'am. Gets between your parts. Ride for two credits?"

Giga looked at Riff. The captain nodded, reached into his jeans pocket, and pulled out a couple coins. He slipped them into the camel's saddlebag, and the animal knelt in the sand. Giga climbed into the saddle.

"Thank you, sirs!" the camel said. "Are you sure you'd like to go straight to the Holy Knights of Sol Asylum? For only twenty credits, I'd be glad to serve as your tour guide. I can show you the Leaning Obelisk of Mareka, visit the Halls of Ghosts in the Temple of Ra, and stroll along the Ereef River where you can see the cranes and ibises. Perhaps even a moonlit walk through the City of the Dead, and--"

"Just to the pyramid, please," Steel said.

The camel tightened his lips, raised his head, and began to trot toward the pyramid. Giga, clad in a white kimono embroidered with palm trees, bounced upon his hump.

Steel, Riff, and Lenora walked alongside.

"Talking camels!" Lenora whispered. "Are your adventures always so strange?"

Riff sighed. "I thought the talking camel was normal. Does that answer your question?"

They reached the base of the pyramid, and Giga dismounted. A staircase stretched up the craggy facade toward a stone archway a few hundred meters above.

"Care to ride me upstairs?" the camel said. "I can carry you one by one. Only three credits per stair climb. Perhaps afterward, you would like to visit the mystical Alley of Serpents in the city, or see the exotic belly dancers of Keetan, then perhaps taste the delight of Happy Cow's Shawarma at the city docks."

"You have Happy Cow Shawarma here too?" Riff asked. It was their favorite take-out place, its franchises popping up on planets, moons, asteroids, and space stations across the galaxy.

"But of course, sir! There is a Happy Cow Shawarma everywhere." The camel lowered his head. "I lost some good friends there, I can tell you."

Riff shuddered. "I think we'll pass. On everything. Thank you, camel."

The camel looked as if Riff had just told him he only rode llamas. The animal raised his nose, spun around, and trotted away.

Leaving the dunes below, they began to climb the stairs--a space captain in torn jeans, an outcast knight in dented armor, an android with a katana across her back, and a scientist nervously clutching her woolen skirt. Steel doubted that anyone stranger had ever climbed these stairs.

He glanced behind him once. In the distance, Steel could see the palm trees, obelisks, and ziggurats of the city, and beyond them white sails flowing across the river. Suddenly Steel wished they could have taken the camel up on his offer, could spend the day exploring the wonders of this ancient civilization. Yet Steel turned his eyes back forward. He would not abandon his task. The shades swarmed across the cosmos, toppling the cities of Earth. Perhaps he had been banished from his order, but Steel Starfire had still taken a vow--a vow to always live a life of honor, to defend those in need, to fight ever onward.

I swore that vow to the man I now climb to see.

Hundreds of steps up, when they were all wheezing--aside from Giga--they reached the gateway into the pyramid. Hieroglyphs of hawks, serpents, and eyes were engraved onto its stones, and golden statues of jackals stood at its sides. Before the doorway stood the gatekeepers: two burly aliens with the bodies of men and the heads of hippopotamuses. They wore white loincloths, and golden rings encircled their massive, swordlike teeth. With their plump hands, they gripped spears.

"Tawerets," Giga whispered, turning toward her companions. "Native life forms of the planet Athemes. The tawerets believe that they were sired twenty thousand years ago, during a romantic encounter between the Sky Goddess Isanish and the river god Heras, a hippopotamus thought to have created the river by shedding his tears. The tawerets' average lifespan is fifty years, and they reach sexual maturity at fifteen. Their dental formula is--"

"Thank you, Giga," Riff said. "Nice on the fly information there."

She grinned. "Happy to comply, sir!"

The tawerets slammed down the butts of their spears. The aliens stood seven feet tall, and their jaws seemed wide enough to swallow men whole.

"Who comes to the Holy Knights of Sol Asylum?" one rumbled, voice like boulders slamming together.

Lenora stepped forth. "It is I, Lenora Rosetta, daughter of Lord Kerish Rosetta. With me are Riff Starfire, captain of the *HMS Dragon Huntress*, and Giga, his loyal companion. With us too is Steel Starfire, a knight of--"

"He is no knight," rumbled the second taweret. The great hippopotamus jaws opened wide, revealing teeth like meat cleavers. "We know of Steel the Heretic. Our tales tell of him, the rogue whom our lord banished."

Steel forced himself to remain calm. He stared at the towering aliens. They were taller than him, wider, stronger, but his strength came from deep within, from a faith that no banishment could shatter.

"I was banished," he said. "Yet I still took the vows of knighthood, and I still have honor in my heart. You will step aside. You will not turn back the daughter of your lord."

The tawerets raised their spears. "The heretic dares speak! We will slay you. For the glory of the Knights of Sol, our gods, we will--"

"If the knights are your gods, then I am your goddess!" said Lenora. Her cheeks flushed, and her chest heaved. She stepped even closer. "Step aside. Do it now, or my father will hear that you attacked his only daughter. Stand back!"

The two hippopotamus heads swiveled on their necks. As large and beefy as the aliens' humanoid bodies were--and those bodies put most wrestlers to shame--the heads were almost comically large. Their jaws snapped shut, and their eyes narrowed. Finally the tawerets nodded, stepped aside, and knelt.

"Enter, visitors, to the depths of shadow and secrets. Enter our dark world, and may the haunting terrors within spare your souls."

"So . . . sort of like entering the bathroom after Piston used it," Riff whispered. Steel did not even crack a smile. They entered the shadows together.

A hall loomed before them. The walls, floor, and ceiling were carved of polished bricks, and embers glowed in iron braziers. Murals covered the walls, depicting the Ereef river, its water full of sailing ships and crocodiles, its banks lined with rushes. Upon the ceiling sprawled a fresco of knightly starships descending from the sun, as tawerets knelt among rushes, worshiping the alien visitors. Real, living tawerets stood along the walls, spears and shields in their hands, their hippopotamus eyes staring with suspicion as the companions walked by.

The hall led them toward a balcony overlooking a vast round chamber. The place was so large the *Dragon Huntress* could have flown loops here without grazing the walls.

"The prisoners," Riff whispered, pausing on the balcony.

Steel stared down with hard eyes. "The justice of Lord Kerish Rosetta."

Lenora covered her eyes and turned her head away. Only Giga seemed undisturbed; the android stared with fascination.

"I count four thousand, three hundred and twelve prison cells, sir," she whispered to Riff, wonder in her voice. "Of course, you might want to count the Two-Headed Vegan Swamp Reptiles as two prisoners, in which case, you should add twelve to the count." Her eyes widened. "Look, sir! Do you see the big slimy green one in the back? That's Boss Ruko himself, notorious godfather of the Gerisha crime family of Betelgeuse, while--"

"Thank you, Giga," Riff whispered, voice weak. "I think I know enough."

Steel stared into the spherical chamber. Thousands of cells lined its walls, twenty stories tall, lined with bars. The prisoners languished within--humans and aliens of all kinds. Some wore straitjackets. Others were chained to the walls. A few were unrestrained and hopped around madly, cackling. One alien, a purple thing with many eye stalks, was banging a mug against the bars. Another prisoner, a young woman with pink hair, dangled her legs between the bars while playing a harmonica.

"Where's Dee?" Lenora whispered. "Where's my brother?"

"These are only the low-security prisoners, ma'am," Giga said, turning toward Lenora. "The most dangerous criminals are kept far below this place, buried past many guardians." The android lowered her head. "Forgive me, ma'am, but Dee Rosetta has been classified as a Priority One prisoner. He's been locked in solitary confinement for the past few years. Did you know that the average prisoner in The Holy Asylum only keeps his sanity for two hundred and seventeen days in solitary confinement? You see, the dungeons are designed to--"

Riff placed a finger against her lips. "Giga, no more information even on the fly, all right?"

She nodded, smiling sweetly. "Happy to comply!"

Two prison guards approached. These ones were shorter and slimmer than the guards outside. They had the bodies of women, clad in white and gold muslin, and jackal heads with shining black eyes. Wavy daggers hung at their sides.

"We're here to see my father, Lord Kerish Rosetta," Lenora said. She repeated her little speech from the gateway.

The jackal-headed guards nodded. They spoke in soft, feminine voices. "Come with us, daughter of our lord."

The jackals took them through a small, shadowy archway and up a winding staircase. They climbed past many prison cells. In one, a group of rough-looking gruffles hooted and jeered. In another, what looked like a living tree was struggling to break the bars with his roots. In a third cell, a shapeshifter leered, turning into Riff, then Steel, and finally Giga, taunting them all the while with mad laughter.

Finally the Alien Hunters reached a towering stone doorway. More hippo-heads stood here, these ones armed with mean-looking guns. The brutes shuffled aside, allowing Lenora, Giga, and the Starfire brothers to enter a chamber.

Steel unconsciously clenched his fists.

In the room, behind a thick stone desk, sat Lord Kerish Rosetta.

CHAPTER SEVENTEEN
THE ASYLUM

Kerish Rosetta, warden of the Holy Knights of Sol Asylum, was a beefy man with pink jowls, a barrel chest, and a yellow mustache. His eyes were small, blue, and shrewd, his nose bulbous and veined. He wore a fine suit of plate armor filigreed with gold, and his sword hung at his side.

The chamber was as stern and austere as the warden. A golden sunburst hung upon the wall, sigil of the Knights of Sol. Portraits of the great knights of old frowned from picture frames--haggard, mustached men with eyes that moved to glare at those who looked upon them. Two taweret guards stood around Lord Kerish, helmets on their hippo heads, their breastplates jeweled.

As the Alien Hunters entered the chamber, Sir Kerish slowly placed down the quill he was holding. When Steel stared at the scroll on the desk, he saw that Kerish had just signed an inmate's death warrant.

"Father!" Lenora said. "I've come for your help."

Fire kindled in Kerish's eyes. His cheeks flushed and his mustache bristled.

"How dare you walk into this place?" he hissed.

Lenora sucked in breath and raised her chin. "I am your daughter! I--"

"Silence!" Kerish roared. He leaped to his feet, surprisingly fast for a man of his girth. His chair crashed down behind him. "I was not speaking to you, child." Slowly, he turned those burning eyes toward Steel. "How dare this vagabond, this heretic, this sinner, this wretched space scum step upon holy ground?"

Steel had expected this. He had fought bloodthirsty skelkrins, beasts of claws and fangs with unending appetite for human death. He had faced the armies of the Singularity, killer robots bent on cosmic domination. He had faced ghosts and watched his friends fall to their darkness. He had carried the pain of his banishment for so long, and so much new pain weighed upon him, that Steel had not thought Kerish could still hurt him.

Yet those words dug into his chest like dull daggers.

"There is nothing holy about what goes on within these walls." Steel raised his chin. "The Knights of Sol took vows to defend the galaxy. Not to play god on alien planets. Holy ground?" Steel shook his head. "The only holy ground to me is the Earth I swore to defend. The Earth I came here to fight for."

Lord Kerish drew his sword. He pointed the blade at Steel. "You are no knight! Your vows are worthless. Just like you are. You swore to serve the knighthood, yet you challenged my leadership, you--"

"I challenged your leadership out of love for the knighthood!" Steel said. "You were consorting with the Cosmian Order, a race of alien-worshippers who would have seen the skelkrins conquer the Earth. What did the Cosmians promise you, Kerish? A palace over the ruins? A kingdom of ash? You might have torn off my sigil, Sir Kerish, but the only one to forsake his vows is you."

Kerish roared and swung his blade.

Steel drew his own sword and parried.

The blades slammed together, showering sparks. The taweret guards opened their jaws wide, bellowed, and prepared to thrust their spears. Riff raised his gun and Giga drew her katana.

"Enough!"

The voice rang through the chamber, deafening. Steel turned, surprised to see that it was Lenora who had shouted so loudly. Clutching her skirt, the scientist stared around with narrowed eyes.

"Enough," she repeated, voice softer now. "We've not come here to fight you, Father." She stepped toward the beefy man and pulled down his sword. "This is no time to resurrect old grievances. A danger spreads across the cosmos. The shades have destroyed the observatory at Kaperosa, and they attack the Earth, crumbling cities, haunting the ruins. Father . . . we believe that Dee has information about them. That he can help." Her voice dropped further, becoming almost a whisper. "We've come to see him."

Kerish's rage did not abate. If anything, his daughter's words seemed to stoke the fire in his eyes. He pointed a finger at Lenora. It shook with fury. The knight's jowls were now practically crimson.

"Yes, I know of these shades. Creatures from a higher dimension. It is Dee's work that summoned these demons. For years, the boy has been studying what he calls the fourth dimension, speaking of traveling into that realm. I locked him in this prison to keep that heresy in check. Yet I was too late. The demons are summoned. Now they swarm across the cosmos." Kerish bared his small, sharp teeth. "And you want to help him, Lenora? No. I will not allow it. Dee will remain in his cell, alone, where he will rot. He will never harm another soul."

Lenora gasped. "Father! Dee is a scientist. He's not to blame. He can help! If you're looking to blame someone, blame me." She lowered her head. "I was studying the black hole from which the creatures emerged. If anything, it was my poking that prodded them. Please, Father." She stepped toward him and placed a hand on his shoulder. "Please. For me. For your daughter. Let me speak to your son."

"I have no son!" Kerish roared, shoving her back. "I will hear no more of this. Leave! Leave this world now, before I have you all arrested."

The hippo-headed guards stepped forth. One grabbed Riff with massive hands the size of hams. Another grabbed Lenora. Both struggled, crying out. Steel shouted that he would not step aside, not without a duel to the death, and Lenora cried out about the shades, and Riff threatened to blast the prison apart, and all the while Kerish swore to sign their death warrants right here and now.

Finally, it was Giga whose cry drowned the other voices.

"Article fifty-seven, section G!" she cried.

Kerish froze, mustache bristling. "What?" he demanded.

The android shoved herself free from the guards who held her. "Article fifty-seven, section G," she repeated and smoothed her kimono. "In the Humanoid Alliance Charter concerning the dealings with interstellar prisoners. The charter that still binds you to Earth rules." Giga smiled. "The clause clearly specifies that no prisoner shall be kept in solitary confinement for longer than thirty days." She tilted her head. "Didn't you say that he's been in solitary for years now? In fact, scanning the prison's systems . . ." Metallic clicks rose from her. "Dee Rosetta, Prisoner 43712, has been kept in solitary confinement for 957 days now. In clear violation of article fifty-seven, section G."

They all gaped at her.

"Well, I'll be," Riff whispered.

Giga looked at him. "Sorry, Captain. You told me no more infodump. Did I do bad?"

"You did wonderfully." Riff turned toward Kerish. "Well, what of it? We have here a clear violation of Humanoid Alliance law. Dear Giga here--she's an android, in case you haven't noticed--has a continuous connection to cyberspace's major blogs and news sources. You wouldn't want her to send out a press release about these little infractions, would you? I'd hate to see the Humanoid Alliance bureaucrats launch an investigation. Terrible amount of paperwork. Trust me, I know. We break their laws all the time."

Sir Kerish finally found the air to speak. His words blustered out with a spray of saliva. "Are you blackmailing me, boy?"

Riff wiped off his face. "Say it, don't spray it. And yes. I am blackmailing you. Thought that was obvious, really. Surprised you had to ask."

Lenora stepped forward before Kerish could attack again. She spoke softly. "Father, please. Just let us see Dee this one time. Let us talk to him. For Earth, Father. To save the cosmos. Help us fight these demons."

Kerish's mustache drooped. He seemed torn between his pride and the knowledge that he had lost. Finally he sucked in his gut, thrust out his chest, and raised his chin.

"Very well. I still have a soft spot for my daughter, it seems. I find it difficult to refuse her. For you, Lenora, I will agree to a short visit. My guards will take you to see your brother. But after your visit, you will leave this planet. Forever."

As the companions left the office, Steel glanced back at Sir Kerish, and he glimpsed pure hatred in the man's eyes. There was murder in those eyes. But those eyes weren't staring at Steel for once.

Clenching his fists and grinding his teeth, Sir Kerish was staring at Giga.

* * * * *

Surrounded by guards, Lenora and the Alien Hunters walked down craggy tunnels, plunging deep into the prison pyramid.

They left the great chamber of cells above. They delved into the dungeons, moving through corridors and stairways that drove deep into the darkness. Torches crackled on the walls, lighting frescos depicting ancient starcrafts exploring distant worlds, gods with the heads of animals, and aliens with twisting necks and the heads of monkeys.

Countless guards filled the place. Tawerets with hippo heads stood everywhere, armed with guns and spears. Women with the heads of jackals patrolled the halls, their scimitars bright. Silent warriors in white linen, men and women with the heads of hawks, stared with gleaming yellow eyes, holding khopeshes. Crocodiles growled on leashes. War monkeys wore spiked armor. Finally, overseeing the natives, Knights of Sol--the human masters--stood in polished steel, swords in their hands.

Every staircase, chamber, and corridor was filled with these soldiers. An entire army buried inside the pyramid.

There must be hundreds of warriors here, Riff thought as they keep walking deeper into the crypt. *How dangerous has Dee Rosetta become to need so many guards?*

Again, Riff thought back to his youth. He remembered the scrawny, brainy boy the other kids would pick on. In one memory, a few neighborhood children had hollowed out a chocolate bar, filled it with salt, and given it to Dee to eat. The spectacled boy had accepted the treat with glee, eaten it all, and hadn't seemed to even notice the salt; he had just been glad to find friends.

Riff sighed. *And now he's buried in this pit, an army of knights and Ancient Egyptian aliens guarding him. Probably thinks they're his friends too.*

After walking what seemed like kilometers, the corridors finally ended at a stone doorway. Several guards stood here, thin men with the heads of cobras.

"Enter," hissed one guard. His forked tongue flicked. "Enter and speak to the prisoner. You have ten minutesss."

The guards got to unlocking the cell. First they spun a massive gear the size of a man. The door opened, only to reveal a second door. The guards then unlocked a hundred small padlocks, and the second door opened too, revealing a third door. Here, upon the stone, were engraved ancient runes. The guards chanted prayers, the runes glowed, and the third door creaked open. Asps in baskets guarded a fourth door; they were soothed only when the guards chanted soft songs. Riff counted ten more doors, each secured with a lock or trap, before finally an inner door made of iron blades dilated, revealing a shadowy chamber.

"Step inside," hissed the serpentine guard.

Riff nodded. "Might not want to close all the doors while we're in there, or we'll be inside for ten hours instead of ten minutes."

He entered the cell. Steel, Lenora, and Giga followed. One of the doors clanked shut behind them.

Riff stared around and gasped.

"Shenanigans," he whispered.

A bed, a small desk, and a television set stood in the room. The TV was showing a rerun of *Space Galaxy*, Riff's favorite show--a classic episode where the captain fought a reptilian humanoid. The walls were built of the same bricks as the rest of the pyramid, but instead of hieroglyphs or murals, countless mathematical equations covered them, drawn with chalk.

"No, no, this is wrong," rose a voice from under the bed. "You're supposed to grab him by the neck. The neck! Not the head. Everyone knows reptilians have thick skulls. The neck, damn it! Oh . . . too late." On the television set, the reptile broke free and tossed the captain into a gorge. "Every damn time. You'll never learn."

Riff peeked under the bed. The shadowy figure of a man lay there on his stomach, watching the show.

"Hello," Riff said.

"Shh!"

"Sorry." Riff closed his mouth.

"Not you," said the prisoner. "That damn Captain Carter. He shouldn't be talking on his communicator. Doesn't he know the Raelians are approaching? I've watched this episode a thousand times, and he never learns."

"He'll get away at the end," Riff said. "He'll escape through the caves, fight off the stone creatures, and sneak back onto the *Lodestar*."

The prisoner turned toward Riff, and his eyes widened. "You like *Space Galaxy* too?"

Riff pointed at his T-shirt which bore the show's logo. "Seen every episode."

The man leaped out from under the bed. His hair was ruffled, and his glasses perched crookedly upon his nose. Dee Rosetta looked the same as always.

"Riff Starfire!" he said. "I know your face."

"Dee Rosetta," Riff said with a smile.

Dee turned toward the others and gasped. "Steel Starfire! And . . . Lenora, my sister!" He shook their hands emphatically, then turned toward Giga. "And what have we here? Hmm . . ." He tapped the android's cheek. "Human Interface Android. Class T, model 75 . . . B?"

Giga smiled sweetly. "75 C-i, sir."

"The C-i! Of course!" Dee hopped for joy. "I worked on your vocal chords, did you know? Back before they locked me up in this joint. Sing me a scale."

"Happy to comply!" Giga sang a little tune.

Dee clapped. "Beautiful! Lovely. Happy to comply! That was my idea for a catch phrase, did you know? Programmed it right into all the 75 models." He turned toward Lenora. "You don't suppose Father would let me have a Class T 75er in here, would he? Even the older models, the dumb ones that don't say much." He sighed. "It sure gets lonely in here. By the stars . . . how long has it been?"

Tears shone in Lenora's eyes. She stepped closer and embraced her little brother. "Too long, Dee. Too long."

He held her awkwardly for a moment, then leaped back and jumped into the air. "No, no!" he shouted at the television. "You're not supposed to fire your photons! Don't you know their shields can soak them up?"

Keeping his eyes glued to the television, Dee sat on his bed. One episode ended and another began.

"Dee . . ." Lenora spoke softly and wrapped her arms around her brother again. "We don't have long. We came here for your help. We need to--"

"To build a four-dimensional engine, one capable of transporting a three-dimensional starship into the higher plane, allowing you to combat creatures who appear as ghosts in our world." Dee kept watching his show. "Should be possible to do by bending spacetime as a Euclidian space rather than a relative space, essentially the same concept as a hyperspace engine only applying geometrical formulas to the warping of the external fabric."

"Yes. I think." Lenora narrowed her eyes. "How did you know?"

"Damn it, man!" Dee leaped to his feet. "Every damn time, you let that girl onto the ship. Can't you see from her glowing eyes that she's an Orianite who's only after your minerals?" He sighed and turned toward Lenora. "Why else would you be here? Building such an engine has been my life's work. Even harder to do than the vocal chords of an android. It's all on the walls, if you'd like to build one yourself."

Dee gestured at the thousands of mathematical formulas scribbled across the cell.

"Two minutes left!" boomed a voice from outside.

Riff winced. "Does anyone have a camera?"

Steel shook his head. "Not me. Lenora? Giga?"

The android smiled. "I do have a photographic memory, sir. But I don't understand these calculations well enough to build the engine myself. Piston might take a stab at it, but--"

"Piston?" Dee said. "Who's that?"

Giga tilted her head. "Our gruffle engineer, sir. He--"

"Engineer?" Dee scoffed. "No no, my little siren of the beautiful voice. No engineer can build such an engine. Don't you have a Euclidian multiple dimensionalist aboard your vessel?"

They all shook their heads.

Dee sighed. "Well then, I'll have to build the engine myself."

"One minute!" boomed the voice from outside.

Riff cringed. "Can you build one within a minute? Ideally small enough to fit into my pocket?"

Dee considered. "Possibly. Hmm. Maybe not within a minute, though. How big are your pockets?"

"Thirty seconds!"

Steel groaned. "So this was all for nothing?"

Dee cracked his neck. "Well, I suppose we'll have to escape then." He walked toward the television set, pushed it aside, and revealed a gaping tunnel. "We can crawl through here. Should take us right out to freedom."

Lenora's eyes widened and she gasped. "What--a tunnel! You had a tunnel all along? Why didn't you escape then?"

Dee shrugged. "Just completed it this morning. Wanted to finish watching my *Space Galaxy* episodes first. Good timing."

Behind them, the cell doors began to clank as the guards worked at unlocking them.

Riff stepped toward the tunnel. "Dee, go! You enter first."

"But this episode just started and--"

"Go!" Riff grabbed the man and shoved him into the tunnel. Steel, Lenora, and Giga followed. Riff leaped into the tunnel last, pulling the television back into place before he slid down, plunging into darkness.

CHAPTER EIGHTEEN

THE GOLDEN SCARAB

Romy swayed her hips on stage, her belt of coins jingling. She wore her serpent tiara, bracelets jangled around her arms, and she had painted on thick mascara, giving herself Eyes of Ra. In her hand, she shook a timbrel.

"I am Pharaoh Romy, ancient seductress of the orient!" she announced.

Across the tavern, the crowd roared their approval.

The Scarab's Lair was a small tavern, not much larger than Romy's attic back on the *Dragon Huntress*. Hieroglyphs were painted onto the walls, featuring hawks, snakes, ibises, sphinxes, and many other characters--an ancient comic strip, Romy surmised. Stone jugs stood behind the bar, full of ale and wine, and peacock feathers rose from obsidian vases.

A hundred people or more crowded the place. Alien musicians--men with the heads of crocodiles--sat on the stage behind Romy, playing drums and harps. Serving girls with jackal heads moved through the chamber, clad in white tunics hemmed with golden coins, pouring wine from silver vessels. Taweret soldiers in bronze armor, beefy men with hippo heads, waved tankards of ale at the dancing Romy, hooting.

Finally, among the aliens, sat the scientists rescued from Kaperosa. At first, when Romy had shepherded them into the tavern, they had glanced around nervously, then huddled in the corner to talk about boring things like math and science and other stuff that made Romy's head hurt. But once she had started swaying on stage, and once enough booze filled the scientists' bellies, they finally relaxed. Now they too drank deeply, sang, and pounded their fists on the tabletops with the beat.

"Dance with me, Piston!" Romy said, reaching down from the stage toward him.

The gruffle glared up at her, clutching a mug of ale. Foam coated his beard. "Get off that stage, Romy! You're embarrassing yourself."

She shook her head, casting sparks off her hair of flame. She gave a little pirouette, tripped on her tail, and fell. With a quick flap of her wings, she was up and dancing again, and the crowd cheered.

"Dance with me, Prince of Egypt!" She reached down and grabbed Piston's beard. "Come on. They want to see a dancing gruffle."

Piston roared. "A dancing gruffle? I'm not a performing monkey."

"A monkey!" Romy's eyes widened. "Do you think I can be a monkey? Are there any aliens here with monkey heads? Can they turn me into one?" She looked around the tavern. "Does anyone know how to turn me into a monkey?"

She saw people with the heads of hawks, snakes, hippos, crocodiles, and jackals, but the only monkey she saw was a capuchin on a leash. Abandoning her dream for now, Romy kept dancing, hips swaying to the beat, the fire crackling on her head. Somebody handed her an ale, and she drank deeply. She had lost count of how much she had drunk today. More than she could count--which wasn't saying much, granted--but until she passed out, it wasn't enough.

She was drinking another mug, and her dancing was becoming more erratic, when the shrieks rose from outside.

Romy frowned and blinked.

"Quiet!" she shouted at the windows. "Romy the Desert Queen is dancing."

Yet the shrieking continued from outside, so loud it drowned even the music inside the Golden Scarab tavern. Humans and aliens turned toward the windows. Romy tried to peer outside, but with the haze of incense that filled the tavern, she could see nothing but smudges. The whole damn tavern was spinning too, which wasn't helping. The sound grew louder outside, accompanied by the roar of engines, then by the screams of aliens.

"Romy, those are starship engines!" Piston shouted. He hopped onto the stage and grabbed her arm.

"Oh hai, Piston!" She patted his head. "Come to dance with me at last?"

The gruffle might have only reached Romy's shoulders, but he was wider and stronger, and he yanked her right off the stage.

"Hey!" she cried.

Both humans and aliens were staring out the windows and crying out in fear. Through the dusty panes of glass, Romy saw swaying palm trees and fleeing people.

As Piston dragged her across the tavern, Romy managed to grab a mug of ale from a table and guzzle it down. Then they burst outside into the blinding sunlight.

Romy blinked. "My eyes hurt."

Piston gasped. "By the gods of rock and metal! Shade ships!"

Squinting, Romy stared up at the sky. Past the tips of obelisks, the soaring columns of temples, and a sandstone sphinx, she saw them. Tesseracts. The ships of the enemy. They soared down from the sky, the sun at their backs, engines shrieking. Palm trees and reeds bent along the river, and the boats swayed.

"Ghosts," Romy whispered.

As she stood on the hot cobblestones, the tesseracts swooped toward the city and blasted out dark fire. The ghostly flames washed over a temple. Statues of men with hawk heads collapsed. Columns cracked. The roof caved in. Priests fled, only for ghosts to leap from the tesseracts and tear them apart. More screams sounded behind Romy, and she spun around to see a tesseract blast dark fire against an obelisk. The pillar cracked and slammed down, crashing into homes.

Aliens ran down the streets, crying out in fear. The scientists fled. Palm trees burned, and more tesseracts kept appearing in the sky, roaring down their ghostly fire.

"To the *Dragon Huntress*!" Piston shouted. "Come on, Romy, we'll fly her together."

Romy nodded. "We'll take Fred."

She ran toward the camel who was tethered outside the tavern. His true name was long and complicated and made her tongue hurt, so she had called him Fred. He stood laden with the essentials Romy had purchased in the market that morning: silken scarves lined with tassels, a parrot in a golden cage, a few jeweled daggers, magical potions, a monkey's paw, and three sacks full of chickpeas. It was a wonder Fred could still stand.

"Hurry, Fred, take us home." She beat her wings, soared, and landed on the saddle.

The camel groaned. "You're the last straw, Romy."

"No I'm not. That'll be Piston." She reached down, grabbed the gruffle, and yanked him up.

Grumbling all the while, Piston managed to settle into the saddle behind Romy. "Gruffles weren't meant to ride camels, damn it."

Fred moaned. "And we camels weren't meant to carry gruffles. Or demons. Or half the market of Athemes."

"Hurry, Fred!" Romy said. "Gallop! Gallop like the wind!"

Wobbling, the camel raced through the city, hooves thumping against the cobblestones. The city denizens ran alongside, wailing in fear. The tesseracts still flew above, and ghosts swarmed everywhere, claws stretching out to rip at flesh.

Leaving the tavern behind, they raced through the city market. Stalls lined the roadsides, selling everything from spices to weapons to exotic pets. A cart overturned, spilling dates and figs. Ahead, a wagon bearing silken scarfs caught flame. A ghost swarmed through a shop, shattering olivewood sculptures and vials of potions. Rugs fell and tangled around legs, sending shoppers falling to the ground.

One ghost leaped from a rooftop, sailing down toward Romy, a smoky spirit only half in this world. Romy thrust her pitchfork, impaling it. The creature shattered into a thousand black strands that fell like burnt scraps of paper. A second ghost leaped from an alleyway, and Piston swung his hammer, cleaving its head. Beneath them, Fred kept running.

"Time to ditch the dead weight!" Piston said.

Romy whined. "But I like the stuff I bought."

Piston grumbled. "I mean you--fly above us!"

"But--"

"Now!"

Romy moaned. She hated flying with her own wings. Too much ale and honeyed dates meant even more weight than usual to lift. But she obeyed, flapping her wings and rising from the saddle. Fred ran beneath her, still bearing Piston, and to Romy's chagrin, the gruffle was now tossing the sacks of chickpeas off the saddle.

She was going to object when another ghost flew toward her. Romy wailed and thrust her pitchfork. More shades raced through the alleyway, overturning carts. Sacks of spices spilled, filling the air with the aroma of cumin and cardamom. Statues of gods fell and shattered. Jugs, plates, and vases of tin, porcelain, and precious metals rolled across the cobblestones. Fred kept running, pushing through the sea of shades, as Piston swung his hammer.

Finally they burst out from the market. They raced across a boulevard. To their right, tesseracts fired upon a towering sandstone temple. Statues cracked and fell. To their left, ghosts swarmed a massive sphinx the size of a mountain, chipping at the stone. The nose crashed down, burying a fortune-teller's stall. Romy's wings ached, but she forced herself to keep flapping them. She pressed the button on her pitchfork, blasting out fire at the shades.

The damn things were everywhere. One's claws ripped across her leg, shedding blood. She screamed and lashed her own claws. Another beast landed on her back, and its fangs dug into her shoulder. She wailed, shook it off, and bit with her own fangs.

"You might be ghosts, but I'm a demon. And everybody knows that demons outrank ghosts."

Her hair crackled, her pitchfork shot out flame, and blood filled her mouth. She flew onward, tearing through the enemy.

I'm done being afraid, Romy thought. *I used to fear you, to flee from you, but I've got a belly full of beer and a pitchfork full of fire.*

A battle raged below. Platoons of tawerets charged down the streets, hippo jaws opened wide. They blasted green electricity from their jeweled spears, knocking shades back. A thousand anubis warriors--women with jackal heads--yipped and charged in chariots. They fired arrows tipped with blue lightning, and they swung golden sabers. Men with hawk heads leaped off temples, glided over the streets on wings of silk and wood, and dropped balls of clay. The missiles exploded on impact, tearing shades apart.

Yet despite their efforts, the ghosts would not stop swarming. The corpses of natives lay strewn across the roads. More columns cracked. Ships sank in the river and palm trees burned. The tesseract ships flew above, unopposed.

Fred kept running below, and Romy kept flying above, and finally they burst out of the city into the open desert. They raced across the sand toward the pyramids. Shades were flying here too, climbing the pyramid slopes, battling the taweret guardians. Between the towering structures rested three *Dragon Huntresses.*

Romy blinked, rubbed her eyes, and brought the world into focus until only one ship stood before her. Damn ale!

Piston leaped off the saddle and bounded into the airlock. Romy tried to fly in after him, but somehow she managed to splatter herself against the hull. Piston reached out, grabbed her wing, and yanked her into the ship.

"I'll kick-start the engines!" the gruffle said, leaping down into the engine room. "Go fly this thing."

Romy saluted. "Aye aye, sir!"

She raced down the hall, only to slam into another wall. She moaned and shook her head, seeing stars. She kept running and stumbled upstairs on hands and knees. Finally she crawled onto the bridge. The whole chamber swayed around her.

I'm never drinking again.

She dragged herself forward, crawled into a chair, and grabbed the controls. The engines roared below.

"Up!" Romy said, tugging joystick and throttle.

The *Dragon Huntress* lurched backward.

Romy groaned and shoved the joystick forward. The ship drove through the sand, digging a rut.

"Damn it, you clod!" Piston's voice rose through the communicator. "Up! Fly up!"

Romy beat her wings and flew toward the ceiling.

Oh wait, he means the ship.

She flew back into the seat and grabbed the controls again. Damn it, she should know this! She had flown the *Dragon Huntress* before. But back then, Twig had guided her hands, and she hadn't been full of ale. Romy cringed. Through the windshield, she could see tesseracts flying near. She yanked the controls madly and hit buttons at random. Finally the ship roared skyward, blasting smoke.

A tesseract flew toward her. Black fire roared out and slammed into the *Dragon Huntress*. The ship spun, sputtering smoke. It took all of Romy's concentration to level their flight-- and to hold her bladder.

"The red button," Romy muttered, remembering. She hit it. Plasma roared out of the *Dragon Huntress* and crashed into a tesseract. The ghostly ship tore apart, raining down metal cubes that thumped into the sand.

"I think I got the hang of this!" Romy said.

She flew toward the city, determined to blast the enemy apart.

Countless tesseracts--with her spinning head, it was hard to see how many--seemed to notice her. The impossible ships shrieked like steam, charged toward her, and fired their guns.

Roaring out fire, the *Dragon Huntress* crashed into their ranks.

CHAPTER NINETEEN

THE OLD GUARD

"And don't you think, Riff, that in season twelve, episode four, scene three, that when the Raelian Spacehawk activated its antimatter cannon that Captain Carter should have responded with a classic B-cluster maneuver?" Crawling through the tunnel, Dee snorted. "I mean, it's textbook Defensive Flying 101, and in season four we clearly see it performed in the background during the Jarasu battle."

Riff crawled ahead of the rumpled prisoner. "No, it suits Carter. He was always reckless. Never one to do things by the book. That's why Pascal was a superior captain to the *Lodestar*."

"Gods! Put me back in my cell, man!" Dee tugged his hair. "I refuse to be rescued by a Captain Pascal fan."

Behind them, Steel groaned. "What are you two talking about? What ancient battles? I have studied all great space battles and--"

"*Space Galaxy*," Riff said. "A television show."

"A *religion*!" Dee said. "Saying that *Space Galaxy* is just a show is like saying that *It Came from the Sea!* is just a movie. In any case, Riff old boy, you are clearly delusional. I will remind you that in the appendixes to *Space Galaxy IV*--and I refer to the original movie series, not the dreadful prequels--Captain Carter is seen entering the Academy during the tenure of Professor Halivian, where one would presume that--"

"Enough!" Lenora said, crawling behind them. "Boys, if you don't shut up about your stories, I'm going to bang your heads together."

They closed their mouths and crawled onward in silence. The tunnel was narrow and rough--Dee had carved it with his spoon--but it soon opened up into a smooth shaft. This new tunnel was constructed of polished sandstone bricks engraved with hieroglyphs. It too was narrow and dark, but tall enough to let them stand and walk.

"Where are we?" Riff said.

"In the heart of the pyramid," Dee said. "In the holy passageways. See, the tawerets--those surly fellows with the hippo heads--worship the Knights of Sol as gods. When the knights asked them to build a prison, they used the same design as their other pyramids, tombs to their kings."

Riff passed his hands over the hieroglyphs lining the tunnel. "And these tunnels are part of every pyramid?"

Dee nodded. "Normally a pharaoh is buried within each pyramid--right about where I was buried. These inner tunnels are constructed to let the pharaoh's spirit rise from his body and fly off to the sky." Dee chuckled. "My father sealed off my cell. But I knew that if I dug through the wall, I'd find these passageways. Now all we have to do is crawl onward, pass the booby traps and guardians, and reach freedom."

"Booby traps?" Riff gulped. "Guardians?"

"Of course." Dee nodded emphatically. "You don't think the architects would dig a tunnel right into the holy of holies but leave it undefended? Still . . . an easier escape than the main passageway the guards took you through. Should be a cakewalk. You did bring your book of ancient incantations, right? To ward off the curses?"

Riff groaned. "It's in my other pants." He looked over his shoulder. "Steel, we might have trouble ahead."

The knight glanced behind him. "We might have trouble behind us too." Footfalls sounded in the distance. "I don't think the television set stopped the guards for long, not even with your *Galaxy Seed* show on."

"*Space Galaxy*!" Dee said. "You're talking about a classic, sir, about--"

"Enough!" Lenora said. She pointed ahead. "Let's move, fast! Run!"

They raced along the tunnel. It began to slope upward, and Riff imagined the spirit of an old pharaoh traveling here toward his final resting place in the sky. He just hoped his own final resting place wasn't here in the darkness. The only light came from Steel's sword and Lenora's flashlight. All the while, the sounds of pursuit rose behind them: thumping boots, clanking armor, roaring hippopotamuses, yipping jackals, and hissing snakes.

The tunnel bent at mad angles, rising, falling, zigzagging. Hope was rising in Riff that the tunnel was deserted when he saw the jagged metal pieces ahead. He skidded to a halt. The others crashed into him.

"What is it?" Giga whispered, leaning around him. She shuddered. "Was it once . . . another android?"

"I don't know," Riff said.

Light kindled in Giga's eyes, casting two beams like flashlights. The light revealed a chamber ahead, its floor strewn with rusty old metal parts: gears, springs, blades, bolts, and countless other pieces. Cobwebs and dust covered them, and frescos of ancient machines covered the walls. Tattered ropes lay on the floor. Beyond the debris, a dark doorway led into another tunnel.

"The booby traps," Dee whispered.

Riff breathed out a sigh of relief. "Looks like we're not the first to have escaped through here. Whoever previously walked here, they smashed whatever traps had once filled the chamber." He squinted but couldn't recognize what the machine had been; too much dust and cobwebs covered the parts. "Whatever this trap was, it was shattered long ago. Let's keep going."

With the sounds of pursuit close behind, the companions stepped into the chamber.

Riff led the way, gun raised. Giga walked a step behind, katana drawn. The Rosetta siblings entered next, while Steel brought up the rear. At the back of the chamber, Riff could see another tunnel. They tiptoed over the debris on the floor, scattering cobwebs, leaving footprints in the dust.

"Captain," Giga whispered, and her voice shook. "I think these things were androids. I . . ." She tilted her head. "But I don't see circuits. Only . . ."

Her foot brushed against a gear. It was only a tap, but the rusted bronze piece clattered across the floor, raising a ruckus. It tore through cobwebs, scattered a host of screws, knocked over a spring, and finally thumped down.

The companions froze.

The chamber began to rattle. Bolts and sprockets and gears vibrated and bounced on the floor. Dust flew. The cobwebs tore. Metal rods rolled.

"Earthquake?" Steel said.

Riff shook his head. "The chamber isn't moving. Just the pieces."

Steel glanced behind him. "Guards getting closer. Come on!"

They all began to run again, heading across the chamber. Before they could reach the opposite tunnel, however, the pieces strewn across the floor leaped into the air.

The companions froze and gasped.

Before them, metal rods, wheels, and plates snapped together. Screws turned. Bolts slammed into place. Springs coiled up and gears began to turn, raining dust. Limbs of metal spread out, tipped with chipped blades. Crystal eyes, set into bronze skulls, blazed with light. Three automatons, taller than men, loomed before the companions, blocking the exit. Gears spun behind metal ribs, ticking, and springs moved along their arms.

The creatures unhooked rusted jaws made of bear traps, and their howls echoed in the chamber.

"Robots," Giga whispered.

"Clockwork men," Riff muttered.

The three Alien Hunters raised their weapons and fired together. Riff's gun fired plasma. Steel's longsword beamed out searing light. Giga's katana lashed out lightning. The blasts slammed into the automatons, but the machines kept clanking forward, shedding rust and cobwebs with every step.

"Company behind us!" Lenora shouted.

Riff glanced over his shoulder and cursed. Anubis warriors were entering the tomb, having traveled here from Dee's cell. Behind them, the hippo-heads were roaring. Riff blasted plasma their way.

He spun back toward the automatons, but not fast enough. One of the clockwork robots charged toward him, and rusty claws lashed across Riff's chest. Blood dripped and stained his *Space Galaxy* shirt.

"They desecrated the holy sigil of *Space Galaxy*," Dee whispered, then roared with rage. The disheveled scientist lobbed himself forward, kicking at the rusty robots, fighting furiously.

"Riff, get rid of the automatons, I've got the guards!" Steel shouted. The knight thrust his blade at an Anubis warrior. The jackal-headed woman swung her scimitar, parrying the blow.

Riff fired his gun again, and the plasma melted the inner gears of an automaton. The creature fell and kept crawling across the floor, spilling bolts and springs. Another automaton leaped toward Riff, and he fired again, knocked it back. A third robot leaped toward Lenora, grabbed the scientist, and bloodied her thigh. Lenora screamed and fell, helpless to stop the machine attacking her.

"No," Giga whispered. "No, I will not let my fellow robots do this. No!"

With the rustle of silk and the flash of steel, Giga leaped into the air. She somersaulted, kicked off the wall, and landed behind the automatons. As the rusty machines kept advancing, Giga reached into their innards. Her fingers worked in a fury, moving gears, unscrewing and tightening bolts, and shifting springs. She moved so quickly her hands were but a blur.

"More guards breaking in!" Steel shouted, swinging his blade. "We have to get through!"

Riff glanced over to see a dozen prison guards entering the hall. A towering warrior with a hawk's head opened his beak and cawed. The jackal-heads yowled. The burly tawerets chomped on Steel's blade with their hippo jaws, trying to shatter it, and one grabbed the knight's arm.

When Riff glanced the other way, he still saw the automatons blocking his passage.

Trapped, he thought and fired his gun at a guard. The taweret fell, only for another to replace him.

"Done!" Giga said. "Go, robots! Attack the guards. Slay them!"

She pulled her hands back. Rust coated her fingers. Their inner gears rearranged, the automatons clanked forward. Shedding dust and cobwebs and loose bolts, the machines walked right past the Alien Hunters and the Rosetta siblings. They reached the prison guards, howled, and attacked.

The automatons' fingers, made of bronze blades, slashed at the guards. Their bear-trap jaws bit. Their gemstone eyes beamed out light that seared through armor.

"Run!" Riff said.

As the machines crashed against the guards, the companions ran. They leaped over the last loose bolts, barged into the far tunnel, and vanished into the shadows.

"What did you do there, Giga?" Lenora cried, clutching her wound as she ran.

"Ancient programming," answered the android.

Dee laughed. "Wonderful creatures, the 75 C-i's. Did I mention that I helped create them?"

As the guards' footfalls sounded behind, they kept racing up the tunnel, traveling through the veins of the pyramid.

* * * * *

They ran for what seemed like kilometers. For a long time, the sounds of battle rose behind them, but finally the screeches of the automatons died, and once again the prison guards were pursuing.

"How much farther, Dee?" Riff shouted.

"Almost there," Dee answered. "The tunnel will take us to the top of the pyramid. That's where the pharaoh's soul was said to escape his tomb and rise to the sky."

Indeed, the tunnel was steeper now, an incline that left Riff sweating and breathing heavily. He couldn't imagine how Steel, in his plate armor, was feeling. Lenora was limping, her thigh still bleeding; Giga helped her run. Riff's own wound was bleeding, an ugly scratch across his chest.

When Riff thought he couldn't take another step, the tunnel opened up into another chamber.

He paused, panting, and stared.

"Wait," he said to the others. "Careful."

They all froze in the doorway, breathing heavily, and stared into the room. Several sarcophagi lay here, the stone coffins carved into the shapes of humans with animal heads. Smaller sarcophagi shaped as cats, dogs, and snakes stood in alcoves in the wall. The sound of pursuit rose louder from behind.

"I thought this wasn't an actual burial pyramid," Riff said.

"It's not," Dee said. "But every pyramid claims the lives of several workers. Slaves, usually, crushed by stones, worked to death, sometimes beaten by their masters. When they die during their labor, they're buried within the pyramid, given that final honor."

"Well, their final rest is going to be disturbed." Riff stepped into the chamber. "Come on, hurry everyone."

They entered the chamber. They had only taken a few steps when the sarcophagi's heavy stone lids began to rattle.

Riff sighed and charged his gun. "Why am I not surprised this happened?"

He had taken another step when the stone lids dropped, hit the floor, and cracked. From a dozen sarcophagi they rose: rancid mummies, their shrouds tattered and drooping to unveil the desiccated flesh within. The mummies' mouths opened, revealing yellow teeth. They had the heads of various animals, and worms crawled within their eye sockets. On the walls, the smaller sarcophagi opened, and animal mummies emerged.

Riff fired his gun, blasting a hole through one mummy. The decrepit man kept advancing, the hole in his torso smoking, and reached out clawed fingers. Steel swung his sword, casting out a disk of light, slicing through two mummies. The tops of their torsos slid off and hit the floor. They kept crawling forward, snapping their jaws, while their legs walked on their own. Giga leaped, bounced off the walls like a pinball, and swung her katana, cutting off mummy limbs. Even Lenora and Dee fought, kicking the mummy cats and dogs that raced toward them.

Yet all their weapons didn't stop the mummies. The corpses raised their severed arms and reattached them. They kept advancing, reaching out their claws, snapping their jaws.

"We can't kill what's already dead," Steel muttered as he lashed his blade.

Riff shook his head. "No, but we can still push through them. Steel, help me lift this thing."

The brothers knelt and lifted one of the heavy sarcophagus lids. The stone was engraved into the shape of a man with a crocodile's head. Lenora and Dee struggled to lift another lid, while Giga lifted a third lid--the largest one--on her own.

Together, they charged forward, knocking mummies aside with their stone shields. The beasts fell back and slammed against the walls. The stone lid drove against them, crushing them against the walls, snapping their old bones. The creatures disintegrated into dust.

"Kill the criminals!" rose a voice from deeper in the pyramid. "Kill them all."

The companions dropped the stone lids, leaped into the far tunnel, and kept running.

The tunnel was so steep now, Riff could barely keep running. He thought he could smell the hot, dry air of the desert. They were getting close. From behind, he heard pounding footsteps, yipping beasts, and clattering blades--getting closer, closer. The companions kept running.

Shadows stirred across the walls, and cackling laughter echoed.

"The walls are coming alive!" Lenora said.

Riff cursed. Across the tunnel's brick walls, the hieroglyphs were awakening. Crocodiles, falcons, cobras, warriors--all peeled themselves off the wall and charged toward the companions. Riff fired his gun. Steel and Giga swung their blades. A painted falcon, a living hieroglyph, swooped toward Riff. He blasted it with his gun. A snake slithered across the ground, painted gold, and Lenora stomped on it. Golden scarabs leaped up, and Steel sliced them with his blade. They kept running, charging through thousands of the painted enemies. Their tiny beaks, teeth, and claws tore at them, further ripping Riff's shirt, bloodying his skin. He kept firing, kept running, and all the while the guards pursued.

Finally Riff could see it--light at the end of the tunnel. He ran with new vigor. The light grew stronger. A gust of dry wind blew, scented of sand.

We're almost free. Almost outside the pyramid. We're going to get out of here--run to the Dragon Huntress, *blast off this planet, save the cosmos, find Nova and Twig, be together again.*

He ran with every last drop of strength in him. This nightmare--of ghosts, of creatures in the dark, of Nova gone-- would all soon end.

The light grew brighter. He could see it ahead: an archway exiting the pyramid. The blue sky.

"Almost there!" Riff shouted. "Light ahead. Freedom--"

No.

His breath shook.

Oh gods, no.

He skidded to a halt. His companions froze around him. They stared ahead, blood dripping, weapons raised.

In the archway, the sun at their backs, stood a group of knights. Among them, sword raised, was Lord Kerish Rosetta.

CHAPTER TWENTY

MAN OF HONOR

Steel stood in the tunnel, armor cracked, wounds bleeding, sword raised. He stared ahead at his old mentor, refusing to look away, refusing to cower.

Kerish stared back, his blue eyes livid in his puffed, red face. His mustache bristled. His lips peeled back in a snarl. He seemed almost like one of the native aliens, a man with the head of a beast, his the head of an enraged hog.

There he stands, Steel thought. *The man I once admired. The man I sought to be like. The man who let me join his order only to cast me aside.*

"Stand aside, Sir Kerish," Steel said, voice calm. "No more blood needs be shed this day."

Kerish took a step deeper into the tunnel, his sword held before him. Six knights stood behind him, their own blades drawn. The sun blazed at their backs, and in the distance, Steel could see the city along the river. The enemy had reached this world too, he saw. Their tesseracts screamed across the sky, and their smoky soldiers flowed across the desert.

"Now you are truly disgraced," Kerish said, pointing his blade at Steel. "I banished you from my order when you dared doubt my wisdom. Now you try to smuggle out one of my prisoners. Your punishment will be more than exile this time, Starfire, but death. And I will mete out your sentence myself."

"One of your prisoners?" Lenora shouted. She stepped forward, clung to Steel's arm, and glared at her father. "He is your son! Your son, Father! His name is Dee. Your only son. And you locked him up here, all because . . . all because he's not a knight like you. All because you can't understand the things he studies, because--"

"You too will die, girl!" Kerish roared. "He is no son of mine. You are no daughter of mine. You are traitors, all of you! Heretics! And this." Kerish's voice trembled with rage, and he pointed at Giga. "This *machine*, this abomination of life, walks among you. A sinner. A foul demon of metal."

Giga tilted her head. "Cannot compute, sir. I am more than a machine. I am life."

"You are a perversion!" Kerish shouted. "You all are, every last one of you. Now your time of death has come. Men! Slay them. Slay them all."

The knights advanced, blades at the ready.

"No!" Steel said, voice ringing through the tunnel. He stepped forward, placing himself between the knights and his companions. "I will not let blood spill here. Not as an enemy of darkness attacks outside. I no longer carry the sigil of Sol upon my breastplate. But honor still beats in my heart, as it does in the hearts of my brother and friends--even this android that you scorn. Honor once beat in your heart too, Kerish. Do not let your pride blind you. Join me, Kerish. Fight with me. Against the dark enemy that flows outside, slaying the innocent even as we speak. We were once brothers-at-arm! Fight at my side again."

Kerish stared at Steel, silent, rage in his eyes. And suddenly all those memories flowed back into Steel. Suddenly he was a youth again, a boy courting a girl. He was making love again to Lenora under the stars. He was standing alone under those stars, cursing the sky, howling in his pain, as Lenora flew away to explore the cosmos, as he remained with the life he had chosen. He was donning his armor for the first time, holding his first sword, speaking his vows. Kerish was knighting him, then banishing him. All that old sweetness, pride, pain--it all flowed into Steel again. It had all led to this day.

He raised his sword.

So it has come to this . . . the battle I was always meant to fight.

With a roar, Kerish pointed his sword forward. Light coalesced across the blade, then blasted toward Steel.

The beam slammed into Steel with the power of a shattering sun.

He took a step back. His armor cracked and fell in pieces. Heat washed across him. Yet he refused to fall.

Steel thrust his own blade, casting out light.

The beam drove toward Kerish, but the lord swung his sword, parrying the light, deflecting it toward the wall. The tunnel cracked, and a chunk of stone fell.

The other knights blasted out light. Riff fired his gun and Giga leaped, katana flashing. As the battle raged outside, so did the battle of Steel's life flare inside the tunnel. With light. With blood. With broken promises and broken lives.

The battle I should have fought years ago.

Kerish swung his sword at Steel, and he parried. The blades clanged, sparked out light, shattered more stones. Another blast of light slammed into Steel. The last piece of his armor fell, leaving his chest bare, bleeding, burnt. No longer a man of metal, shielded behind an armor that hid his body and soul. Just a man mourning. A man who had lost too much. A man exposed.

"I believed in you once," Kerish said, face twisted with rage, but there was something new to his eyes. There was pain. There was sadness. "I thought of you as my son."

Steel drove his blade forward. Kerish parried again. Light blasted from the swords, cracking the walls. Boulders fell. The others fought around them, weapons firing and flashing.

"You were a father to me!" Steel said. "I chose to follow you. To join your order. To let the woman I love fly away."

"And you betrayed your order!"

"No! I would not betray my vows." Steel's eyes burned, and he fought in a fury, slamming his blade again and again at Kerish. "You turned to evil, Kerish. I banish you now. I exile you as you exiled me. You are no knight. I strip you of your sigil."

Eyes stinging, throat burning, Steel thrust his blade with both hands. The sword slammed into the sunburst sigil on Kerish's breastplate, tore through the symbol, and finally clove the armor in half.

"You are banished," Steel whispered.

As the battle raged around them, Kerish stared down at his shattered armor, then raised his eyes to stare at Steel.

"You love her," Kerish whispered.

Steel's fist trembled around Solflare's hilt. "I love Lenora. Yes, I--"

"The android," Kerish said. "You love her. I see it in your eyes. You love a machine. You love a perversion of life, a sin. So I will make you suffer."

His face gone pale, Kerish raised his sword and blasted out an inferno of light, a supernova of heat and sound and blinding energy.

The white beam tore the air, blazing over Steel's shoulder.

Giga screamed.

Steel turned around to see the light slam into the android, tossing her back.

He stared, frozen for an instant, a mere heartbeat, terror gripping him.

Giga lay on the ground, moaning, a hole in her chest. Torn cables crackled inside her. Her legs twitched. Her eyes flicked up and met Steel's gaze.

"Sir," she whispered.

Steel stared, unable to breath, unable to move.

Giga.

His eyes dampened.

Giga, the woman he had flown through hyperspace for, pulling her back from the jaws of the Singularity. Giga, the woman who had pulled him from the wreckage of the *Dragon Huntress*. Giga, the woman he loved.

Arigato, she had whispered to him in the depths of hyperspace, the Singularity reaching toward her, his arms around her.

My lady, he had replied. His damsel to defend. His woman to love.

"Giga!" Riff cried, but knights held him back. Lenora and Dee stared in horror, knights grabbing their arms, tugging them away.

"Goodbye," Giga whispered, gazing into Steel's eyes. "Goodbye, my knight."

Kerish pointed his luminous sword at Giga's head.

"Now the abomination is cleaned," Kerish whispered and thrust his blade.

Armor fallen, body burnt, honor and duty and love pulsing through him, Steel leaped into the air.

He vaulted between Giga and Kerish.

The lord's beam of light slammed into Steel's chest.

Steel tossed his sword.

He hit the ground by Giga, a hole in his chest.

His blade flew through the air and drove into Kerish, through the crack in his armor and into his heart. The burly lord crashed down, the sword impaling him.

Steel lay on the ground, his wound cauterized, smoking, driving through him.

"My lady," he whispered, reaching out to clasp Giga's hand. "Are you all right?"

"Steel!" The voice filled the tunnel, hoarse, torn with pain. Riff leaped forward and knelt by him. "Steel! Oh gods, Steel. Oh gods. Don't move. I--"

But his brother's words faded. A soft song of angels seemed to fill the world, all other sounds--the cries of battle, the screams of dying, the shrieks of war--all fading, all forever silenced.

"Riff," Steel whispered. "Lead them onward, my brother, my captain."

Tears filled Riff's eyes. He was shouting something, trying to bandage Steel's wound. Giga knelt above Steel too, her chest pierced but her life spared. He had saved her, Steel knew. He had given his life for her.

"I go now," Steel whispered, and a smile rose on his lips--a rare smile, a smile he had almost forgotten. "I travel now to the light of Sol. To see Mother, Riff. To dine in the halls of afterlife, a knight again, my honor reclaimed."

"Don't leave," Riff whispered.

"Don't die," Giga said, tears flowing down her cheeks. "Please, my knight. I love you. Don't leave me."

He clasped their hands. His brother. The woman he loved. Even the other knights crowded around, staring with tears in their eyes, perhaps at last recognizing that here lay a true knight, their true lord.

"Steel," Lenora whispered, stepped forward, and caressed his cheek. "Please, Steel, please. Live." She leaned down, tears flowing, and kissed his forehead. "Live."

"I have loved you, my lady," Steel whispered, voice weak now, trembling, fading away. "I love you all. Always. Love is the greatest strength, mightier than sword or star, brighter than the sun. Carry my love forever in your hearts. My friends. My family. Farewell now. Farewell."

"Steel!" they cried, holding him, weeping above him.

I saved them. Now I rest. Farewell.

He could no longer see the tunnel, no longer see the battle, the struggles of this cosmos. All he saw was light, and all he heard was the heavenly song, calling him home.

CHAPTER TWENTY-ONE
LAST FLIGHT

Riff stepped out of the pyramid, carrying the body of his brother.

He stood upon the tip of the triangle, a kilometer above the sand. The sun beat down. The river flowed in the distance, spreading out carpets of green. The shadows of the enemy flowed over all life.

Yet that life lost meaning to Riff. The sun could no longer light his way. The sky no longer beckoned. He did not weep, did not cry out hoarsely. He did not tremble or fall. As he stood outside the tunnel, gazing upon the world, more than anything he felt emptiness.

It was feeling nothing at all.

He's gone. I can't believe he's gone.

How would he ever fly between the stars again? How would food ever more have flavor? How would laughter ever more flow through him? How would love ever light his heart, or the joy of friendship warm him?

Nova and Twig are gone. Steel lies dead in my arms. Let the suns across the cosmos stop shining. Let every star go out, one by one. I feel nothing. I am empty.

The cosmos was but a shell, meaningless, an illusion shattered, all of life but a piece of paper, thin, torn, fluttering in the wind.

It felt to Riff as if he floated above his body. As if, looking back at his life, all those memories--joy, terror, love--had been only dreams. Flickers so quickly gone. Beads of light so elusive they were as sparks in an endless, dark ocean.

Now they were gone.

He's gone. I can't believe he's gone.

Giga stood at his right side, tears streaming down her cheeks. Dee and Lenora stood to his left, holding each other, crying silently. But no tears could fill Riff's eyes. No grief ached in his heart. Perhaps he was too stunned to feel grief. Perhaps this loss, this shattering tragedy, tore all of his reality apart, leaving room for nothing but nothingness.

Air blasted his face, and a hot, burnt smell filled his nostrils. The tesseract ships were flying near, twenty or more, casting out dark beams. The streams slammed into the pyramid around Riff, shattering bricks, and the air itself seemed to burn.

Do I die here with you, Steel? Riff looked down at his brother. Steel's face was serene in death, smiling softly, his eyes closed. *Do I join you now, little brother?*

A roar pierced the world.

Engines blasted fire.

A jet of plasma tore through the sky, ionizing the air, and slammed into two tesseract ships. The vessels crashed down. Breathing fire, sounding her roar, the *Dragon Huntress* swooped toward the pyramid. The airlock opened, and Piston stood within, reeling out cables.

"Hurry, inside!" Piston cried.

They grabbed the cables. Giga helped Riff hold onto Steel, carrying his body into the ship. Dee and Lenora followed, and the *Dragon Huntress* soared--with fire, with tears, with cries of grief.

Piston stared at Steel's body, shaking, tears flowing into his beard. Romy ran into the airlock, stared with wide eyes, then fell to her knees and wept. The ship kept soaring, fire roaring, blasting the enemies away, and still rising until they breached the atmosphere, leaving a dying planet behind. Leaving their joy, their innocence, their hope to ever achieve victory.

He's gone.

They streamed through the darkness of space, but the stars did not shine, and Riff knew they would never shine upon him again.

Let them go dark. Let the night fall. Let the lights vanish, one by one. My brother is gone.

* * * * *

They stood on the main deck, four Alien Hunters where seven had once stood.

Captain Riff Starfire, still in his old jeans, his chest bandaged, his head lowered.

Piston Bergelgruf, so strong yet now trembling, tears flowing.

Romy, for once no smile on her face, her tail drooping, her eyes wide with shock.

Giga, a hole still in her chest, a hole perhaps forever inside her.

With them stood Dee and Lenora Rosetta, silent, eyes huge and haunted, holding each other.

Twiggle Jauntyfoot, one of Riff's closest friends--vanished. Nova Tashei, the woman Riff loved--kidnapped. And Steel Starfire, his brother, the pillar of his life--lying serene in a coffin before him.

How do I do this? Riff thought. *How do I let him go? How do I find Father and tell him? How can I keep flying without him? Without them?*

He looked at the others. His last companions in the world. He spoke softly.

"I've never known proper words like Steel did. I've never known holiness, honor, ceremony. And I don't know what to say now. But I know love." His voice caught, and his eyes stung. "And now I know loss. So now I say goodbye."

"Goodbye, Steel," Romy whispered.

"Goodbye, laddie," Piston whispered, placing his trembling hands upon the coffin.

"Goodbye, sir," Giga said, voice so soft they barely heard.

Lenora could not even speak. She fell to her knees, wrapped her arms around the coffin, and sobbed silently. Her brother knelt beside her, his hand on her shoulder.

Riff placed his hand on the coffin. "You will always be my compass, my anchor, the pillar of my life. You will always be my brother, the soul I loved more than any other. Wherever you go know, know that we will always love you. Always. Rest now, Steel. You fought for many days. You fought for us, to give us life. Rest among the stars whose light you fought to keep shining."

As Riff spoke, it seemed to him that beings stood around him, glowing gold, not dark ghosts but spirits of comfort, of love, invisible friends soothing him at his hour of pain.

They carried the coffin together into the airlock. They stepped back onto the main deck, and Riff's tears flowed as he pressed the buttons on the control panel. Out the porthole, he saw the coffin glide across space, its flight smooth, peaceful, like a gliding leaf on the wind. They stood at the window together, the last survivors, watching until Steel became a distant light like a star . . . and then vanished.

CHAPTER TWENTY-TWO
REUNIONS

They sat in the sticky food court of Horsehead Space Station, the cosmos crumbling around them.

The rusty station floated in the Orion nebula, a distant outpost of the Humanoid Alliance on the border of alien territory. Outside the window, Riff could see the *Dragon Huntress*'s head, charred and scratched. The inside of the space station wasn't much prettier. The outpost offered a place to refuel, buy supplies, and find something resembling a meal. Cleanliness was obviously not of much importance out here. Rust covered the table, and graffiti scrawled across the walls. The neon lights flickered, and a mouse scurried underfoot.

"Eat, lassie," Piston was saying.

Romy lowered her head. "I'm not hungry."

Riff stared at his own meal. He too struggled to find an appetite. They had all ordered from Happy Cow Shawarma--it was that or Tony's Tentacle Emporium--but Riff guessed that there was more cardboard in his meal than cow.

He pushed his shawarma aside. "I'm not hungry either. As soon as Dee gets back with supplies, we're blasting out of here."

He raised his head and looked at the monitor mounted onto the wall. News reports kept flashing in from across the cosmos. Tesseract ships besieging the planet of Ashmar. Shades flowing through Haven and Gruffstone. Earth surrendering, only for the shades to ignore the pleas of mercy and keep toppling cities. The cosmos unraveling.

"We woke something in the black hole," Lenora whispered. She sat beside Riff, her own meal uneaten. "What have we done, Riff?"

He reached across the tabletop and held her hand. "We'll fix this, Lenora. I promise. We'll fix Giga. We'll fix up the *Dragon Huntress* so that she can fly into the fourth dimension. And then we'll fix this whole crazy cosmos."

He meant his words to sound comforting, yet they sent even more fear into Riff's own heart. If Dee was right, if he could build a four-dimensional engine . . . the *Dragon Huntress* would fly into the black hole. Into that dark land that still haunted Riff's dreams. To face the Dark Queen. Perhaps he would come to miss this grungy space station.

"Got everything!" Dee said, barging into the food court. He ran toward them, carrying a box of supplies. "Everything I need to build my masterpiece."

The scientist's spectacles hung precariously on his nose, and his hair stood on end. He upended his box onto the tabletop, scattering cables, screws, bolts, circuitry, and other gizmos.

"Got what I need here to patch you up, Giga," he said.

244

The android smiled. A hole still gaped open in her chest. "Thank you, sir."

Riff couldn't help but wonder. If Kerish had attacked Giga a second time, blasting another hole into her, would the android have survived that too? Had Steel, leaping to block the attack with his body, died in vain, died to protect a robot that Dee could have patched up with a few cheap materials?

I cannot believe that, he thought. *I have to believe that Kerish's next blow would have shattered the central circuits in Giga's head, erasing her memories, her personality, who she is. I have to believe that Steel's death saved her. Saved us.*

"Dee," he said. "You and Piston fix Giga, then install the Euclidian engine upgrade. Then you stay here with Lenora and wait for us. The Alien Hunters--the four that remain--are going to fly into the black hole. We're going to blast it up. Then we're going to come back here for you."

Lenora leaped to her feet. "What? No!" She gasped. "I won't let you just . . . just fly into the black hole without me!"

"Yes you will." Riff fixed her with a steady stare. "And that's final. You and Dee are not flying into Yurei with us. This is a job for the Alien Hunters, and only the Alien Hunters."

"Riff!" Lenora walked around the table and grabbed him. "I've spent years studying that black hole. Years! I can't let you fly inside, to see what's in there, when I can go with you, study and--"

"We're not going to study it. We're going to blast it to bits." Riff's voice softened. "Lenora, after what happened on Athemes, I . . . I can't let others die. I can't put you and Dee in danger. My crew and I are trained to deal with this. Stay here. Where it's safe. Please."

"He might be right, sister," Dee said. He pointed at the monitors. The news broadcast had ended, replaced with an episode of *Space Galaxy*. "Good place to watch some quality programming."

Lenora sighed, then embraced Riff. "Be careful, you brave, crazy fool. Don't do anything stupid."

"You mean, aside from flying into a black hole?" He smiled, his arms wrapped around her. "You and Dee are the bright ones. Maybe it's time for the stupid to make a stand. It's my time to shine."

* * * * *

With supplies and a full tank of fuel, the *Dragon Huntress* left the station and entered the deep darkness between the stars.

Piston and Dee donned space suits, hovered outside the ship, and worked at assembling the new engines--engines that would jolt the ship up a dimension through Euclidian space. While they worked, Riff sat alone on the bridge, playing an old guitar he had picked up at the space station, a scratched acoustic instrument that had seen better days.

Nova used to sit here to his left, Steel to his right. Both gone. Head lowered, he played "Moonshine Blues" by Bootstrap and the Shoeshine Kid. The same song he used to play at the Blue

Strings club back in simpler days. He missed those days so much he ached.

I left Earth with people that I love . . . and I lost them to the darkness of the cosmos.

That night, when Riff lay down in bed, he could not sleep. Too many memories. Too much sadness. Too much pain. He lay on his back, awake, gazing up at the dark ceiling, and he didn't know if he'd ever find peace again.

I miss you, Nova. I miss you, Steel.

As he lay in shadows, a knock sounded on his door. A moment later, the door creaked open, firelight fell upon him, and Romy tiptoed into the room. She wore purple pajamas, and tears dampened her eyes.

"Captain?" she whispered. "Did I wake you? I can't sleep."

"I was awake," Riff said.

The demon stepped closer. "Can I sleep in your bed tonight? The crew quarters are empty. Piston is still working on the engines, and Giga is on the bridge, and . . . and I'm scared there alone."

Riff patted the mattress, and Romy climbed into bed beside him. Soon she was snoring, drool dripping down her chin. Riff watched her sleep. When the demon wasn't blabbering, singing, muttering, or chirping away, she seemed almost a precious thing, a dear friend. A soothing presence.

Thank you for being here, Romy, he thought and stroked her fiery hair. She mumbled in her sleep, wincing, perhaps with pain or memory. Riff kissed her cheek and stroked her hair until her face smoothed, and she slept calmly.

Before Riff himself drifted off to sleep, he thought that he could feel that presence again, the twin souls he had felt during the funeral. He thought he could almost glimpse gold, almost feel Nova's breath against his neck, almost hear Twig's laughter. He fell asleep and dreamed that they lay here with him, forever flying with him through the darkness.

* * * * *

They returned to it at the end.

As the cosmos unraveled, the *Dragon Huntress* glided toward the black hole in the center of the cosmos. Toward Yurei. The dark eye. The lair of the queen.

Gliding here, still many kilometers away, space seemed almost peaceful.

That peace would soon shatter, Riff knew.

His remaining crew stood with him on the bridge. Piston hefted his hammer. Romy clutched her pitchfork. Giga stood calmly, her katana slung across her back. They were all who remained upon this ship, and they all stared through the windshield at the black hole. Their destination.

Giga shifted closer to Riff and slipped her hand into his.

"Are you ready, sir?"

No, Riff thought. No, he wasn't ready. How could anyone be ready for this? How could he ask his crew to fly here with him? To enter the darkness?

He stared at the black hole ahead.

Yet enter the darkness we will, or the light will forever dim.

"I've asked you all to fly with me here," Riff said to his crew. "And you all agreed. Out of loyalty. Out of fear for the cosmos. Out of courage. Out of love for those we lost." Pain clutched Riff's chest. "Piston's going to turn on our new engine now, and I'm not sure what will happen. We're going to enter a higher plane of existence, to fly through four dimensions, not only three. Whatever we see, hear, feel--it will overwhelm us. Confuse us. We must be brave, no matter what strangeness we see through this window, no matter how shocking this new reality is."

"I've seen Piston eat," Romy said. "Nothing can shock me anymore."

"Why you--" Piston began, blustering, and made to grab the demon. She leaped back, squealing.

Riff sighed. "Even outside a black hole containing an evil queen and her ghost minions, somebody on the *Dragon Huntress* is going to bicker. I need you ready now. Ready to face the darkness. Ready to fight . . . whatever's in there. We're going to fly into Yurei." He clenched his fist. "And we're going to blast our fire onto its queen."

They looked at him, eyes soft, afraid, yet brave. And he knew they would fly with him to the edge of the cosmos if he asked.

Piston stepped closer and patted his arm. "We're with you, laddie. Always."

Romy leaped onto Riff, almost knocking him down, and squeezed him. "I'll always fight with you, Captain. You have my pitchfork. And my teddy bear!"

Giga only had to look at him, didn't have to say a thing. Riff saw the love and loyalty in her eyes, and he knew that she too would always fight at his side.

"All right, let's get going!" Piston said. "No time like the present, I always say. Romy, you clod! Join me in the engine room. You can help me calibrate the Euclidean hyper-dimensional warping coils."

Romy blinked. "I . . . can." She nodded. "Almost positive."

The pair wandered off the bridge, leaving Riff and Giga alone.

"We're with you, Captain," Giga whispered, squeezing his hand. "Always. We will all fight for you."

"Not for me," he said. "For Twig. For Nova. For Steel."

The rumble of the engines filled the ship. The floor rattled. The hula dancer swayed and bulldog bobbed on the dashboard. Riff's hand tightened around Giga's.

The black hole loomed outside, twisting, coiling, bulging out like a bubble, staring at them.

"Euclidian engine heating up, sir!" Piston called through the communicator. "We're entering four dimensions!"

Riff held his breath, nearly crushing Giga's hand.

Outside, space changed.

The stars burst into streaks--not streaming lines like those in hyperspace, blurred as the ship roared by, but the lines of their orbits, coiling across spacetime like a silver cobweb. Thousands of visions of the *Dragon Huntress* stretched ahead of them, a path of reflections like slides strewn across space. A stone ring flowed around the black hole--the planet Kaperosa stretched across its orbit.

"We're gazing upon the fourth dimension," Giga whispered. "Across the three dimensions we know . . . and across time itself."

Riff stared ahead at the black hole. In its center, he could now see a planet, a charcoal world, invisible in three-dimensions, appear now as a pupil in the dark eye.

"There it is." He stared with narrowed eyes. "The world of the shades. The home of the Dark Queen. The--"

"Riff."

The voice spoke behind him. At first he thought it was Giga who had spoken, but she never used his name.

I know that voice.

Riff caught his breath. Slowly, he turned around.

He could find no air. His eyes dampened. He could not believe what he saw.

"Riff," she said again, smiling tremulously, tears in her own eyes.

He leaped toward her. She laughed and wept and crashed into his arms.

"Nova," he whispered into the embrace. "Nova. Nova. Nova."

She laughed and mussed his hair. "Did you forget to talk?" Yet even as she mocked him, her tears flowed, and she wrapped her arms around him.

"How can this be?" he whispered. He touched her cheek and golden hair, stared into her green eyes, felt the softness of her armor. "How can you be here?"

She blinked, tears spiking her lashes. "I was always here, Riff. Always at your side. Stuck in the fourth dimension. I could see you, see everyone, but you couldn't see me. When you slept, I slept at your side. When Steel . . ." She lowered her head. "I was there too. Watching. Standing at your side. Always."

"I love you, Nova."

She laughed as she wept. "I love you too."

They kissed--a long, deep kiss that made Riff forget the blackness outside, forget his pain for just that moment of pure joy. Nova was back. Light shone again in the world.

When finally their kiss ended, Riff tilted his head. "You know, Nova . . . you sleeping in my bed, watching me, invisible all the while . . . that's creepy, really. That's stalking."

She groaned and punched his chest. "Hush, you. Just because I just kissed you doesn't mean I'm afraid to clobber you bloody."

"Just kiss me again instead."

And she did.

"Captain, sir!" Piston came barging onto the bridge. "The clod's back, the little one! And--Nova! Oh, lassie!" The gruffle ran toward Nova and pulled her into his wide arms. "You too!"

Twig raced onto the bridge behind Piston, leaped into the air, and crashed into Riff's embrace. She laughed and mussed his hair, and he laughed too, holding her in his arms.

"Twiggle Jauntyfoot!" he said. "Were you stalking us too?"

She nodded, grinning. "You need to stop kicking in your sleep, sir. You nearly knocked Nova and me off the bed."

Riff's eyes widened. "You mean, you both-- in my bed-- while I slept--?"

Twig shrugged and leaped back to the floor. "With those scientists aboard, it was the only place to sleep." She laughed. "Good to be back in three dimensions, sir. I'm famished. Nova, let's go eat. Real food!"

Nova nodded. "Better make it quick though, Twig." She glanced out the windshield. "We're getting close to that black hole."

"One last meal," Riff said. "All of us. Together. In the kitchen. One more hour together before night falls."

Floating through space, they entered the kitchen and crowded together. They warmed up the old frozen pizzas--a delicacy they had been saving. As they ate, they shared stories of Steel, speaking of the time Romy had slipped on his armor, of how Steel's mustache would flutter in his sleep, and how Twig had once stuck magnets onto his breastplate. They laughed as they told their stories, missing him, feeling some comfort together.

One last hour together, Riff thought, smiling as he sat among his friends. *One more hour of laughter.*

CHAPTER TWENTY-THREE
INTO THE BLACK

They all stood together on the bridge. Six Alien Hunters. Six survivors in a crumbling cosmos. Six misfits to save the light.

The black hole loomed before them, a planet lodged in its throat. Yurei. A goddess of darkness.

Engines roaring fire, wings spread wide, the *Dragon Huntress* shot through space toward the shadow.

With blazing fire, with clattering metal, with the last hope of the galaxy, the starship charged into the black hole.

The panels rattled madly. The seats swayed. The bulldog bobbed so madly his head fell off. The Alien Hunters clutched the controls, struggling to remain standing. The roar of bending metal filled the ship. Outside streamed a typhoon, a blackness tugging them forward, squeezing them, spinning them madly.

"It's tearing us apart, Captain!" Piston cried.

"It's squishing us!" Romy wailed.

Riff gritted his teeth, staring ahead. He pointed. "Giga, keep us flying. To the Dark Planet. Focus on the planet."

"Happy to comply!" she replied cheerily.

Rising, falling, caught like a leaf in a storm, they wobbled through the black hole, charging toward the planet. The charcoal world hung before them, not spread out like Kaperosa or the stars outside, but a solid ball of stone, never moving, eternal. It didn't even seem a planet at all, but darkness made solid, shadows coalesced into a world, a lair.

The lair of the queen.

A chunk tore off the *Dragon*'s wing.

A heat shield tore off the hull and spun madly through space.

"We got to turn back, sir!" Piston shouted. "Or this black hole will rip us apart like a wolverine on a rabbit."

"Negative!" Riff shouted, voice nearly drowning under the roar. "Giga, keep flying! To the planet! Faster, all power to the engines."

"Happy to comply!"

With a deafening howl, with blazing light, with a jolt that cracked the windshield, the engines roared into higher gear. Fire blasted out behind them. The ship screeched forward, crashing through the vortex, howling with an almost organic sound, a true dragon in all her glory.

Fire.

Lights.

Sparks of all color.

Finally shadows. Silence.

Riff exhaled shakily, realizing he had been holding his breath. They floated through clear space, in silence.

"Are we dead?" Romy whispered.

"I don't think so," Twig whispered back.

Romy bit her lip. "If we're dead, can we go to Hell? I'm a bit homesick."

"We might not be far off," Riff said, staring ahead through the windshield.

The Dark Planet loomed ahead, covering nearly his entire field of vision. A rocky black world. Craters and canyons marred its surface, and jagged mountain ranges rose across it like spine ridges. Gray clouds flowed around it like smoke around a charred corpse. Staring at this barren landscape, Riff felt it. The dark presence he had felt in his nightmare, as if the planet itself were alive, sentient, mocking him. Woven of evil.

"Captain," Giga said, tilting her head. "Sensors show that the planet isn't made of matter. Not atoms as we know them. As if it's . . . formed of concentrated dark matter. It's causing my calculations to break."

Riff nodded. "The entire black hole broke Lenora's calculations. Whatever's here is something new. Something we've never seen before. Something perhaps more dangerous than anything we've ever faced." He managed a wry smile. "Let's go poke it with a stick."

Giga nodded, suddenly not seeming particularly happy to comply, and guided the ship onward.

As they flew closer to the Dark Planet, it seemed to Riff that canyons and mountains formed faces on the surface, cruel demonic masks that beckoned him onward. Then clouds enveloped the ship, hiding all, clinging to the windshield, dancing like women of shadow.

These aren't clouds, Riff thought, belly clenching. *It's a living creature. A vast, living thing enveloping the world.*

"Approaching the surface, Captain," Giga said. "Still no sign of enemy ships."

Nova clutched her whip. "They must know we're here. It's a trap."

"Thank you, admiral," Riff said. "But I don't yet see a giant block of cheese."

Finally the clouds parted, revealing the rock land--surprisingly close. The thruster engines blasted out steam, and the ship leveled off.

"Keep us flying, Gig." Riff stared ahead, eyes squinting. "Just above the surface."

"What are we looking for, sir?" the android asked.

"A hill," he said softly. "A hill that's a thousand hills. And a rose."

They kept flying over the surface. Still no enemy ships attacked. Still no shades flew toward them. Nothing but the barren landscape, the smoke, the hills, and everywhere the visions of time--a jumble of reflections, the sky and ground and mountains spinning, bending around them.

"Run a scan for life forms," Riff said, staring ahead with narrowed eyes.

"Happy to comply! Scanning . . . scanning . . ." Giga tilted her head. "Picking up a very small signal, about a hundred kilometers away. Not much larger than my hand, sir."

The rose, Riff thought. He remembered it from his dreams. A frail flower, struggling to bloom upon a black hill, its petals falling. A flower he had crawled toward in his nightmare, knowing he had to save it, had to stop the evil from crushing it, and that evil flowing all around him, a living being in the air.

What was the rose? Riff did not know, but again that urge to save it filled him. It was important; he had felt it. Perhaps it held the answers to this place.

"Take us there, Gig," he said. "And keep the *Dragon*'s fire warm."

"Where is everyone?" Nova whispered. She squinted, examining the landscape. "The tesseract ships, the shades . . . did they truly leave their planet undefended?"

Piston grumbled, hefting his war hammer. "Could be they sent all their troops across the cosmos already, thinking the black hole is defense enough."

"Getting closer to the life form, Captain." Giga's voice was calm, her face serene. "A hundred kilometers away. Ninety-nine. Ninety-eight . . ."

Riff grabbed his gun. The memories jabbed him full of pain. *Scream, Starfire . . .*

The voice spoke in his mind again--the voice of the Dark Queen. Silky. Cruel. A voice like a serpent slithering through a garden. Was it a voice in his memory, or the queen speaking to him again, reaching out from the wastelands into his mind?

Come closer, Starfire . . . come to me and shatter in my arms.

Visions floated outside, images of time, of futures that could be. The *Dragon Huntress* crashing. The Alien Hunters grabbed, tortured, torn apart upon the dark earth. Riff ignored them. Just possible futures. Different paths.

Yet your path is already written, Starfire. A path of pain.

He clenched his teeth, ignoring the voice.

"There." He pointed. "A hill."

The hill the shades had shown him. The heart of the planet.

"Life form on that hill, Captain," Giga said.

Riff shuddered. The hill cast out a thousand reflections, spreading out, twisting, looming, swooping from above. "Can you zoom in, Giga? Put it up on the head-up display."

"Happy to comply!"

The HUD crackled to life upon the windshield, zooming onto the hill. There Riff saw it. Growing from the hilltop. A single red rose in a world of black and gray. The rose seemed to call to him, fragile, begging, dying . . . struggling to reach out to him, to survive the miasma.

"Fly to it, Giga."

"Happy to--"

A screech rose across the landscape, filling the bridge. The windshield rattled. The floor shook. The Alien Hunters grimaced and covered their ears. The shriek rose louder and louder, finally forming words.

"Welcome, friends! Welcome to Yurei, the realm of the Dark Queen."

The clouds and smoke swirled ahead, rising into a storm, taking forms. The dark swirls danced like women, swaying, intoxicating, laughing, their eyes black coals, shining and staring into him. With shrieks, the banshees charged toward the ship.

"Giga, fire!" Riff shouted.

The *Dragon Huntress* blasted out her flame.

The plasma flew through the air, driving through the smoke. The miasma parted from the heat, then coiled back together, forming the shape of hands the size of crocodiles. The smoky fists slammed into the ship.

Scream, children . . . scream for me.

The *Dragon Huntress* jerked in the sky. The hull dented. The windshield rattled. The giant astral hands gripped the ship. A mouth yawned open before them in the clouds, and gleaming black eyes--like two spheres of tar--opened above. The creature laughed, woven of the storm, large enough to grasp the *Dragon Huntress* like a child grasping a toy. Its laughter rolled across the land, and again Riff felt it--evil itself taken form, coiling across him, filling his belly, invading his nostrils.

"The Dark Queen," he whispered.

"I am Yurei!" she cried, lightning flashing across her. "I am your mistress, your goddess, your torturer. Worship me. Beg me to die."

Giga drew her katana and stared forward, eyes raging. "Cannot compute," the android said . . . and fired the cannon again.

The plasma spurted forth, slamming into the queen's eye.

The apparition screamed.

The sound slammed forward, tossing the *Dragon Huntress* into a tailspin. The smoky hands loosened. The ship plunged through the sky, managed to right itself, and soared again. More plasma blasted out, but the queen waved an astral fist, diverting the stream.

A voice rose in Riff's mind again.

Save the rose, boy! You must save the rose!

Riff caught his breath. This wasn't the queen speaking. It was his father's voice. Aminor the magician--the wise traveler--guiding him.

"We're falling apart!" Piston shouted. "The ship won't hold much longer."

"Giga, keep firing!" Nova cried.

"Shades attacking!" shouted Twig.

New shrieks rose outside. The smell of burnt metal filled the air. Through the storm, Riff could see them. The Dark Queen Yurei was lashing her hands, weaving shades out of the smoke, tossing them forward. The beasts swarmed forward, robes fluttering, red eyes burning. They crashed against the *Dragon Huntress*, clawing at the hull, denting the metal, tugging on the wings. The ship spun madly. Riff fell. Outside he saw tesseracts flying forth, blasting out fire that drove into the starship. And always the Queen laughed, jaw opening and closing, a giant of clouds looming above them.

The rose, boy! You must reach it.

As the ship rocked, Riff pulled himself to his feet and stumbled toward the wall. He grabbed one of the space suits that hung there. He pulled it on.

"Where are you going?" Nova shouted.

"To grab the rose!"

A blast of enemy fire shook the ship, tossing Nova against the wall. "You've gone mad. What are you talking about?"

He ran off the bridge. He had to go there alone. Quickly. Hidden in the storm. He fell again, pushed himself up, stumbling onto the main deck and into the airlock.

He opened the outer door.

The storm raged, pummeling against him, shoving him back into the ship. The clouds coiled around him, reeking, hot, the tentacles of the queen.

Riff snarled.

He lit his jet pack.

He roared out of the airlock, blasting fire, and flew through the storm.

The winds gusted around him. The smoke clung to his helmet and suit like a living thing. The landscape rolled around him; Riff felt a little like a flaming sock tumbling through a washing machine falling off a cliff. A shade soared toward him, jaws opening wide, revealing its fangs. Riff fired old Ethel, and the gun spewed out her blaze. The shade burned and fell. Another demonic creature swooped. Riff fired again, shoved down on his jet pack's throttle, and shot forward, dodging the falling corpse.

He saw it ahead. A glimmer of red. A glow soon fading behind the storm. He curved his flight, roaring toward it. Thousands of shades flowed through the typhoon. Wind slammed against Riff. The *Dragon Huntress* soared above him, dipped, tilted, flipped upside down, nearly crashed, then soared again. The blasts of tesseract ships kept pummeling its hull, denting and ripping the metal, and the ship's cannon kept roaring out fire. Flying here outside, it seemed to Riff that the *Dragon Huntress* had become a true dragon, a roaring animal of legend.

More shades swarmed toward him. Riff fired his gun again and again, knocking them back, swerving between them. He could barely see anything but their fluttering cloaks, the smoke that filled the air, and everywhere the Dark Queen--laughing, storming, reaching out hands the size of storm clouds, her eyes like twin black moons above.

There! He saw it again. A dim red glow through the storm. He inhaled deeply and flew. Winds buffeted him. Stones pelted him. One rock slammed against his helmet, shattering the glass, and the storm whipped his face, cutting his skin. He kept flying. He fired his gun again and again until the plasma charges were gone.

Ahead, on the hill, the rose grew.

Its petals glowed, ruby red. The storm seemed not to touch it, yet the flower seemed so frail. One petal tore free, glided down, and crumbled to ash upon hitting the ground.

I'll save it. Whatever it is, I'll save it.

Riff flew in a beeline, eyes narrowed.

A tesseract ship rose from behind the hill.

Riff cursed and tried to swerve.

A blast of dark fire streamed from the enemy warship. Riff dipped lower. He screamed. Darkness and fire spread across him. The blast grazed the top of his helmet and tore into his jet pack.

The *Dragon Huntress* swooped above, raining fire onto the tesseract. The enemy ship shattered and crashed down in fragments.

Riff cried out in pain. Fire had burned his leg. His jet pack sputtered, coughed, and died.

Riff plummeted through the sky and hit the ground with a scream.

He tried to push himself to his feet. He yowled in pain, his leg twisted, burnt. He pulled himself forward, crawling uphill as the *Dragon Huntress* fired her plasma above. Ahead of him, Riff saw countless reflections through time. He saw himself dying, withering to bones. He saw himself holding hands with a dark woman of smoke. He saw the rose planted, wilting, blooming. A thousand futures all around him, a thousand pasts behind him.

He climbed the hill on hands and knees. The smoke flowed around him, laughing, whispering, screaming, filling him with sickness. He kept crawling, bleeding, as the battle raged above. He let the flower's glow guide him.

It needs me. I'll pass through this evil. I'll save it.

The hills seemed endless, growing taller. Riff could barely breathe. The smoke kept filling his mouth, his eyes. The world spun. His blood kept dripping.

He fell.

He slid down.

Climb, brother! spoke a voice in his mind.

"Steel," Riff whispered, hoarse.

Through the storm, he thought he could see a tall, dark figure, wreathed in smoke, standing above. A glint of metal. Steel! A vision of Steel in armor!

Climb, brother.

Eyes burning, face covered in soot, his helmet shattered, Riff climbed.

Each meter was agony. Stones tore into his hands. Burning ash rained onto him. Fire blazed and the shrieks of battle stormed all around.

But the *Dragon Huntress* always flew above, his guardian angel. And the rose forever shone before him. Evil laughed all around, tearing at him, ripping his skin, but there was still goodness in the world. There were his friends. There was the memory of Steel.

"There are the Alien Hunters," he whispered.

He rose to his feet, climbed through the storm, and reached the hilltop.

The rose shone before him, so fragile, its last petals falling.

Riff fell to his knees.

"I'm here," he whispered.

Daniel Arenson

CHAPTER TWENTY-FOUR

THE QUEEN AND THE ROSE

"You've come to me," the rose said, voice soft and high. "I've called you for so long."

She did not speak in words. She had no mouth. Yet still Riff hear her voice, a voice like chiming bells. As he knelt above her, the rose seemed even smaller than before. So frail. No larger than his hand. Her red glow cast back the darkness, a gleam like rubies in a cave.

"Who are you?" he whispered.

"I no longer have a name. Not one that I can remember." A petal tore free, fell, and turned to ash. "I've been trapped here for so long."

Riff felt her sadness flow into him. She was sharing it with him. He ached. So much sadness. So much despair.

"Why?" he said.

"The Dark Queen. Yurei. She needed life. Life from three dimensions." The rose wept dewdrops. "So she chose me, a flower to plant. A life to funnel all her will through. To use me as a portal, a link to the lower dimensions. I did this." The rose trembled. "It's through me that Yurei sent her armies into the cosmos. It's through my own body that her evil flowed."

266

Riff took a shuddering breath. "I can save you. I can take you with me. I can plant you on a faraway world."

He caressed the rose's stem, careful to avoid the thorns.

"For years, I dreamed of you coming here," said the rose. "I have seen your reflections through time. Digging me up. Taking me in your starship. For many years I wept in joy to imagine my roots seeking through soft soil, my petals rising toward a warm sun, the sky blue, no storm around me."

"Then let it be done." Riff dug his fingers into the ground, loosening the rose's roots. "Let me take you with me."

"It's too late," the rose whispered, trembling, and another petal fell. Only two petals now remained. "She's here."

Creaks sounded behind him.

The storm pulled back, revealing the stars.

Slowly, his hands still in the soil, Riff turned his head.

The storm was pulling inwards, coalescing, forming a crude shape that seemed carved of charcoal. The figure stepped forward, the size of a human, shedding ash, raising smoke. With every step, the figure solidified further, becoming more humanlike. Gleaming black eyes opened upon its head. Its rough body smoothed out, curved, grew limbs. Dark wings unfurled from its back.

Before Riff's eyes, the Dark Queen took the form of a woman. She walked toward him, carved of purest, polished obsidian, gleaming in the starlight. A woman of intoxicating curves, full lips, alluring eyes, temptation brought to life, nude and wreathed in nothing but smoke.

"Yurei," Riff said, still kneeling with his hands in the dirt.

She swayed toward him, the stars in her midnight eyes. Her dark, full lips smiled, a smile promising endless pleasures. Her hands reached out, tipped with claws. She seemed a demon of nightmare.

While Romy is fire and laughter, Riff thought, *Yurei is a demon of shadows and sex and endless mystery.*

"It is I," Yurei whispered, voice silken. Standing above him, she placed her hands upon his shoulders. She perhaps seemed carved of obsidian, but her touch was soft, warm, spreading her warmth through him. She leaned down, her lips brushed his ear, and her voice dropped to a whisper. "The Dark Queen. I have called you for so long, Starfire. You've come to me at last. To join me."

He dug his fingers a little deeper into the soil. "Actually, thought I'd just do a little gardening and be on my way."

Yurei's face changed. Her jaw unhinged, dropping halfway down her chest, lined with fangs. Her eyes blazed with red light. Her cheeks sunk in, clinging to bones, and her hair became living serpents.

As quickly as her rage had flared, it vanished. Her face returned to its former beauty, and her eyes softened.

"Riff." Her voice was soft, and she caressed his hair. "Remove your hands from the soil. Place them in my hands. Rise and rule this cosmos with me."

Riff glanced over her shoulder. The *Dragon Huntress* had frozen in time. It hung in the middle of typhoon, a thousand tesseract ships around it. Shades clung to its wings. In the windshield, Nova was crying out silently, frozen. The storm, the stars, the smoke--all hung perfectly still, casting out a dizzying array of reflections.

Riff returned his eyes to the Dark Queen. "And what if I pull out this rose and claim it?"

"Then we will both die," Yurei said. "Then I will perish, and this entire world will crumble, and the black hole we float in will swallow us all. It is this rose, nameless and ancient, that glues spacetime together. You hold the cosmos in your hands, Riff. How does it feel? To control the destiny of the universe? To feel that destiny in your palms?"

"It feels," he said, "like I got you by a very sensitive area."

For just an instant, that rage flashed again. Then Yurei knelt before him, her hands still on his shoulders. She smiled crookedly, and the starlight gleamed in her black eyes. There was no white to those eyes, no irises, just pure black orbs flowing with stars--tiny universes in her smooth face.

"Join me," she whispered. "Be my mate. My king. Together we will rule the cosmos. You will have power, Riff. Power not only to rule, to dominate, but to heal. To undo tragedies. Mastery not only over space but time as well. Join me, and we can travel back to save your brother's life. We can save your mother's life from the cyborg that took it. We can travel across time together, undoing wrongs, making things right. I know the pain that fills you. I know about all those you lost. Together let us rule over all spacetime! Let us make this a good cosmos."

Now his own rage flared. "Is that why you killed so many people? Is that why you destroyed the Earth? Only to heal it later?"

"I did." She nodded, smoke wafting from her hair. "I've always known you would come here, Riff. When you live in the fourth dimension, you can gaze forward through time. I knew you would come here, hurt, afraid, full of loss. I knew that you would want to fix the past. To heal things. To heal your own soul. And I knew that you would not resist me, that you would join. That you would release this rose and become mine."

Riff looked around him. He saw a thousand futures spreading into the horizons. In some the last petals withered and the planet fell. In others, Riff danced with Yurei, himself a god of smoke, made love to her, sat at her side, a king upon a throne of gold, his crown woven of dark fire. Other futures were vaguer, flickering in and out of existence.

"If you can see the future, why does it flicker?" he said. "If you know that I will join you, why is there doubt and fear in your eyes?"

"No doubt," Yurei whispered. "No fear. What you see is lust."

She caressed him, moving her hand across his thigh, then between his legs, her fingers long, tingling, shooting warmth through him. She leaned forward and kissed his lips, and her kiss was like a blooming universe, a thing of electricity and wonder and endless space. No wine, sunrises, or the splendor of stars had ever filled a man with more awe and joy than her kiss.

"Be mine." Her lips touched his ear. "My king. My mate. Release the rose and rise to rule."

And stars . . . he was tempted.

He hated himself for it . . . but oh, by the old and new gods, he was tempted.

I could have her kiss me every night, he thought. *I can make love to her, explore her secret pleasures. I can rule the cosmos. I can save my planet. My mother. My brother.*

His hands, still buried in the soil around the rose's roots, trembled.

And why shouldn't I? Why shouldn't I take her offer? I can become an emperor! A ruler of infinite power! All of time will spread before me, and I will be its master. Able to heal all hurts. To have everyone bow before me. No longer the captain of one ship but a god.

He began to pull his fingers out from the soil, leaving the rose where it was.

Yurei's lips parted with an eager smile.

Another petal fell, leaving just one red petal upon the rose.

Riff looked into Yurei's eyes again, at the stars within them, the stars he would rule . . .

And he saw the stars he used to fly among.

The stars he used to explore in the *Dragon Huntress*. With his friends. With Nova, the woman he loved--the only woman he loved.

I can save you, Steel, he thought.

His brother smiled in his memory. A sad smile. A smile full of old pain. A smile that made the knight's brown, hound dog eyes fill with light.

And Riff knew then how to save his brother. Knew what Steel wanted from him now.

"For you, Steel," he whispered. "For you, Nova. For you crazy Alien Hunters in your crazy ship."

He took a deep breath, shoved his fingers deeper into the soil, and plucked out the rose.

* * * * *

Riff lifted the soil in his hands, the rose growing from the crumbly pile. The flower trembled.

The Dark Planet shook.

The ground cracked. The storm came back to life with rage, deafening, spinning like a typhoon. The *Dragon Huntress* tumbled above. Boulders fell from the sky.

"What have you done?" Yurei shrieked. The Dark Queen's face cracked, leaking red light. Her jaw opened like a python. Her eyes burst into flame. "What have you done, fool? You've doomed us!"

Her fingers cracked and fell. Her body split open. She broke apart into smoke and rose into the sky, screaming, tugged in a thousand directions.

The black hole churned around them, sucking them deeper. The distant stars outside began to fade.

Riff ran.

He vaulted downhill, holding the rose in his palms. The flower shuddered, seeming ready to lose its last petal.

"Hold on, little buddy!" he said, then hit the communicator on his wrist--he had to use his chin. "Piston, you hear me? Need a lift! Now! Now!"

The *Dragon Huntress* was spinning madly above, dipping, rising again. The shades upon its wings fell, sucked into the distance. Tesseract ships whirred, pulled into tailspins. Shards of stone thrust up from the planet. The storm pulled backward like water into a drain.

"The black hole is closing," the rose said. "It's going to crush us all."

"Not just yet," Riff said.

A crack drove across the earth, a meter wide. Riff leaped over the canyon.

The *Dragon Huntress*'s airlock popped open, and Piston lowered a cable.

"Hang tight, little one!" Riff said to the rose, holding her in one hand. With the other, he grabbed the cable.

The *Dragon Huntress* soared, pulling Riff with it.

"Look!" the rose called out. "Below!"

Dangling on the cable, Riff looked down to see tesseract cages shattering. Scientists spilled out from the cubes onto the trembling surface.

The scientists stolen from Kaperosa, he realized.

"Piston, more cables!" Riff shouted. "Fish 'em up."

As the world rattled and the storm raged, the *Dragon Huntress* dipped again. Men and women grabbed the cables. The ship rose higher, carrying the survivors with them like a boat tugging fish on lines.

The black hole tore up boulders, mountains, ripping the planet apart. Tesseract ships fell into its depths. Shades dispersed into smoke. Piston spooled up the cables, pulling Riff and the others into the ship.

"Get me a vase!" Riff cried.

He raced through the ship, placed the rose in a container, and ran onto the bridge. The others were waiting there. Outside the cracked windshield, the storm was raging. The stars were fading.

"Get us out of here!" Riff shouted.

"Happy to comply!" Giga said. "Kicking engines into maximum speed."

The *Dragon Huntress* barely seemed to move. The engines roared. The ship shook. The ground collapsed beneath them.

"Why aren't we moving?" Riff said.

"The black hole is tugging us back, sir," Giga replied.

"Give us more juice."

"Cannot compute, Captain. Engines at maximum capacity."

Riff's heart sank and his belly lurched. The planet shattered into boulders. The ship rattled.

"Engage hyperdrive engines."

Giga tilted her head. "Dee's four-dimensional Euclidian engine is still running, sir. I cannot compute what will happen if we turn on hyperdrive engines as well, bending spacetime while in the higher dimension."

The black hole was now yanking them backward. Riff could barely see space outside.

"Do it," he said.

"Happy to comply!"

"Fragging aardvarks," Nova muttered. She stepped toward Riff and clasped his hand.

The hyperdrive engines hummed. The black hole began to warp around them. A crack raced across the wall. The hull bent.

With a blast of white light, the *Dragon Huntress* charged forward.

Like a cork from a Champagne bottle, they burst out of the black hole. The stars spread into a million lines. As the Dark Planet disintegrated behind them, the *Dragon Huntress* streamed through the darkness.

"She's gone," Riff whispered, sinking into his chair. "The Dark Queen. The shades. Their world. All gone." He wiped the sweat off his brow.

And so is Steel. Gone. I could have saved him. I chose not to. I . . .

Riff rose to his feet.

"Wait," he whispered.

CHAPTER TWENTY-FIVE

THE WAVES OF TIME

Riff stared out the windshield. Both space and time were warped around him--they flew not only through a curved fabric of spacetime but a higher dimension. The fourth dimension.

"Time," Riff whispered. He spun toward Giga. "Set our course to the desert planet Athemes. We're going back to the pyramid."

"Happy to comply, Captain!"

The door to the bridge slammed open, and Piston barged in, his hair in disarray.

"Captain, the engine room is going bonkers, sir! Pieces falling off in a rain of bolts. We cannot keep the fourth dimensional engine on much longer, sir. It's tearing us apart."

Riff stared out into space, barely comprehending what he saw. It seemed as if they flowed through a tunnel of swirling light--the stars not only warped but showing their entire orbits, reflections in time, a cocoon of light.

"Keep that Euclidian engine in top shape, Piston," he said. "We're going to need it when we reach Athemes."

Piston's eyes looked ready to bug out. "Planet Athemes, sir? We've done our task! We defeated that Yurei lass. Even if I turn off the Euclidian engine now, sir, there's no guarantee I can fire it up again."

"Then keep it running." Riff nodded. "We're not leaving four dimensional space until the whole ship collapses."

"Which might not be far off," Piston muttered, tugging his beard. "Aye, sir. I'll keep our engines running for as long as I can, sir, but no promises it'll be much longer. Not with that wrench the clod dropped into them. Twig! Twig, you clod, where are you? Help me calibrate that Dee lad's engine, or we're likely to shatter into a million pieces of space debris."

The gruffle lolloped off the bridge, muttering and calling out for Twig.

Riff returned his eyes to space. Darkness and light, time and space, swirling all around him. Inside him, his reality spun just as madly.

Yurei said I can rule space and time with her. I don't need to rule them. I just need to fly through them for a bit longer.

Nova walked up toward him. Her catsuit of golden *kaija* fabric whispered with every step. She placed a hand on his shoulder, and her eyes were soft.

"Maybe we should listen to Piston," she said. "The ship is breaking apart. Steel would not want us risking our lives for him."

"The ship will stay together." Riff nodded. "We haven't survived so much--the blasts of skelkrin fire, the fleets of the Singularity, and a goddamn black hole squeezing us--to disintegrate now. I have to believe that."

Nova placed her arms around him, holding him close. "I miss him too, Riff. But even if we can reach Athemes, even if we can travel along time . . . we don't know if we can change things. And even if we do change time, we don't know how it'll affect our present. Twig explained it to me. Paradoxes. I didn't understand her then, but I think I do now. If we save Steel . . . none of this might have happened. Not us flying into the black hole. Not you killing Yurei and saving the rose. Not us flying back to Steel. A loop in time. A paradox."

Riff placed his arm around her waist. They stood together, facing the windshield, staring out at the tunnel of light.

"My father explained to me once that time is like a beach." The memories of the kindly old man filled his mind. "Always changing. Sometimes the waves are high, sometimes the water is calm. Sometimes the sea is golden in sunrise, and sometimes deep green, sometimes gray in a storm. It's always changing. Fluid. And we can navigate through the sea of time. We can find our way home."

The ship gave a mad jolt. The dented hull rattled. The windshield rattled, the crack upon it expanding.

"Won't find our way home if our windshield shatters," Nova muttered.

Sitting beside them, Giga tilted her head. "Cannot compute, ma'am. There is no wind in space. Do you mean the front fused silica viewport panes?"

Nova groaned. "For the millionth time, Giga, I call them windshields."

Riff returned to his seat. With the engines rattling, his chair vibrated--rather soothingly, he thought.

If we die, he thought, *at least I'll die getting a good massage.*

* * * * *

They were racing across the ship, rolls of duct tape in hand, when Giga's voice rose through the communicator.

"Captain! Arriving back at the planet Athemes, sir."

Riff stood in the kitchen, slapping duct tape onto a hole in the hull. He ran into the corridor and saw Nova emerging from the kitchen, where she had been taping other breaches. They hurried back onto the bridge. Here, too, strips of tape covered the ship--holding together loose control panels, the hull, and cracks in the windshield. It seemed like the *Dragon Huntress* was now more duct tape than metal.

Best damn material in the cosmos, Riff thought. *Never go into space without duct tape.*

Giga smiled at him from her chair. "Ten seconds before I shut down hyperspace engines, sir. Might give us a jolt. Nine. Eight. Seven . . ."

Riff leaped into his chair and clutched the armrests. Nova occupied the third seat. Piston and Twig were down in the engine room, and Romy was still up in the attic with a roll of tape-- probably eating it. The lights swirled outside.

"Remember to keep our Euclidian engine on," Riff said.

"Happy to comply! Three. Two. One."

With a shuddering sound, the hyperspace engines shut down. Spacetime uncurled around them, forming solid lines again, though those lines still twisted at odd angles; the ship still flew in the fourth dimension.

For a few seconds, the *Dragon Huntress* sailed smoothly.

Then the ship jolted like a rowboat running into a humpback whale.

The seats tore free. The hula dancer flew through the cabin. The windshield, the control panels, and the hull all rattled. The duct tape twisted; if not for its miraculous powers, the ship would have fallen apart.

"Captain, sir!" Piston's voice rose through the communicator. "Euclidian engine rattling down here like a terrified skeleton. She don't got much more power in her, sir."

"Fragging aardvarks," Nova cursed. "Nearly broke every vertebra in my spine."

Riff pulled himself back to his feet. He stared outside. "There it is. The planet Athemes. In the fourth dimension."

With time spread out before them, Riff didn't see the planet as a sphere. It appeared more like a series of rings--thousands of reflections showing its orbit around its star. The stars themselves appeared as curved lines of light, like a photograph of night with camera shutters left open for hours.

"Captain, sir!" Piston barged into the bridge. "I cannot keep this darn Euclidian engine running much longer, sir. It's crushing the ship like a Carinian stone beast squeezing a lemon, sir."

"Just a bit longer, Piston," Riff said.

Piston grumbled and stormed off the bridge. "There ain't enough duct tape in the cosmos to hold this ship together."

Riff stared down at the stretched-out ring of stone, the planet spread across both space and time. "Giga, can you take us down to the pyramid?"

"Cannot compute, sir. There are infinite pyramids below."

"Take us down to the one we fought in. To the tunnel where Kerish . . . where . . ." His throat caught. "Where we were."

Giga looked at him, eyes soft. She nodded and spoke in a whisper. "Happy to comply, Captain."

Whining miserably, the *Dragon Huntress* limped down toward one of the planet's reflections. As they entered the atmosphere, the ship's whining rose to a scream of protest. Fire blazed. Riff ran through the cabin, patching up extra cracks. Finally they flew in clear sky. All around them, Riff could see the reflections of time--a thousand years of storm and clouds, a thousand generations of forests rising and wilting below. To his left, he could see vague streaks of the old *Dragon Huntress*--the one that had visited here days ago--gliding down toward the city.

They clanked down toward the pyramid--the craggy one with the iron tip. The Holy Knights of Sol Asylum. Riff could see the pyramid being built, rising, crumbling with age. A hundred battles spread around them, past and future. Among the reflections floated the images of the tesseract ships--now long gone--battling the old *Dragon Huntress*, Romy at the helm.

The new *Dragon Huntress*--dented, scratched, patched together with tape--glided toward the pyramid's crest. There, in the tunnel's mouth, Riff saw them. Lord Kerish and his knights. And behind them . . .

Myself. Steel. Giga.

The ship began to rattle madly. Riff fell. He clutched the control panel.

"Captain, it's tearing us apart!" Piston cried through the communicator.

"We're creating a paradox already!" Nova shouted.

Riff crawled across the shaking floor. "Giga, bring us closer. Bring the airlock right to the tunnel."

"Happy to comply!"

Riff stumbled down the corridor. Through a porthole, he saw a chunk of wing collapse. Smoke blasted out from the ship. Bolts rained. Crawling, he reached the main deck and made for the airlock.

"Connecting airlock to tunnel, sir," Giga said through his communicator.

Riff tugged the airlock door open, fell downstairs, and banged against the outer door. It swung open, and he tumbled into the pyramid's tunnel.

The reflections still filled it--Kerish thrusting his blade, tossing light against Giga, and Steel jumping, taking the second blast against his chest, falling, dying in Riff's arms. The pyramid itself trembled as the *Dragon Huntress*'s Euclidian engine rumbled, threatening to collapse any second.

"Engine dying, sir!" Piston shouted.

Riff swayed through the shaking tunnel. He approached the reflections, trying to grab them, to find the right one.

Time is like a beach . . . ride the wave, son.

There! He saw it. The right reflection out of the thousands. Kerish thrusting his blade, the light beaming against Steel.

An explosion rocked the tunnel.

Fire and light flared.

"Euclidian engine dead, sir!" rose Piston's voice.

The reflections began to fade.

Riff shouted, leaped toward the flickering image of Kerish, and shoved the knight's sword aside. The light streamed out, missing Steel, slamming into the ceiling . . . then fading . . . fading . . . all going dark.

Fire.

Ruin.

Piston's hands grabbing him, pulling him back.

Crashing metal and flame and shrieking sky that spun all around . . . then sand and sunlight and shadow.

CHAPTER TWENTY-SIX
A LAST FAREWELL

In his dreams, he traveled through time.

He was a boy again, his mother gone, his father off on his quests, and he wandered the dregs of Cog City. He grew into a young man, a bluesman in a seedy bar, playing guitar for boozehounds and bootleggers. He stood on a stage in Ashmar, playing his music for a young princess with hair of gold, with laughing green eyes, with lips that loved to smile, with a soul that lit his life. He traveled among the stars, the captain of a rickety old ship shaped like a dragon. With friends. With those he loved. With a brother.

He lay in the sand, the sun and moon moving above, time coiling, stretching, then finally gathering into the one dot, one luminous pinpoint of light.

The present.

The now.

A place of calm, of healing.

His eyes fluttered open.

The sun shone upon him, soft and gentle. The reflections were gone from the sky. All pain, all fear, all anxiety--they seemed to have flowed away, leaving him serene, at peace, at one with the present and the sky and the--

"Wanna wrestle?" Fire flashed, wings beat, and Romy leaped onto him. Her tail wagged furiously, and she grabbed and twisted his arm. "Wrestle me, Riff! I'm Romy the Rowdy! You can be Riff the Rabble-Rouser, and we can find lucha libre masks, and--"

"Get off!" He groaned and shoved the demon aside. "Stars above."

He pushed himself onto his elbows and looked around him. He exhaled slowly. All his serenity vanished, and fear flooded him.

He lay on the sand below the pyramid. Around him spread the wreckage of the *Dragon Huntress*. A shattered wing thrust up from the sand. His captain's chair lay toppled over. The kitchen sink stood atop a dune, split in two. An engine smoked, half buried in the sand. A million little pieces--bits of the hull, bolts, screws, cables, wires--lay in piles. The ship hadn't just crashed like on Kaperosa; it had completely fallen apart.

Riff leaped to his feet. "Nova!" he shouted. "Twig! Piston! Giga!"

His heart thrashed and his belly clenched. Oh stars, were they--

"Twig!" he cried out. He ran forward. The halfling was limping over the dunes, clutching her head.

"My brain hurts, sir," she mumbled, sand in her hair.

Grumbles rose from behind Riff. "He ruined it! The star-headed lad ruined my beautiful ship. Oh, precious lassie." Piston emerged from behind another dune, lifted a chunk of circuitry, and wailed. "She's dead, sir. The dragon's dead."

Riff kept racing through the wreckage. Tears of relief filled his eyes. "Nova! Giga!"

The two came limping toward them. Nova's armor was scratched, tattered, and ashy, but it had protected her body.

Giga was showering sparks, and her leg twisted at an odd angle, but the android was very much alive. She held a sparking computer in her hands, the size of a shoebox.

"The *Dragon Huntress*'s brain," the android explained. "Well, my brain too, given that I'm only an interface."

Romy's eyes widened. "I want to hold my brain in a box too!" She turned toward Nova, tail wagging. "Nova, can you get me a box for my brain?"

"Sorry, Romy, all out of matchboxes," the ashai said.

Riff looked from side to side. Still the fear pulsed through him. He rummaged through the wreckage, seeking him, and his fear grew. His breath shook.

"Is he gone?" he whispered. "Is he . . ."

A voice rose behind him, deep and soft. "By my honor, the starship has fallen."

Riff spun around, and tears flooded his eyes. His body shook. Warmth blazed through him.

Steel came walking through the wreckage, clad in cracked scraps of armor, ash staining his gaunt cheeks and long, brown mustache. His brow furrowed.

"Brother, are you all right?" the knight said. "What happened? My memory is vague."

Riff ran through the wreckage, grabbed his brother, embraced him, and laughed. "You're alive, Steel! You're really here, aren't you? Not just a reflection."

The others ran forward too. They all leaped onto the brothers, hugging them, hopping up and down, laughing. Twig jumped right onto Riff's shoulders and sat there. Romy beat her wings and tried to sit on Twig, and the whole pile collapsed, and the Alien Hunters fell onto the sand. They rolled apart, still laughing.

"I am very much alive," Steel said, brow still furrowed, eyes still confused. "Though I remember . . . almost like falling asleep, and a dream, and . . ." He shook his head and exhaled. "A memory that's gone already. Riff! We must fix the starship or find another. We have to fly to the black hole. To stop the Dark Queen, and--"

"Way ahead of you, brother." Riff laughed again and fell back into the sand.

He gazed up into the blue sky. Ibises flew overhead, and the scent of the desert filled his nostrils. Up on a dune, a camel stared down at them, shook his head in wonder or perhaps disgust, then turned and trotted away.

* * * * *

As the sun set outside, the Golden Scarab Tavern shone with light. The sound of laughter, jangling coins, and music filled the common room. Dancers with jackal heads, clad in silk and jewels, swayed upon a stage, much to the delight of the ale-soaked patrons. Musicians with the heads of serpents played timbrels, drums, and harps. The cook--a massive man with a hippo head--stood in the kitchen, roasting kebabs. A thousand candles shone, and the voices of the customers rose in a murmur, itself a song.

Romy kept trying to leap onto the stage and dance too, but with ten beers in her belly, she kept slipping and ended up drooling on the floor. Piston seemed determined to join her--the gruffle was downing ale after ale, taking a break from drinking only when a new platter of kebabs arrived. Nova was shouting at Piston for stealing her drinks, while Twig was regaling Riff with an old story from Haven. Giga stood on a tabletop, her brain in a box at her feet, rattling off facts about Athemes's history of camel husbandry. Everyone was ignoring her.

Only Steel was quiet. The knight sat at a back table, nursing a cup of wine. The cook had placed a platter of kebabs before him. The rich, fatty lamb steamed upon a bed of wild rice and mushrooms, its aroma heavy, but Steel had no appetite.

He stared over his meal at Lenora. She sat across the table from him, her food too untouched. As soon as Steel had hailed her, she had left her hideout at Horsehead Space Station, hitched a ride back to the desert, and met him here. Now she gazed at him with soft, hazel eyes, her brown tresses framing her face.

For the first time, Steel noticed that thin crowfeet were stretching out from those beautiful eyes. That a single white hair was growing on her head. Suddenly he was aware of how real time was, how frustratingly slow yet fast, how it locked them--mere three-dimensional beings--along its track forever. Sixteen years had passed since that day two youths had parted. And yet Lenora had never seemed more beautiful to him.

He reached across the table and placed his large, calloused hand upon her small, soft one. He smiled at her thinly. She smiled back. For a long moment they said nothing. Yet there was so much that Steel wanted to say. So much that he didn't know how do.

"Lenora," he finally said, voice sounding too hoarse to him. "I am so sorry for your loss. I was hoping to find your father alive and well too after the engines shattered. When I found him gone, I mourned him. I cannot begin to imagine your pain."

She nodded and lowered her eyes. "Yes, I mourn him too. I hated him at the end. For what he did to Dee. To you. I hated him, and yet I grieve for him. Is that strange, Steel?"

He shook his head. "It's our nature to grieve for what we lose." He stared into her eyes, not talking about her father this time. And he thought she understood.

"Sometimes it feels like the cosmos is full of grief." She looked around her and sighed. "And yet this is a time of joy, a time of music, of dancing, of laughter."

Romy had finally found a wrestling partner--Piston was trying to pin her down and grab the leg of lamb she had stolen from him. Twig was cheering for the demon, while Giga was hiding her laughter behind her palm. All around them, the natives of Athemes--men and women with animal heads--were singing, laughing, and telling joyous stories.

Steel returned his eyes to Lenora. "What now?" he whispered. "What happens to us?"

Sweet sadness filled her smile. She squeezed his hand. "There is so much left to learn in this cosmos. There is another black hole in our galaxy, right in the center, larger than Yurei. A team has been working in a station orbiting it, and they offered me a position. It's a five year gig, and . . . I don't know, Steel. I haven't yet given them an answer." Her eyes softened. "And what of you, Steel? Back to saving the galaxy?"

His smile too felt sad, a smile that made his eyes sting. "The Lord Commander of the Knights of Sol himself hailed my communicator only this morning. He offered me my knighthood back. A seat on his council. He heard of what transpired here, and he wants me at his side, to help him rebuild Earth."

Lenora gasped and her eyes lit up. "That's wonderful, Steel! I'm so happy! I--"

"I turned him down," Steel said.

She gaped at him. "Steel!" She covered her mouth. "But . . . why?"

He looked outside the window. In a cobbled lot stood the wagons they had hired, piled high with bolts, circuits, and sheets of metal. Now the sadness left his smile, and he returned his eyes to Lenora.

"We're going to rebuild it. The *Dragon Huntress*. She will fly again. And she is my home now. And I have a new knighthood now." He pointed at his freshly forged breastplate. Instead of the old sunburst sigil, letters were engraved over his heart, spelling *Alien Hunters*.

She laughed, though tears fell from her eyes. "So I was right. Back to flying around, saving the galaxy. I suppose that means that . . ." She lowered her head.

Steel rose from his seat and walked around the table. She rose too, and he embraced her. They stood together among the noise, the laughter, the candlelight. She laid her cheek against his breastplate, and he kissed the top of her head.

Time is like that, Steel thought. Impossible to rewind. He could not change the past sixteen years. He could not change whom they had become--she a scientist, he a hunter of the skies.

But he could still feel sadness. And as he embraced her, that sadness embraced them too.

Finally Lenora touched his cheek, tears on her lashes. "Goodbye, Sir Starfire, Defender of the Galaxy."

"Goodbye, Lenora, always my lady, always my love. We will meet again someday under different skies."

As the musicians played and the patrons laughed and sang, Steel kissed his lady.

A time of triumph, he thought. *A time of sadness. A time of joy.*

CHAPTER TWENTY-SEVEN

THE DRAGON HUNTRESS

They stood in the courtyard between palm trees, gold-crested obelisks, and sphinxes of sandstone, staring at the greatest wonder in the city.

Before them she stood, gleaming in the sun, her hide silvery, her head raised proudly, her wings spread wide.

"The new *Dragon Huntress*," Riff whispered.

Piston thrust out his bottom lip and nodded appreciatively. "They did good work, the hippo-heads. Good engineers, they are. Could do without the hieroglyphs they had engraved onto the hull, though."

A line of hieroglyphs indeed appeared upon the ship, each of the seven Alien Hunters depicted as an animal. Riff was pretty sure that the scorpion was Nova, and that the bat was Romy. He was less sure about the others, but he liked to imagine that the lion was him. Beneath the hieroglyphs appeared letters in Earth's common tongue, painted gold: *HMS Dragon Huntress*. Beneath them, in silver, appeared the words: *Alien Hunters Inc.*

Riff turned toward his fellow Alien Hunters. He took a deep breath and began a pre-prepared speech.

"We are seven, yet there is an eighth among us, a great huntress of the sky. From fire and ash, the *Dragon Huntress* is reborn. She will rise as a phoenix. Our great mother, companion, guide. The new dragon will be a new home to us, a ship to sail to the farthest reaches of the cosmos, to explore wonder and secrets, to fight our enemies--together, a family, sharing bonds of fellowship and love and--"

"I think I'm the lion," Romy said, still staring at the engraved hieroglyphs.

Twig tugged one of the demon's bat wings. "You're the bat. I think I'm the lion."

Romy rolled her eyes. "You're probably the puppy."

"That's a wolf," the halfling said. "I like wolves."

Romy mussed the halfling's hair. "Cute little puppy pup."

"I'm not a pup!" Twig growled and leaped onto the demon.

Piston roared and tried to separate the two "clod-headed scoundrels." Nova tugged her hair with frustration, and Steel crossed his arms and glowered.

Riff sighed. "So much for my inspiring speech," he said to Giga.

The android smiled at him. "I thought it was a good speech, sir, but you did seem lost a bit at the end."

Riff opened the airlock, and the staircases unfolded, leading into his new home.

"After you, Gig?"

She nodded. "Happy to comply."

Giga entered their new starship, her kimono--the black silk embroidered with silver dragons--rustling with every step. Riff and the others followed.

The new main deck looked just like the old one. A dart board hung again on the wall. Pillows topped the couches. A new goldfish swam in a new bowl. There was even a board of counter-squares on the coffee table. On a side table, a rose bloomed in a clay pot, its petals glowing.

Romy flounced onto the couch and yawned. "This is my new place. Everyone--attic!"

Piston groaned and grabbed the demon. "Hush, you. Up! Into the attic, demon."

Romy wailed, and soon a fight broke out again, everyone shouting and wrestling. Riff sighed and left them behind. He walked down the corridor, passing along the rebuilt rooms. And each place was a place of memories. His bedroom--where he would sleep with Nova every night. The shower--where he had made love to her, the hot water steaming around them, after battling the alien spiders. The kitchen where he and his friends had shared so many meals and laughs. The crew quarters where he had slept, side by side with his friends, that time Giga had been possessed and locked in his chamber. The escape pod where he had kissed Giga, then shot down to fight Grotter on a forested world.

So many memories here, he thought, trailing his fingertips across the walls. *So many memories of pain and fear . . . yet joy too.*

For years, the Blue Strings had been his only home. Now he had a new home. A new family. One he would not give up for all the power in the cosmos.

Yurei tempted me with a galactic empire, but everything I need is here inside this giant, creaky dragon.

He entered the bridge. The control panels gleamed. The hula dancer and bulldog bobble heads, retrieved from the wreckage, stood on the dashboard again. Three beige chairs faced the windshield. Riff sat down in the middle one, the suede creaking. Steel sat to his right, Nova to his left, while Giga took position by a control panel.

"Nice to look out a windshield without any cracks," Nova said.

Giga tilted her head. "Cannot compute, ma'am. There is no wind in space. Did you mean the front fused silica viewport--"

"I meant windshield!" Nova cracked her whip. "We fly through the atmosphere too, you know, and there's wind there. Fragging aardvarks."

"No more fighting," Riff said. He turned toward the android. "Let's test the speakers on this new boat."

She smiled. "Bootstrap and the Shoeshine Kid, sir?"

"You know me too well."

"Happy to comply!"

The soulful sounds of Bootstrap's guitar filled the cabin, accompanied by the Kid's ivory tickling. To the sound of "Moonshine Blues," the new *Dragon Huntress* roared and soared into the sky.

* * * * *

The lights were dimmed, the others were sleeping, and Giga roamed the halls of the new *Dragon Huntress*. She could feel the ship connected to her wireless network--a new body. The engines, the cannon, the wings . . . all still felt different, tickly. But as Giga wandered the ship, soaking it in, she smiled.

I will like it here, she thought. *My new dragon body.*

The others, perhaps, would not understand. To them, the *Dragon Huntress* was a starship, a home. But Giga had always been a piece of the ship itself, its Human Interface. To the others, she was just Giga, the sweet little android. But Giga had always known that her true form was different. She was more than a petite geisha in a kimono.

"I am a dragon," she whispered.

She was walking across the main deck when she noticed a tall, silent figure by the viewport. She stepped closer. In the dim light, she saw that it was Steel. The knight was staring outside into the darkness of space.

She approached him. "Sir?"

He turned toward her. "You can call me Steel, my lady. You know that."

She smiled. "And you know that you can call me Giga." She came to stand beside him. "Why do you stand here so often, Steel, looking out at the stars?"

He returned his eyes to the distant lights. "When we look at the stars, we're not really seeing them. We're seeing the past. Light that left the stars years ago. We're looking through time. That is why I look at the stars. To look at memories. To remember . . . her." His voice was soft. "Lenora."

Giga leaned against him, resting her head on his shoulder. "It must hurt so much to lose her."

"I thought that, over the years, I could overcome the hurt of losing her in our youth. Now those wounds feel open. Fresh."

Giga reached up, hesitated, then stroked his hair. White was invading his temples, but the rest was still deep brown, soft around her fingers. "New stars are always born. There will be new love for you, Steel."

For so long, Giga herself had suffered the pain of lost love. She remembered how she had kissed Riff outside the escape pod. How she had loved him, dreamed of him at nights, how much it hurt when he had chosen Nova. Perhaps her words to Steel were true for her, as well. Perhaps new love could still bloom. She thought of other memories: how Steel had saved her from the Singularity, and how she had saved him from the wreckage on Kaperosa. And those memories warmed her.

Silently, she slipped her hand into his. His hand was so much larger than hers, coarse, rough, a hand that had wielded a sword for so long.

Let me bring you some healing, Steel. Let us heal each other.

They stood together, watching the stars, creating new memories.

* * * * *

Riff yawned and lay back in bed. "Well, that was a nice little adventure. Think I'll sleep for a week."

Nova leaned over him, frowning. She grabbed his shoulders. "You're going to stay awake for a week at least. We have some catching up to do."

"Hmmm . . ." He nodded. "You're right. I did miss a few *Space Galaxy* episodes."

She growled, gripped his hair with both hands, and kissed him hard on the mouth. "Shut up and ravage me."

He considered for a moment, then nodded. "Okie dokie."

He had dimmed the lights, and he was pulling off Nova's armor, when the door to their bedchamber slammed open.

"Captain, sir!" Romy burst into the room. "Sir! Sir. A message came in, and--" The demon froze, her eyes widened, and she gasped. "Are you two . . . wrestling? *Without me?*"

Nova cursed and pulled a blanket over herself. Riff sighed and thumped onto his back.

"Romy, knock. Knock next time." He groaned. "What do you want?"

"Werewolves!" the demon said. "Alien werewolves from outer space! They're attacking Mars! The message just came in. They invaded a golf course, and they're digging up all the grass, and--" She paused and tilted her head. "Do you think there's such a thing as werepoodles? Do you think they're tasty? I'm hungry. I think we should take this mission."

Riff groaned. "Oh shenanigans. Werewolves on Mars." He stretched and rose from bed. "I'm not even surprised anymore. Fine! We'll fly over."

Romy grabbed his hand. "Come on. Come on! To the bridge. Let's set course right away. Oh, and will you wrestle me?"

"Not if he wants to survive the night," Nova muttered.

They stepped onto the bridge together. Yawning, Piston and Twig wandered in, both in their pajamas.

"What's all this ruckus about, you clods?" Piston grumbled.

A huge yawn stretched Twig from toes to fingertips. Little wrenches were sewn onto her pajamas. "You're all so noisy. Let a halfling get some beauty sleep."

Steel and Giga entered the bridge next, walking close together, and shared a glance and smile.

"Looks like we're heading to Mars," Riff said. "Something about alien werewolves. Seems normal enough." He yawned. "Gig?"

The android smiled. "Setting course to Mars, sir. Happy to comply, as always."

"You lot are mad," Piston muttered. The gruffle lolloped off the bridge, grumbling all the while. "Damn kids won't let an old gruffle sleep. I'm too old for this nonsense, I am. Damn young ones with their werewolves and flying around all night long. Twig! Come on, you clod, we better calibrate the engines you keep dropping wrenches into."

Twig raced after him. "Maybe they're out of tune because you keep getting your beard caught in the gears."

"My--my beard--?" Piston sputtered. "Why you little, halfling-brained clod!"

The two vanished down the corridor, their voices fading.

Riff sighed and sat in his seat, still wearing his pajama pants. Nova stood beside him and mussed his hair.

"No rest for the weary, eh?" she said.

"I'll sleep when I'm dead," Riff replied.

His choice of words shot painful memories through Riff. Nova--vanished into the black hole. Steel--dead in his arms. What danger did they fly to now? What more loss would he endure? As he looked out at the stars, he prayed to whoever might be listening: *Let us never know more heartbreak. Let us know only joy, only adventure, only love.*

The hyper-engines roared to life, then eased into a content purr. With a blast of light, the *Dragon Huntress* shot into hyperspace . . . flying toward a new adventure.

THE END

NOVELS BY DANIEL ARENSON

Alien Hunters:
Alien Hunters
Alien Sky
Alien Shadows

Misfit Heroes:
Eye of the Wizard
Wand of the Witch

Dawn of Dragons:
Requiem's Song
Requiem's Hope
Requiem's Prayer

Song of Dragons:
Blood of Requiem
Tears of Requiem
Light of Requiem

Dragonlore:
A Dawn of Dragonfire
A Day of Dragon Blood
A Night of Dragon Wings

The Dragon War:
A Legacy of Light
A Birthright of Blood
A Memory of Fire

KEEP IN TOUCH

www.DanielArenson.com
Daniel@DanielArenson.com
Facebook.com/DanielArenson
Twitter.com/DanielArenson

79272315R00182

Made in the USA
Middletown, DE
09 July 2018